Chasing Clovers

Kat Flannery

CHASING CLOVERS

www.katflannerybooks.com

SECOND EDITION Paperback
June 1, 2018

ISBN: 978-0-9811056-9-7

Cover designed by Carpe Librum Book Design

Praise for
Chasing Clovers

"A compelling story line. A combination of suspense, tension and romance will keep you turning the page until the end."

—Michelle Ferguson, author of *From Away*

"Everything I wanted in a Historical Romance was in this story…Any romance aficionado will love this book and this author."

—Tammy Gaines, NovelOpinion

ACKNOWLEDGEMENTS

The process of writing *Chasing Clovers* took many wonderful people. I would never have been able to get past the first five chapters had it not been for my mother, who asked—no, demanded—a chapter every two weeks.

My sister, Lori-Ann who read countless drafts and re-writes always with a bright smile and encouragement. My best friend, Carrie who over many drinks and thai bites, helped me flush out characters and subplots. My friend, Tammy who read the whole manuscript with a chapter missing and still, loved it. My editor and good friend, Rhonda who took the time and patience to sit with this stubborn Italian girl and make this story what it is today.

Thank you to, Emmie and Alice for your support in anything I do. My friend and mentor, Roberta who over the last six years has pushed me to be the writer I am today. My father, who doesn't like to read and is not fond of romance but sat patiently through all my chapters and offered his advice, thank you dad.

My three sons, Skylar, Seth, and Samuel thank you for eating Kraft dinner, hot dogs, and lots of chicken fingers while I was writing this book. Mommy loves you.

And last but definitely not least, I would like to thank my husband for allowing me to work countless hours on this book without any complaints. For encouraging me to never give up even when my desk was full of rejections. You always believed in me. I love you more than you will ever know.

I truly believe through God all things are possible…and I am proof of that.

I love you all,
Kat

Novels by Kat Flannery

Chasing Clovers

The Branded Trilogy
Lakota Honor (Book 1)
Blood Curse (Book 2)
Sacred Legacy (Book 3)

Hazardous Unions:
Two Tales of a Civil War Christmas
(*by Alison Bruce & Kat Flannery*)

The Montgomery Sisters Trilogy
FERN (Book 1)
POPPY (Book 2)

For every mother who has lost a child.

"Faith, hope and love; but the greatest of these is love."
1 Corinthians 13:13

CHAPTER ONE

Calgary, 1884

The stagecoach pitched to a stop, jostling Livy Green from fitful nightmares of a past she longed to bury and the stranger she was about to marry. Her neck stiff and her back aching, she massaged her shoulders. She straightened and tried to stretch her arms, but the tiny space wouldn't allow it.

A loud sigh blew from her lips when she realized how rumpled her clothes were. Frowning, she ran her hands along her skirt. Nothing but a hot iron would get the wrinkles out. With only two other dresses in her wardrobe, and no time to change anyway, she had no choice but to meet her fiancé looking as she did.

Her stomach dropped. *What if I'm not what he's expecting?*

She peered out the window and wasn't surprised to see a few North West Mounted Police mingling with the other townspeople. Their bright red uniforms stood out like apples on a tree. She reached for her satchel and held it tightly before she stepped out the small door. *You can do this.* She squeezed the handle on her luggage. *You have to.*

Fort Calgary was a bustling town with two hotels on either side of the street, a small dress shop with ladies hats and fabric displayed in the window, and a red-bricked bank on the northwest corner. She watched people walking along the wooden planks and filtering in and out of the shops.

A loud squeal sounded behind her.

Livy jumped. She was almost trampled by a young boy running from his mother. Her heart lurched at the sight of the child. The familiar ache inside her soul willed her to look away. But she continued to watch mother and child until they disappeared inside the mercantile.

She took a deep breath, forced all thoughts of the past out of her mind and scanned the streets again. Her face flushed when she thought of what she was about to do.

Bag in hand, she spotted the blacksmith across the street next to the barbershop. Her stomach twisted at the sight of the saloon two buildings down. The all too familiar swinging doors waved back and forth, taunting her. Two drunken cowboys left the saloon, weaving their way down the boardwalk.

Livy clenched the satchel and tensed.

She turned away, closed her eyes, and took another deep breath. Here she would be the wife to John Taylor—a man she'd never met—and stepmother to his two children.

She took another breath. She would start over. *Again.*

She surveyed the busy boardwalk in search of a tall man with dark hair. Almost every man she saw fit the description he had given her, so she decided to move over to the bench in front of the mercantile and wait for Mr. Taylor to find her. Hands folded together on her lap. She tapped her toe restlessly. Where could he be?

A rough looking cowboy sauntered toward her. His brown greasy hair, and ripped denims were paired with an evil smile.

Livy tucked her chin into her chest. *Oh, please don't let that be him.* She'd seen his type before and knew what they were capable of. The man lingered beside her for a few moments before continuing on down the boardwalk.

She sighed with relief. *How am I going to do this?*

No longer Angel Green, she was now Olivia Green. The past was far behind her, except on those long dark nights that would not allow her to escape it.

She chewed on her bottom lip and stared at the busy street.

Her new life would begin here. She would survive.

She blew out a shaky breath. It was all she knew how to do.

"Olivia?" a male voice asked.

A tall man stood beside her, his hat pulled low so she couldn't see his eyes. He hesitated, then extended his hand. "Olivia?" He had a polite, resonating voice.

She shaded her eyes with a hand. "Livy will do fine." She was uncomfortably aware of his presence as he towered over her.

He smiled and took off his hat. Wavy black hair curled above the collar of his coat and his skin was tanned from the sun. He looked nothing like the dirty cowboy. *Thank goodness.* Instead, he wore a clean flannel shirt tucked into faded denim pants.

"John Taylor. Good to finally meet you. My buckboard is over there." He pointed the way, then peered around. "Where are your trunks?"

"I only have this one."

Her cheeks reddened as she lifted her tattered brown satchel. She held it slightly behind, not wanting him to see the holes and stains on it.

Nodding, he offered his arm. She ignored it. Friendly eyes stared back at her. After what had happened to her in Great Falls, she hated being touched by men.

"Do not be insulted, Mr. Taylor," she said, staring at his boots, "but I'd rather you show me the way instead."

She headed in the direction he'd pointed out earlier. When she heard a low chuckle from behind, she pursed her lips and walked faster. *I need no one, least of all a man.*

In truth, she needed John Taylor more than she could admit.

As soon as she reached the buckboard, she tossed the satchel up onto the seat, gathered her skirts and climbed up. She had sat down when she noticed he was still standing on the walk.

"Uh, Miss Green?" He tipped his hat back, crossed well muscled arms and smiled at her. "That's not my buckboard."

Her face flooded with heat.

If this wasn't his wagon, why hadn't he said something earlier, instead of watching her make a fool of herself?

Her eyes misted. How had she gotten here, in this place, with a man she didn't even know? She swallowed. How could she have thought he was the answer to her problems?

Standing, she clutched the satchel and moved to the edge.

How am I going to get down from this blasted wagon?

Out of the corner of her eye, she saw John Taylor step toward her. She didn't want his help, nor did she want a stranger's hands on her. Determined, she held her breath and climbed down before he reached her.

He shrugged broad shoulders and strode toward another wagon. She watched his massive frame climb up with ease. Reins in hand, he waited for her.

The buckboard looked brand new, the wood oiled so it glistened in the warm afternoon sun. Lumber and a crate filled with supplies were piled in the back.

She set her satchel in back and climbed up beside him. "This is your wagon?"

He laughed, showing perfectly aligned teeth. "Sure is, ma'am."

Instead of waiting for her to sit, he whistled and the team jerked forward. Livy grabbed the side of the wagon and muttered a curse beneath her breath. If he wasn't her intended, she'd give him a tongue lashing he'd never forget.

Once seated, she ran her shaking hands along the front of her skirt and took a deep breath. *Be more civil, Livy.* It wasn't in her best interest to lose her temper and go flying at Mr. Taylor.

She closed her eyes. *Be kind. Smile.*

Her lips lifted at the corners, but then faltered. How could she smile? How was she supposed to be happy when all she felt was empty, incomplete and—worst of all—alone?

The buckboard rolled past shops, hotels, and even though she didn't want to see it, the saloon. Relieved to be putting the town and its harsh reminders behind her, she stared at the fields.

The stage master was true to his word when he had said, "You'll never see a sight like the prairies. It looks like a patchwork quilt, green and yellow with a touch of orange when the sun hits it."

Lost in the array of colors, she stared at the stalks swaying in the breeze. The hot sun beat down on her and she remembered the bonnet hanging around her neck. She placed it atop her head, not bothering to tie it but letting the strings dangle in the breeze.

"Sun gets real hot during the summer months," he told her. "Best to always wear a hat."

Unsure of what to say, she stayed silent.

They had traveled for almost two hours. Livy was grateful when he pulled the wagon to a stop below a large oak tree. Her bottom was beginning to go numb and she needed to stretch.

"I'm hungry. How about you?" John lifted a red blanket and a basket from behind the seat. He jumped down from the wagon and strolled toward the tree. "Coming?"

As soon as her feet touched the ground, she stretched and tried to work some of the kinks out of her sore muscles. Feeling a little better, she moved toward him, who fanned out the blanket and plopped down. Motioning for her to do the same, he opened the basket and handed her a piece of cheese and a slice of buttered bread.

Her stomach grumbled as she bit into the moist bread.

"Mmmm," she hummed.

"Yeah, Alice can sure make good bread," he said before taking a bite of his own.

"Alice? Is that your housekeeper?"

He shook his head. "No, I don't have one."

She was mesmerized at how his work-worn hands transformed into a light, almost feathery touch while he blotted his lips.

"Alice and Hank own the ranch that borders mine. She bakes my bread and watches the children from time to time."

"Oh."

He took a deep breath. "Look, Livy...I know we've only written each other a few times," his dark eyes studied her, "but I hope I made it clear that you'll be cooking and cleaning as well as looking after the children." He took another bite of cheese.

He *had* made it perfectly clear in all four letters she'd received. But she had lied when she told him she knew how to cook. She purchased two cookbooks and read a few pages on her journey, but she had not put any of this knowledge to use.

"Um, that will be fine." She hesitated. "But I must tell you, I have little experience cooking."

He stopped chewing. "How little?"

With nowhere to go and little money left, she lied. "I know enough that you won't starve."

He must have believed her because he didn't question her any more. Instead, he finished his lunch.

"You remember the children's names?" he asked after a while.

Of course she did.

"Ben and..." She didn't want to say the little girl's name. "Em—" She cleared her voice. "Emily."

Emotions that she had kept locked up began to escape. The panic that always came when she thought of her daughter started to crawl up her chest. A sharp pain slashed across her heart. Her throat felt thick and sticky.

She grabbed the flask of water and took a long drink. Her eyes grew moist. She swallowed hard.

"Are you okay?" He touched her shoulder.

Heat from his hand radiated down her chilled body, but she couldn't move away. She was forced to endure his touch.

"I had a piece of bread caught in my throat."

She coughed, lying for the second time in five minutes. This time she didn't feel guilty.

He eyed her for a few seconds. "Are you all right now?"

"Yes." She blinked back tears. "I'm fine, Mr. Taylor."

Only she wasn't fine and wasn't sure she ever would be.

He stood and offered his hand. "Call me John."

She hesitated. Part of her wanted to take his hand, to feel wanted, accepted. But she knew all too well what her touch could lead to.

Her fingers dug into the blanket beneath her. With an impatient huff, he grasped her hand. She felt the calluses on his warm palm and slowly closed her fingers around his, so he could bring her to her feet.

"Em's my little angel." A sad smile lay across his face. "Sweet as the woman who gave birth to her."

He let go of her and she felt the instant cold on her palm.

"I'm sure she is," she said.

The mention of children put her on edge. Most times she'd walk away, but today there was nowhere to go and her mouth had taken liberties yet again.

"Livy, does it bother you that I have children?" The blanket dangled from his hands. "Because if it does, say so now. I won't have a wife who doesn't approve of my kids." His lips formed a straight line, grim and full of displeasure.

"No. I...I like children."

This wasn't a lie. She *did* like children—what she knew of them anyway. She hadn't grown up with any other kids. Living inside a saloon didn't exactly make you front-runner in the friendship corral. Most of the kids she came across either teased her or were afraid of her. And what she knew of having her own children, she'd rather forget.

He would take her back to town and put her on the next stagecoach if she didn't make this right. If truth be told, that's what she deserved. To be alone, a castaway thrown to the slums without another thought.

She tried to smile, but her efforts proved futile. "I'm sorry." She wasn't the least bit sincere. "I'm a little irritable from the long ride. Please accept my apology...John."

"Apology accepted."

Relief washed over her.

"When will we get to your ranch?" she asked.

"You're already on my land. Have been for the last half hour."

When he grinned, she had never seen a more handsome face in all her life. His dark eyes brightened and he seemed to relax before her eyes.

He had said they'd be traveling for another couple of hours.

How big is his spread?

She scanned the fields.

"The T-Bar Ranch is one of the biggest cattle ranches this side of the mountains." The pride in his voice was unmistakable.

It had been so long since she'd felt proud, since she'd been happy. Would she ever feel those emotions again?

"Y-you own all of this?"

He pushed his hat back, grabbed the flask and took a long drink. "Yup, I sure do. Worked my fingers to the bone gettin' it that way too."

"You must be proud."

"Damn right I am," he replied. "I live and breathe this land. It's a part of me. Like my son and daughter, they all sit right here." He patted his chest.

"Your wife must've loved it here."

His expression changed from one of delight to regret. She instantly felt horrible. She knew his wife had died. He'd said so in his letters. She also knew what it was like to lose a loved one, and the emptiness that came with the loss.

"Yes, she did," he whispered.

She couldn't look into his eyes. She didn't want to see the pain that lay in their dark depths.

"I'm sorry."

"For what?" he demanded, disgust on his face. "She's gone and there ain't a damn thing you or me or anybody else can do about it."

One minute he was beside her, the next he was at the wagon.

The rest of the ride was spent in silence.

When the ranch house came into view some fifty yards after the wagon crested a hill, Livy inhaled at the vast picture before her. The large whitewashed house stood two stories tall and a porch wrapped around the entire dwelling. The house and the brightly colored flowers planted along the walk were a welcoming sight.

Two barns were situated to the left of the house. She could hear the clucks from the chicken coop. Fenced corrals with cows penned inside were scattered all around. Cattle sprawled over the land, grazing in the fields. Beyond the house she could see the Rocky Mountains. The mammoth jagged rocks were intimidating yet stunning.

"It's so beautiful," she said, awestruck.

John smiled for the first time since they left their resting point. "Yes, it is. I never tire of seeing it when I come home."

"How could you not? It's perfect."

He stopped the wagon in front of the house, jumped down and came around to help her. Although she attempted to wave him away, his strong hands wrapped around her waist and brought her to the ground.

"Go on ahead and wait for me inside," he said.

Nervous, she glanced up at him and only relaxed when he gave her a kind smile. His hands were still on her waist. As he stared down at her, she couldn't quite make out the play of emotions that flickered in his sable-colored eyes. Uncomfortable with having him so close, she tried to step out of his grasp, but his hands tightened on her waist.

"Mr. Taylor, please." She pressed her palms against his chest. "Let me go."

He didn't move.

"I said let me go."

She shoved him hard and he released her so quickly, she lost her balance and scrambled to correct her footing.

"Go into the house," he commanded, "I'll be in after I put the horses away."

Picking up her satchel, she ran toward the house.

John drove the buckboard to the nearest barn, mentally cursing his behavior. What the hell was he doing? When he'd helped Livy down, he never thought holding her would affect him like that.

He shook his head.

She'd been unsure of him from the moment he'd met her. He'd seen the fear in her eyes every time she looked at him.

He removed the horses' harnesses.

Damn. Why had he sent for her?

He yanked off his hat and ran his hand through his hair.

He knew why. The children needed a mother.

Setting his hat back on his head, he led the horses into the barn. He brushed them and cleaned their hooves before he led them outside to their pen. He smiled when the horses stomped their hooves and whinnied in anticipation of the fresh hay he was bringing to them.

"Here you go, boys."

He watched as the horses munched on the food, his thoughts trailing back to Livy. She was sitting in his house at this very minute, but he couldn't go there yet. What was he supposed to say to her? He wouldn't apologize for his harshness. He felt nothing for her. Never would.

Becky's face appeared in his mind and his stomach turned at what he'd done.

Hanging his head, he took a deep breath. "I'm sorry, Becky."

How would he handle having another woman in his house? Helping with his children? Eating off of Becky's dishes?

"Ahh, shit."

He'd battled back and forth for months before he placed the ad in the paper. He thought he'd prepared for this. It wasn't like he jumped at the first reply either. He'd made sure Livy was the right woman for the job. He asked her questions that he now knew she'd lied about. She didn't really know how to cook, but if that was the worst of her deficiencies, he could deal with that.

But something told him it wasn't.

There was more to Livy Green he didn't know about. She had sent him references from her boss at the mercantile and the woman who owned the boardinghouse where she stayed. She seemed on the up and up, and he had no reason to doubt she wasn't the perfect candidate.

But now that she was here, he could tell she was hiding something more from him. He could see it in the way her green eyes darted warily away from his. And when he touched her, she went stiff as a board and her pretty face lost all color. She was afraid of him and that only meant one thing.

Someone had mistreated her.

He made his way toward the house, his eyes drawn to the oak tree where Becky rested. He'd never love another the way he'd loved her. Regret settled deep inside his soul.

Was he betraying Becky? Would she understand why he'd sent for Livy?

He dug his hand into his pocket and found the heart-shaped locket. He'd given it to Becky on their first anniversary. He carried it with him after she died. It was the only thing he had left of her, and he kept it as close to his heart as possible.

Once inside the house, Livy let the satchel fall with a thump to the wooden floor.

This just won't work.

He had already caught her in one lie and he was bound to catch her in all the others she'd told him. Then what? Where would she go then?

She released a frustrated sigh. She was desperate. Worst of all, she was tired of being alone. Tired of always looking over her shoulder. Tired of the nightmares.

She plopped down on the bench by the door.

She didn't belong here.

She shook her head. "I don't belong anywhere."

She had nowhere to go and little money saved. If she left the ranch, she'd be back to singing for money, a thought that sent shivers up her spine. She couldn't go back to that life. Her stomach knotted as she clasped her hands together. No, she would make it work here. She'd clean, cook—or at least try to—and she'd be kind.

A loud sniffle pulled her from her thoughts.

In the hallway, a young girl clutched a tattered white blanket. She stared at Livy with wide, tearful blue eyes. She was about two or three years old, with thin, stringy blonde hair. She wore a dusty-rose pinafore smeared with dirt.

Livy blinked. "Emma?"

Raw emotions rolled through her, paralyzing her. A piercing, knee-buckling pain zigzagged across her chest. She couldn't catch her breath. Emma's face was there. Her smell. Her blonde, frizzy hair.

Livy covered her face and rocked back and forth on the bench.

Emma...my baby...my darling little girl.

Something touched her knee. Through tear-filled eyes, she saw a small, dimpled hand, so sweet and perfect.

But not her Emma's.

She had to put some space between her and this child, so she ran to the door, flung it open and slammed right into a wall.

Someone gripped her shoulders.

Blinded by grief, she struggled to get free. Misery overwhelmed her, causing her insides to churn. She needed to get away. Fast. She gathered enough strength to shove the barrier out of her way and ran to the railing on the deck. She leaned over and emptied her stomach on the bushes below.

"No tears, Livy," she mumbled. "No tears. The past is that, gone forever."

But it didn't feel that way to her.

She squeezed her eyes shut. She would give her life if she could hold her little girl one more time. To smell her hair, kiss her soft cheeks. A sob escaped as tears streamed down her face.

You are starting over. You have to.

She was still bent over the railing when a cool hand touched the nape of her neck. A cup of water was placed in front of her.

"Drink," John said.

Her heart raced. How long had he been there? Had he heard her? Afraid to look at him, she kept her eyes down and picked up the glass. She took a sip, hoping it wouldn't come back up.

"Motion sickness," she lied to him again. "I...I get motion sickness."

"Uh huh."

He didn't believe her?

She glanced up at him, her hair free from the braid hanging in her eyes.

"It *is* a bumpy ride." He smoothed a loose strand behind her ear. "I'll be in the kitchen when you're ready to come in."

When he disappeared inside the house, relief washed over her. She leaned against the wall and sipped the water. She hadn't expected John's daughter to affect her like that.

"What did you expect?" she muttered.

If she were to live here, she had to find a way to be comfortable around the girl.

She took a few deep breaths, patted her hair into place and strode toward the door.

If she were lucky, she wouldn't see the child again for a while.

CHAPTER TWO

She found John seated at the kitchen table. Well over six feet tall, with wide shoulders and a muscled chest, he made the spacious room seem smaller. She pulled her gaze from his body, and did a quick scan for his daughter. She couldn't help the sigh that escaped when the child was nowhere to be seen.

"I poured you a cup of coffee." He slid the tin cup in her direction. "Can't say that it's hot, but I'm used to that."

He shrugged and his mouth tilted upwards in a half smile.

His eyes followed her as she placed the cup she'd been holding on the side counter. Hands shaking, she pulled the chair back to take a seat across from him.

"Thank you," she said softly, and cradled the mug of coffee between her hands.

He was right. It wasn't hot, but it was warm and she squeezed the cup a little harder. She couldn't keep her eyes from wandering about the neat and tidy kitchen, so unlike the saloon kitchens where she worked.

The window above the wash basin was open to allow the hot breeze to flow through, and the white lace curtains added a woman's touch. It was a small window, but it let the sun in to brighten the room.

The long wooden table they were seated at was in the middle of the room and appeared to be made by hand, John's no doubt. A cook stove stood against one wall and an icebox occupied part of the opposite wall. She took a deep breath and could smell a mixture of lilacs, coffee, and man.

This was to be her new home. A new life, and even if she didn't want to be here, even if she wanted to bolt for the front door and run far up into the mountains she saw earlier, she couldn't. She had to stay. She had to be kind. She had to smile. Livy hadn't smiled—really smiled—since before Emma died. Her stomach pitched, and she took a deep, shaky breath.

She didn't have a choice. It was either this, or go back to the saloons and the dirty cowboys, the memories, and the fear.

"I didn't mean to…" John began in an apologetic voice.

"I think we should start over," she interrupted.

He smiled, easing the tension between them as well as her frayed nerves. "Good idea."

The chair groaned as he stood up. "Your bedroom is upstairs, first door on the left. Mine is across from yours. Ben and Emily's are at the end of the hall. And the outhouse is out back past the garden."

"Okay."

He took his hat off to wipe the sweat from his forehead.

"Alice will be leaving today. She was watching the children for me while I was in town. She can show you where everything is, you'll find her out back in the garden with Emily."

"I will find her when we're done talking."

"The evening meal is at six, and you only have to worry about me and the kids. The men take their meals in the cookhouse."

She had to cook today? Heaven help her—could this day get any worse? She chewed on her bottom lip as her mind raced through the short list of things she knew how to make.

I'll make sandwiches and some canned fruit. That can't be too hard.

"The meal will be ready at six."

John remained a moment longer. Livy, sensing he had more to say, waited patiently for him to continue. Instead, he pulled his hat down onto his head and placed the mug in the wash basin on the counter.

"I've got work to do. See you at supper," he mumbled before he walked out the back door.

She listened as his boots stomp down the steps, and slowly faded away. She sighed.

"Alone at last."

Leaving her cup on the table, she strode out of the kitchen into what seemed like a sitting room. On the far wall stood a shelf full of books. She examined the colorful bindings lined up neatly on each ledge. She'd never seen so many books in her life, and wondered if John had read them all. She ran her hand along the tall and short bindings while surveying the room. A fireplace protruded from the corner. Around the opening sat jagged pieces of brown, grey and rust-colored stone. A sofa and chair on either side. Closing her eyes, she imagined sitting here warm and cozy, a book in hand as the snow fell outside.

"You must be Olivia."

Caught day dreaming, she spun around and saw a short elderly woman standing in the doorway of the room, holding the little girl's hand. Livy's heart skipped and her hands grew clammy. She tried not to look at the child. "Yes, I am."

"I'm Alice." A friendly smile on her wrinkled face, she glanced down at the girl, and tugged gently on her hair. "And this here is Miss Emily."

"Hello," she said, her voice shaking. The child made her uncomfortable, and she could feel her chest grow tight.

She was glad that Alice didn't seem to notice her resistance to the girl. It was better to keep her insecurities, and the way the girl affected her, to herself. If Alice suspected anything, she was sure to ask questions. And Livy had told enough lies for one day.

"Benjamin will be in right away. He's a fine lad too." The woman patted Emily's head.

Livy could see that Alice was very fond of the children. She tried to smile back, but only made it half way. "I'm told I have to cook dinner tonight."

"Yes, six o'clock." Alice motioned to the kitchen. "I started a stew on the stove for you. All you have to do is add the vegetables Emily and I dug out of the garden."

She sighed with relief. She wasn't keen on sandwiches and was sure John would want more than that for his evening meal.

"That was very kind of you," she said.

With no idea how to cook, she was sure she would make a mess of things tonight on her first try. She'd already decided to stay up half the night reading her new cook book, in the hope of finding a few easy recipes. With luck, she wouldn't kill any of them.

"How about a cup of tea?" Alice suggested.

She was hesitant, but the more time she spent with the older woman, the more comfortable she became. Besides, it would be nice to have another woman to talk with.

In the kitchen, she noticed there was a steaming pot of tea on the stove, and once again was relieved. She had no clue where anything was and didn't have the energy to search through all the cupboards for their tea.

Alice took care of everything. She put two cups on the table and carefully poured hot water into them. The child never left her side, but peeked around the woman's skirt.

Seated once again at the kitchen table, she inhaled a deep, calming breath. She wished the girl would go outside and play. It was difficult to be around John's little girl—to look at her.

"Tell me, where did you come from?" Alice asked politely from across the table.

She'd come from everywhere.

"Well, I was living in Fort McLeod."

She lived in the dirty trading post town for six months when she spotted John's ad in the local paper. Before that she'd been in Great Falls Montana, but she planned on keeping that part secret.

"Fort McLeod," Alice said, raising her eyebrows. "I've heard tales of how rough and scary it can be there. With Fort Whoop Up a few miles north, it isn't any wonder."

She stiffened. This was true. Fort McLeod was a rough town, with two saloons a trading post and that was about it. No respectable woman lived there, unless she was married. And Livy was neither.

"It wasn't that bad. I didn't live there for long."

"Well, you're here now." She patted Livy's hand.

Yes, I am, even though I've lied through my teeth to get here.

After their visit, Alice gave the girl a hug, promising to come back soon. "Now you be good for Miss Green."

The child nodded as they stood on the porch saying their farewells. She waved, as Alice's buggy pulled away. A part of her longed to go with her. To escape the life she was now destined to live.

"Are you gonna be our new Ma?" asked a high pitched voice from behind her.

She turned and spotted a boy no taller than her waist standing in the doorway of the house. He wore jean overalls and a black cowboy hat that was too large for his head. If it wasn't for his ears, the thing would surely fall past his eyes to rest on his nose.

"You must be Benjamin," she said. It was much easier to look at this child. In fact she had no problem at all.

He stood and stared at her with the same dark brown eyes as his father's. "Can ya cook?"

What was with the men in this house? All they cared about was filling their bellies. "Well," she said, hesitating, "I can cook a little."

Who are you kidding? You can't cook at all.

He wrinkled his face. "I'll just eat with the men, till ya get the hang of things."

"You'll do no such thing." John's voice came from behind her, and she jumped.

When had he gotten here? These people were like ghosts, surprising her at every moment.

"Ahh, Pa," the boy said, "she said she can't cook."

"No, she said she hasn't done much cookin'," John corrected.

"Same thing."

"Mind your manners, son. She'll need a few days to get comfortable."

"Actually," Livy interjected, "Alice made a nice stew, and it's on the stove now. Me and—your sister and I have vegetables to clean and add to it. So there will be a nice supper tonight."

John smiled at his son. "See? You like stew. There's no need for you to eat with the hands."

"Well," Ben said, squinting, "if Alice made half of it, it can't be that bad."

"That's my boy."

They spoke as though she weren't standing there. Something she was used to. While growing up in a saloon, no one ever paid her any attention. It wasn't until she'd grown old enough to sing for money that all eyes were on her—and not in a good way.

She shuddered at the awful memories invading her mind.

"Are you cold?" John asked.

"Yes." *Another lie.*

"There are some sweaters hangin' on the back porch. Feel free to use them anytime."

"Thank you."

John bent and picked up the girl. "How's my Angel today?"

The familiar name caught her off guard. She almost answered, and was relieved that the girl's giggle stopped her.

He tickled his daughter, nuzzling his chin into her neck.

She hadn't heard the child utter a word yet and was startled at the innocent sound overflowing from her petite mouth.

"Papa, don't twickle me." She wiggled in his arms to get free from his grip.

He put her down and playfully swatted her behind. "You go help Miss Livy with supper."

The girl squealed and ran into the house.

His dark eyes rested on Livy. "You find everything you need?"

"Yes, thank you." She averted her eyes. He made her uncomfortable, but not in the same way the men in the saloons had. She didn't feel the need to flee and cower in her room. It was something else, something she'd never experienced before.

"Come on son, I'll race ya to the barn."

The boy hopped off the porch and ran ahead of his Pa, laughing merrily.

"Cheater," John yelled before chasing after him.

She watched the father-son moment. A gnawing ache wrapped around her heart and squeezed until her breath caught in her throat and she had to look away.

When Livy entered the kitchen, she couldn't help but notice the girl. Emily had pushed a chair over to the counter and was ready to help clean the vegetables.

She stopped and took two deep breaths before she spoke, refusing to look at her. "Do you know where the aprons are?"

The girl jumped down, opened a drawer, and pulled out two cloth aprons. She took one and put it on. The child remained motionless.

"You can't put it on yourself?" she asked, concerned that she would have to help her—touch her.

The girl shook her head.

"All right, I'll help."

After the apron was tied, she let the girl shell the peas into a bowl while she chopped potatoes and peeled carrots. Once she was done, Livy tossed the vegetables into the steaming pot, and grabbed the bowl of peas. Five peas rolled around inside the bowl. Emily had eaten the rest and now stood on her chair, sucking on a shell.

She stirred the five peas into the stew. "Alice said to let it simmer for the next hour."

She placed the pot at the back of the stove as Alice had instructed. She wiped her hands on her apron and headed for the door, intent on unpacking. A loud crash, followed by a piercing cry reminded Livy of the child in the kitchen. She ran back into the room. Emily lay on the floor, crying. Blood seeped from her mouth.

Livy stood frozen. *Help her.* But her legs wouldn't move.

Guilt washed over her. This was her fault.

Staring at the girl, she didn't know what to do.

"Come on, little girl, get up."

Emily didn't move.

Livy's face grew hot, and her hands began to shake. "Please, please get up." Her resolve faltered. The barriers that kept the pain locked far away were breaking down.

Tears streamed down the girl's face and into the blood smeared on her chin and lips. "It hurts. I want my Pa."

Livy took a half step toward her. Visions of Emma filled her mind, and she glanced at the child whimpering on the floor. She had been unable to help her daughter—unable to make everything better. Her heart beat rapidly. *Oh please, oh please, someone help me.* She grew frantic. Her skin crawled, and her chest constricted. Emma was in her mind, in her heart, in her soul.

The girl stopped crying and stared up at her. Her long lashes wet with tears as her eyes, blue and honest, stared into Livy's.

I'm being horrible.

Battling her inner turmoil, she rushed over to the basin and wet a cloth. She placed it on the girls lip. "Put this on it for a while to take the swelling down."

Mentally exhausted, she lifted the girl from the floor and put her on a chair.

"I," Emily hiccupped, "want my Pa."

"Sit here for a few minutes while I go upstairs to get my cook book." Needing to escape, she ran upstairs gasping for breath as another attack seized her lungs.

Take deep, even breaths, in through the nose, out through the mouth. She clamped her hands over her eyes to stop the tears that wanted to come. Never again would she hold her daughter in her arms and wipe her tears.

"Stop it, Livy, just stop it," she screamed to the empty room. She scratched her neck to stop her throat from closing. She was angry at the little girl who lived when hers had not. Angry at God for taking her daughter. Angry that she didn't have the strength to wrap her arms around the child and comfort her.

She stopped pacing, lifted her satchel up off the floor and dug fitfully through it until she found her cook book. Clutching it in her hand, she forced her feet to walk back downstairs.

She peeked into the kitchen. The child was fast asleep with her head resting on the table. She blew out a breath as she quietly entered the kitchen.

For the first time, she really studied the girl. One chubby little hand held the cloth, while the other rested under her head. Her blonde hair spread across her small back and Livy watched as her lips opened and closed while she slept peacefully.

Her stomach turned at the shame she felt. *She's a little girl Livy. She has nothing to do with your loss.* She reached out to touch the girl. Eyes filled with tears, she bit her bottom lip. Her hand hovered above the blonde head when she pulled back. Cheeks wet, she fled the room leaving Emily where she slept.

CHAPTER THREE

The evening meal went reasonably well, considering all she had to do was prepare the vegetables. Elbow deep in soapy water, she washed up the last plate and set it aside to be dried. She grabbed the tea towel and went about the task. She couldn't stop her mind from straying to the girl lying helpless on the floor. She knew she'd been cruel. Instead of comforting the child, she'd fled the room. Her inability to be around the girl was something Livy hadn't expected.

She was prepared to marry John Taylor. Prepared to be around his children. Or so she thought. Ever since Emma's death, she hadn't allowed herself to be around many children. Not a smart thing to do, she realized that now.

When she decided to take his proposal and move west, she honestly thought she'd be able to look at his children without resentment. She knew she'd never be able to love another child the way she loved Emma. But she was sure she'd be able to at least like them. The boy, Benjamin didn't bother her. It was the girl—the sweet, innocent little girl—like her Emma.

She couldn't look at John's daughter without thinking of Emma. Without wondering how this child lived when hers had not. She was at a loss as to how to fix it. And the worst part? She didn't know if she had the strength to try.

When John saw his daughter's split lip, Livy thought she was done in for sure. He asked her what had happened, but before she could tell another lie, the child told him about how she'd fallen, and how Miss Livy had made it all better. Astonished, she couldn't understand why the girl had not told John how cruel she'd been.

While he knelt to inspect the wound and kiss it better, he mouthed a 'thank you' to Livy. Shame twisted inside her. Unable to stand the scene any longer, she left to get some air.

She knew she had crossed the line today and was worried he would see her indifference toward his daughter and ask her to leave. With nowhere to go, she was hopeful things would work out.

Since her fall, the girl hadn't so much as looked at Livy, out of fear, she was sure. That she was the sort of person a child would fear made her feel ill. Why hadn't the girl told John how she fell, and it was Livy's fault? Guilt ridden, she thought it best if she didn't have too much contact with the girl, for now anyway. She knew she couldn't avoid her all together, or John would start asking questions she wasn't prepared to answer.

"The kids are fast asleep."

Startled when John came up behind her, she dropped the plate she'd been drying onto the floor, shattering into tiny pieces at their feet. "*Damn,*" she whispered under her breath.

As she bent to pick up the broken glass, he remained standing and stared down at her. Was he angry at her for swearing? She had no clue what to do. *You should watch your mouth—that's what you should do.* He was still looking at her, and her face heated. "I'm sorry."

"No, it's not your fault. I scared you." He knelt beside her, and began picking up the jagged glass.

She moved slightly to the left, her body all too aware of how close he sat.

"I guess I should make some noise before I come into a room, huh?" His full lips tilted into a smirk.

"It might help."

His dark eyes evaluated her, making the room feel cramped and closed in.

She inched away from him again.

He held a piece of the plate in his hand and rested his elbow on his knee, "You know, you wouldn't look half bad if you smiled."

He grinned wider.

She stiffened at the insult. "Excuse me?"

John's brow furrowed.

"Now don't go gettin' your chaw in a knot. I meant that you're kind of pretty as is. I can't imagine what you'd look like with a smile on your face."

He chuckled.

She clenched her jaw. Fury radiated from every pore in her body. After the day she'd had, this seemed to be the icing on the cake. She squeezed her eyes shut. She hated being teased. She'd grown up with it all her life, and couldn't help but feel angry. "I don't see how a broken plate would prompt one to smile, Mr. Taylor."

"Ah, hell. I'm only playin' with you, Livy."

"Well, play all you want to, Mr. Taylor, but it won't be at my expense." She stood, untied her apron and tossed it over the back of the chair. "I'm sure the rest of the plate will find your humor hilarious."

Chin held high, she marched up the stairs, smiling when she heard him swear, hoping he cut himself.

Angel curled her exhausted body into a tight ball on her bed. The pain in her abdomen was beginning to fade. Her long brown hair, loose from its braid, clung to the sweat on her temple. She had no energy left to wipe it away. She took a shaky breath once the ache had subsided, and let her head rest lightly on her pillow. It wasn't but a few minutes when another piercing spasm sliced through her stomach, jolting her upright. Angel moaned and clutched her midsection. Veins of throbbing torment snaked slowly around her back and seized her whole middle.

She bit her bottom lip to muffle the cry she knew would burst from her dry lips. But her efforts proved futile as a loud scream erupted and her eyes clouded with tears. Her stomach felt as if it were about to explode. The hard, swollen mound protruded from the damp white cotton nightgown she was wearing. The door to her room opened, and Doctor Simms entered quietly and calmly. He placed his large hands on her stomach, and she nearly jumped off the bed from the pressure.

"It's almost time," he said to her, pushed up his sleeves to wash his hands at the basin on her dresser.

Angel's breaths came in short, quick puffs. Her hands instinctively searched out the sheet on either side of her, ready to tear it from the straw-filled mattress. Her crotch felt heavy and it pulsed with urgency. A gush of liquid burst from between her legs and soaked the bed beneath her. An uncontrollable urge to push took over. She sat up and pulled her legs inward. She drew in a deep breath, pressed her chapped lips together and pushed with all her might.

The doctor was in front of her now, and nudged her shaking legs farther apart. "A few more pushes and the baby will be out."

The agony of it all was too much. She didn't know if she could stand the pain any longer. Her tired body was hot and sticky, and her legs felt numb. Her stomach tightened again, and she couldn't help but push. Her crotch burned—the pressure from the baby's head unbearable.

The room blurred, and her head started to spin. She panicked, fearing she was going to die. Her life was ending, and she would never see her baby's face. Her middle was going to tear in two. She pushed again. Her body stretched and ripped, allowing the small life to come through. She ground her teeth together and groaned loudly.

A baby's cry pierced the quiet night. she reached down, touching the baby girl that had slipped from her womb. Shiny and wet, she was the most beautiful thing Angel had ever laid eyes on. The pain gone, she examined her daughter, now cradled in her arms. Pink lips quivered as the baby mewled. Angel bent to brush a light kiss on her damp forehead.

The doctor handed her an old yellow blanket. With shaky hands she began to clean her daughter.

The room was lit by one lamp, casting the room in an orange glow. Calm and serene, Angel glanced out the window. All she could see were the white fluffy snowflakes that stuck to the glass. She snuggled closer to the bundle in her arms. She was warm, and for the first time in her life, truly happy.

"I've got your money, Doc." Her voice was hoarse from the long labor. She rummaged under her pillow and grabbed a brown tin. Inside was the money she'd been saving. Not much there, she counted out a few coins and handed them to the doctor.

Shaking his head, Doctor Simms spoke clearly, "It's already been taken care of, Dear."

Angel glanced up confused.

"Sam."

The bartender and owner of the Saloon had paid for her delivery? Angel knew she shouldn't have been surprised. He'd felt guilty about what had happened to her and wanted to somehow make it right.

"Me and little Emma," she said her daughter's name for the first time, "we plan on getting out of here and starting fresh someplace else." She watched as the doctor's kind blue eyes moved around the tiny room. She owed him and Sam so much more than her thanks. They had both helped her when no one else had, or wanted to.

The room she rented upstairs at the saloon was a far cry from the white house the doctor called home. Her cheeks flushed with embarrassment when she noticed the bawdy gowns that she had to wear scattered across the floor. Her life had no meaning before this day, and she was determined to give her daughter the life she never had. Emma whimpered, and Angel gazed down at her child. The love she felt for her daughter came instantly.

Doctor Simms shrugged into his coat, and said quietly, "You'll do right by her. Chances are he'll be passing through here again soon, and he'll come looking for you." He stared directly into Angel's eyes. She saw pity in their kind depths.

"When you leave here, don't ever come back." He gave her one last look, and left the room.

She heard the doctor's warning and her body shuddered. She knew the doctor was right. He'd come back. He said he would, and as sure as Monday followed Sunday, he'd come looking for her. Emma cried and she gently rocked her baby back and forth while humming the lullaby Sam had taught her.

Livy woke, her nightgown drenched with sweat. She lifted trembling hands to her lips. She had dreamt of Emma again, holding her, touching her, kissing her. Now fully awake, she tried to remember what her baby girl had looked like, but her face would not appear in her mind.

"No, no, no," she cried, burying her head into her pillow. "Don't let me forget," she sobbed harder.

She couldn't remember Emma's smell, or how her hand felt when she'd hold on to Livy's finger. What color was her hair? What color were her eyes? She didn't know—couldn't remember! Her heart beat loudly inside her chest as uneven gasps blew in and out of her mouth. The room began to spin and her vision blurred. She needed to get a hold of the short breaths filtering up from her lungs.

She sat cross-legged on her bed, concentrating on her breathing. *In, out. In, out.* Until her pulse slowed to its regular beat. But the ache deep inside her soul lingered, and the piercing pain continued to shoot across her chest. Her face wet with tears. She laid her head back onto the pillow. Closed her eyes, and willed her daughter's face to appear.

John woke to Livy's cries. He wondered if he should go to her. "And do what?" he spoke aloud to the empty room. He didn't know her well enough to barge into her bedroom, and as sure as there was fire in hell, he knew he'd not be welcome. Not after he'd insulted her last night.

As much as he didn't want to admit it, he'd thought she was quite pretty. Even though it annoyed him, he hadn't stopped thinking about her all day. He felt sorry for her. She'd said in her letters she had no family left. So he knew she was alone. Maybe that's why she seemed so empty all the time, so lost. Maybe she missed her Ma and Pa, or had a brother or a sister who had died. He thought on it and decided to ask her. See if he could help—sometimes talking to someone did.

When Becky died, he'd talked to God. He was the only one worth talking to, and at the time, the only one there to listen. He rubbed his chest. He sure missed her.

Three years had passed since the night little Emily was born—the happiest, yet saddest day of his life. While he watched his little girl slip into the world, he also watched his wife slip out. Since then he'd thanked God a thousand times over that he'd had the chance to tell his wife one last time that he loved her. He rolled over and lightly touched the locket on the table beside the bed.

Emily never knew her Ma, and he hoped Livy could fill the void in his little girl's life. He sighed. His son struggled too without his Ma around, and often woke with nightmares. Livy would be good for him too. But his daughter needed a woman, especially when she got older, and he was grateful that Livy had answered his advertisement. He hoped he wasn't betraying Becky by remarrying. The question lingered in the back of his mind several times a day since he'd sent for Livy. Becky was the only woman for him, always would be. No one else came close.

The rising sun peeked through the blue curtains, and cast sapphire and grey shadows throughout the room. It was time to get out of bed. He yawned and stretched his arms above his head. He was always working, and he was tired of it. Rubbing the sleep from his eyes, he couldn't remember the last time he'd taken a day off or had any fun. On a ranch this size there was always something to be done. He was glad he had Clive, his foreman, to ease some of the heavy load.

They had grown up together in Calgary. Clive had left for a few years, but had come back, knocked on his door, and asked for a job. He couldn't have been happier. It was after Becky had passed, and he couldn't get out of bed. He'd relied on Clive in those days when he didn't leave his room except to get another bottle of whiskey. His body gave an uncontrolled shake. Now he didn't touch liquor. Couldn't. Made him sicker than a dog. Doctor said he'd die if he drank any more. Besides, he had two kids to look after, and had disappointed Becky enough by succumbing to the amber juice that left his head foggy and his body numb.

His mind already filling with chores that needed to be done today, he decided to give up on getting any more sleep. Sighing, he got out of bed, dressed, and headed downstairs to start the coffee.

CHAPTER FOUR

Livy waited until she heard John go out the back door before she ventured downstairs. Her growling stomach and the smell of coffee lured her to the kitchen. Eyes still puffy from crying, she got out a mug and poured some of the hot brew. Lifting the cup, she inhaled the aroma. The scent always calmed her nerves, and after the night she'd had, she needed it.

She thought of the dream. It reminded her that he was still out there somewhere, and she may never be safe from him. He had almost found her twice after Emma had been born. And both times she had escaped just in time. She didn't know if he still searched for her. It had been a little over a year since she saw him last.

There was a time when she didn't care if he found her or not, when she wanted him to. Dying would've been her only escape from the reality of Emma's death. But the memories of what he did to her—what he took from her—always haunted her. She'd forever be looking over her shoulder wondering if he'd find her and break her into pieces all over again.

She took a deep breath and picked up the cookbook on the table. She fingered through the pages for an easy recipe. A half hour later, after reading, and re-reading the instructions for making pancakes, she decided to hunt for the ingredients. She lined them up on the counter and began preparing the batter.

Thirty minutes and several swear words later, she had a plate of steaming pancakes ready to be served, the burnt ones hidden on the bottom. She placed them on the table, and saw that the children were already sitting quietly, waiting for their breakfast.

"Oh, I didn't even hear you two come down." This didn't surprise her. They were like their father, quiet as Indians ready to raid.

"Yeah, well, we smelled the pancakes," Benjamin said, his dirty blonde hair messed from a night's sleep.

"I hope you're hungry." She looked at the boy.

"I sure am," John replied from behind her. This time he didn't startle her, she heard him washing up on the porch and had expected him through the door any minute.

"I'm hungwey too, Papa," Emily protested.

"I bet you are, Angel." He gave Livy a wink before he sat down at the table. "You're growin' up awful fast."

"No she ain't," Ben disagreed, "She's the same size as she was last year."

"Am not." Emily pouted.

"Of course you're not, Angel. Ben here is just jealous because he hasn't grown much this past year himself." John gave his son a warning look. "Isn't that right, Benjamin?"

"Yeah, I s'ppose."

"That's better." John picked up his knife and fork. "Now let's dig in. I'm starved, could smell these pancakes a mile away." He gave Livy another wink.

She hoped he had something in his eye, refusing to acknowledge his attention. Her face heated, and she took her seat.

"Well, eat while it's still hot." She motioned toward the steaming flapjacks.

The Taylor's were seated around the table. They took turns passing the pancakes and syrup around until everyone's plate was full. Pleased that she'd actually made her first meal, she smiled at her accomplishment. After slathering her own pancake in syrup, she took a bite. The pancake was horrible. She gagged and picked up her coffee—John did the same—and they took a long swig.

Face red, she said. "They're a little salty."

John took another bite, and choked it down. "Maybe a little, but they're still edible."

"No they ain't Pa, they're horrible." Ben made a face as he pushed the plate away.

"Benjamin Taylor," John yelled.

She put up her hands to stop him from saying more. "No, Ben's right. They are horrible. I can't even eat them."

"See," Ben said to his father. "Ma used to make good pancakes."

"Ben." John's eyes deepened with sadness.

Livy wiggled on her chair. She wanted to flee the kitchen. It was another reminder that she didn't belong here. Her feet fidgeted underneath the table. A strong yearning for Emma swept over her, and her heart ached to feel the one comfort she had ever known.

"I like 'em," Emily piped up, breaking the uncomfortable silence, syrup dripping from her chin.

John laughed and gazed at his daughter, the sadness gone from his eyes. "Well, you eat 'em up pumpkin."

She chewed happily as she took another bite.

"How about some toast?" John asked Ben and Livy.

She stood. "I can make…"

"NO." Both John and Ben shouted.

John was already up at the counter. "I'll make the toast."

"I think I can make some toast," she muttered.

"Never doubted that you could," John said placing some bread over the stove to heat, "but you slaved over the pancakes already this morning, so I'll make the toast."

She knew he was being nice, and he thought she'd ruin the toast as well. She shrugged. He was right, she'd never made toast before either, and wasn't about to push her luck.

The dishes done, and the kitchen clean, Livy decided to go out and see what was in the garden. Out on the porch she was blasted by the putrid smell of cows. She placed her hand over her nose to block the awful stench.

"You get used to it," Ben said, from behind her.

She turned and saw the boy sitting on the step whittling away at a piece of wood. "Does your Pa let you have a knife?" she asked, concerned.

He scowled up at her. "I'm not no baby."

"I never said you were. I thought maybe he didn't know."

"He gave it to me." Ben didn't look up. The short blade sliced away little pieces of wood to lie around his feet.

"Oh, I see." She didn't. But she wasn't his mother. Her vision blurred—she wasn't anyone's mother. Blinking back the tears, she pointed at the square patch off to the side of the house. "Is that the garden?" she asked, changing the subject and pushing thoughts of Emma aside.

"Nope, those are weeds."

She knew he thought her daft, but she didn't care. "Well, Mr. Smarty Pants, where is the garden, then?"

He lifted his hand and pointed a few feet ahead of them. "Right there."

Well, now she was sure he thought her daft. She glanced in front of them. Lifting her skirt, she went to inspect the bountiful fare. She stared at some tall green stems.

"What are you standin' here for?" Ben asked, beside her now.

"Well, I'm not sure what everything is."

He gave an exasperated sigh, lifted his hand and pointed to the green vine-like stems on the end. "Those are peas. Next to them are carrots, and then beans, radishes, onions, lettuce, and potatoes. The ones at the very back is corn."

She took a mental note of everything he said. "Did you plant all these?"

He bobbed his head. "Me and my Pa did."

She scanned the garden. It was quite vast and must've taken John and Ben weeks to plant.

He turned and ambled over to the porch, picked up two buckets, and handed her one. "These are what we put them in when we pick 'em."

Taking the bucket from him, she headed into the garden, starting where Ben had said the peas were.

"Wacha makin' for supper?"

She hadn't gotten that far. "Um…what would you like?"

"I like roast. So does Pa." He eyed her. "But it's hard to make."

She took a deep breath and ignored his last comment. "Okay, roast it is." Heaven help her, she had no clue. "Ben, what kind of vegetables do you like with your roast?"

He shrugged. "Potatoes are good, and Em likes carrots."

The mention of the girl's name caused Livy's spine to stiffen. She had often called her daughter by that nickname. She ground her teeth together. Tightened her grip on the bucket, and forced the painful memory to the back of her mind.

"Ben, Ben, let's skip!" Emily yelled, bounding around the corner of the house, rope in hand.

"Later, I'm busy in the garden," he hollered back.

"Me help too." She dropped the rope and ran over to Livy. "Me help too, Miss Liby." She pulled on Livy's dress.

Refusing to look at the child, Livy tried to dismiss her, and continued picking peas. But Emily tugged harder on her skirt. Her body rigid, she wanted to tell the girl to leave her alone and go away, but she knew what might happen if John found out. Taking a deep breath, she pulled all her fears and frustrations inside. "Yes, you can help."

Her bucket was full of peas and carrots, and the weight of it all had her bending over while she walked. Ben's bucket was half full of potatoes. They hauled them into the kitchen to be cleaned and cooked. A task she was sure she could do. After she put the bucket on the counter, Livy searched the cupboards and icebox for the roast, but came up empty handed. Drawing back the curtain, she called out the kitchen window to Ben. "Where would I find a roast?"

He rolled his eyes, jumped off the porch, and ran to the middle of the yard.

He pulled open a door, and disappeared into the ground. The cellar was outside in the yard. She should've known.

Reaching inside the bucket, she began pulling out the potatoes and dunked them into the bucket of cool water beside her on the counter. A couple minutes later, Ben bounded through the back door carrying a slab of meat. He slapped it on the counter with a bang, and then he was out the door, running across the yard, before she could say thank you.

Staring after him, she didn't quite know what to make of the young boy. She didn't seem to have much of a problem being around him, like she did his sister. He seemed like a good kid. "Humph," who was she kidding? It wasn't like she had any experience to know.

A loud scraping sound came from behind her. She spun on her heal and watched Emily push a chair up to the counter. She had decided yesterday to ignore her, but could feel her conscience tell her otherwise.

She rummaged through her cookbook in search of a recipe. This was her second day here, and she was trying to cook a bloody roast. Was she crazy? Why couldn't Ben have asked for something easier, like soup and sandwiches? She moaned. Even pancakes had seemed an easy task, and still she had messed them up.

The girl stood beside her on the chair, waiting for Livy to tell her what to do. How was she supposed to tell her what she didn't know? She was almost to the end of the book, and still she hadn't found anything that said *roast* in it.

"A lot of good that was. That thing cost me a whole dollar." She tossed the book onto the counter.

A soft knock at the kitchen door interrupted her rant and she went to see who it was. A tall black man stood in front of her, holding a cowboy hat in his large hands. He gave her a wide smile, his white teeth contrasting with his dark skin.

"May I help you?" she asked, peering around his broad frame to look for John.

"No ma'am." His smile grew bigger. "I'm here to help you."

"I beg your pardon?" She never allowed herself to be alone with men, not after that night long ago.

"Mr. Taylor. He sent me down. I'm Ezekiel, I cook for the all the hands on the T-Bar."

"Oh." She breathed a sigh of relief when she realized why he'd come. "Your help will be most appreciated."

She smiled up at him, and stepped back to allow him into the warm kitchen.

Ezekiel was so tall he had to duck his head to get inside. He placed his hat on the table and went to the basin, pulled up his shirt sleeves and washed his hands.

She waited until he was done, and followed suit.

"Zeek, Zeek!" Emily hopped up and down on her chair.

"Hello, sprite." He patted the top of her head. "You gonna help?"

"Yup."

Ezekiel addressed Livy. "What we makin' today?"

"A roast." She pointed at the slab of meat still sitting on the table.

Ezekiel slapped his hands together. "Okay, a roast it is."

"Um…Ezekiel?" she hesitated, "I've no idea what to do with it." She was done lying about how little she could cook. Being truthful was the way she was going to learn.

His warm smile told her he didn't judge her, and for that she was relieved. For the next hour Ezekiel showed Livy how to prepare the roast, and how to get the fire up in the stove to cook it.

"Remember to open the damper." He reached over the stove to turn the knob. "Cause if you don't, you'll fill the house with smoke."

Her mind was full of so many things that she hadn't thought to write anything down. A few minutes later the roast was in the oven and the vegetables were cooking on the stove. Ben came in and announced he was hungry for some lunch. She had no clue what to cook for him, and searched frantically around the kitchen. Ezekiel suggested she heat up the leftover stew from yesterday. He smiled his approval when she placed bread and butter on the table as well.

"Well, it's time for me to go. Those cowboys don't like it when they have to wait to eat either," Ezekiel chuckled, picking up his hat.

She touched his shoulder. "Thank you, Ezekiel," she said, now relaxed in his presence.

"I can come back tomorrow to help again?"

"Yes, I would like that very much."

"Okay then." He plopped his hat on his head and headed back to the cook shack. She stood on the porch and watched him go. A warm breeze blew down from the mountains to caress her face, but all she smelled were the cows and chickens. Would she ever smell anything else? She covered her nose with her hand. The children had been fed and were in the field playing tag, so Livy thought she'd take a walk around.

She stepped off the porch and crossed the yard. To the left was a corral with a few cows penned inside. She watched the enormous animals saunter lazily inside their pen. Next to the corral stood a red and white barn with paint chipping off the door. Careful not to get her shoes muddy, she lifted the hem of her skirt and went inside.

Four saddles sat on top of what appeared to be a fence, but with wooden planks angled out on either side. Weathered wool blankets were draped at the end of the make-shift fence. Long ropes, short ropes and all sorts of tools that Livy had never seen before hung on the far wall. She made her way farther to the back where a few horses lounged inside rickety wooden stalls. The back door stood open, and she went through.

Behind the barn there were more cattle, separated, and relaxing inside corrals. A group of cowboys stood around one of them, and Livy thought she saw John among them. Curiosity getting the better of her, she strolled toward them.

The men tipped their hats as she drew nearer and moved to make room for her at the fence.

"Who you bettin' on Ma'am?" one of the cowboys asked.

She was unsure which one had spoken to her. They all resembled each other in their dirty cowboy hats and denims. And compared to her, they were huge.

"Pardon me?"

She wrapped her arms around her middle, placing a barrier between her and the men that stood so close by.

"Are you gonna bet on the boss, or Rusty?" He pointed to a man beside John at the other end of the corral. "You see, I'm takin' old Rusty 'cause he rides them bulls all the time."

"You're crazy, Gill," another cowboy yelled from somewhere Livy couldn't see. "The boss'll win."

"You wanna make a friendly wager on that?" Gill shouted back.

"Sure do."

The men started to yell out bids, betting everything from horses to money. Livy stood in the middle of them. Feeling uneasy, she backed away from the crowd. Then she spotted the bull. He was by far the largest animal she had ever seen.

Her stomach dropped as the black beast snorted and pawed at the ground. His shiny black coat glistened in the sun, and his horns were curved and pointed. The sharp spikes were meant to do damage. Her eyes sought out John, who stood outside the other end of the corral. Was he insane? That bull was sure to kill him.

She stood frozen as the one they called Rusty made his way up onto the fence. The men grew quiet as he climbed over the fence, and leapt onto the beast's back. Rusty's hands grabbed onto the rope around the bulls neck, and he held on while the animal bucked and kicked at the air.

The longer he stayed on, the louder the shouts got. He flew off and landed hard on the ground. Rusty got up quickly, ran to the fence and vaulted over it before the bull got to the fence.

"Five seconds." Someone yelled.

"Not bad," Livy heard John say. "But you better dig out your five dollars Rusty, cause when I'm done you'll be payin' me."

"Don't be so sure, Boss." Out of breath, Rusty sat on the ground.

She watched John as he stepped up onto the fence and waited for the bull to come near. It all happened so fast. He jumped onto the bull, and it took off running. Soon it bucked and spun, but he stayed put.

The bull rammed headlong into the fence, came away from it and rammed into it again. The cowboys jumped back, as if the animal might come through. She watched horrified as he was tossed around like a rag doll. The hands shouted and whistled even louder than before. Her stomach turned, but she couldn't look away. John held on while the bull tried everything to get him off his back.

When she was sure he'd never let go, he jumped off, landed on his feet, and ran to the fence. The bull chased after him, and stopped just before John's legs cleared the top rail.

The cowboys ran to their boss, each one patting him on the back.

"Pay up, Rusty." John took his hat and slapped some of the dust off his pants.

With a scowl on his face, Rusty dug into his pocket and handed John his five dollars.

"Your lady came to watch, Boss." Gill snickered, as he passed by John. "You gave her quite the show."

Livy observed John from a few feet away while he spoke to the men that had gathered around. "Fun's over boys, back to work," he ordered. John pushed his hat low on his head as he sauntered toward her. He stopped a few inches away from her body.

He was way too close for her liking, and she stepped back. He took a step forward. "Did you like the show?" he asked her, a cocky smirk on his face.

The man infuriated her. Almost getting killed for sport! He was also too close to her person. Back rigid, her arms tensed ready to defend.

"If that's what you call it," she answered, before turning to leave. He grabbed her hand and pulled her close to him. She could feel his breath fan her face, and even though he didn't frighten her like most men had, there was something about him that made her uneasy. He was tall, wide, and all muscle. She pushed on his chest to move him from her, but he didn't budge. He smelled of leather, animal, and the musty scent that was all him.

"You didn't like the bull ridin'?" He was still smiling.

"No. I think you're crazy to almost get yourself killed over a few dollars."

"Rusty bet me, and John Taylor never backs down from a bet."

Of all the stupid things she'd heard in her life, this had to be one of the stupidest. "Well, a lot of good your bet would've been had you broken your neck."

He shook his head. "Wouldn't have happened."

His conceit grated on her nerves. Who did he think he was? "You're not invincible, Mr. Taylor." She tried again, to turn away from him, to leave. But his grip tightened on her arm. Livy didn't like where this was going. After what happened in Great Falls, she tried hard to never be in a situation where she was alone with any man. She scanned the field for any of the cowhands.

"How do you know?"

"Because, Mr. Taylor you are not God," she hissed.

The mischievous gleam in his eyes gone, he let her go. "No, Ma'am, I am not."

She crossed her arms.

John's lips came closer, almost touching hers.

She shivered.

"Maybe you should get a shawl, Miss Green." He spun away from her.

"Whatever for? It's as hot as Hades out here."

"Because," he called over his shoulder, "You have goose bumps on your arms."

Chuckling, he disappeared behind one of the buildings.

"Damn that man," she muttered under her breath. A profound need to escape from the imbecile who was soon to be her husband she went back to the house.

CHAPTER FIVE

Boyd took a long drag from his cigarette. He'd been watching the bull riding when he saw her come over to the corral. Angel Green. At first he didn't know it was her, but then she turned his way. Her green eyes were unmistakable against the sun's glare. He thought he'd never see her again after their night together a few years ago.

She'd been feisty, fighting him the whole way, until he gave her a few slaps to let her know who was in charge. The thought of it made him hard. He liked it when his women fought. Their cries begging him to stop drove him crazy, and Angel had done just that.

He often thought about all the women he'd had the privilege of taking, their screams lulled him to sleep at night. There had been many. His first offence starting at the age of fifteen, and since then the number had grown rapidly over the years. He liked the power he held over them. He loved to see the shame in their eyes when he'd finished. He had never been caught. He'd leave the scene well before his victim told her husband or father. He was wanted, he knew, but that didn't stop him. It made his game all the more amusing.

He hated all women. His mother included. Good for nothin' whore. He scowled. His father found his mother in bed with another man and killed them both, then turned the gun on himself. He was eight years old at the time. He blamed his mother for his father's death. He was sent to live in an orphanage, where his mind grew sick, and filled with uncontrolled lustful thoughts. He fantasized about forcing all women to have sex with him.

He felt the scar on his cheek. His finger traced the length of it, starting under his left eye all the way down to the corner of his mouth. He smiled. It was his gift from Angel. He pulled on his pant leg to loosen his tight jeans from the bulge that had grown there.

He went back to find her a year later, the memory of their night together still fresh in his mind, but she had disappeared. Talk was she'd had his baby. But he didn't see any child with her now, and the boss never mentioned she had one when he'd told them of his plan to take a wife. Maybe she gave it away. He didn't think she'd keep it anyway. He shrugged. He didn't care. The reason he'd come back was for another piece of her. He didn't know why she'd left, he'd paid her good.

He snickered.

It wasn't like he'd raped her.

He traveled over the years working as a cowhand, but things always ended with him escaping in the night. He had a way of making people uneasy. He smiled. He couldn't control the cravings for unwilling women. Neither went over well with most of his bosses.

If Angel saw him, she'd run and tell Mr. Taylor what he'd done and the huge man would fire him for sure. Not that he worried about it. John Taylor could go to hell. He stared hard at Angel. Oh how he'd love to take her one more time. His hand instantly sought out his groin and he rubbed his palm over the hard swell beneath his jeans.

The shock on her face when she saw him, made his middle pulse. He vibrated. He knew he couldn't have her yet. He'd have to wait, and bide his time. He felt the whiskers on his jaw, and his mouth watered. He stared hard at Angel as an idea came to mind. Making sure no one was looking he pulled his hat low on his forehead, tossed his cigarette, and crept away.

CHAPTER SIX

John was covered in mud from the collar of his shirt to the soles of his boots. He spent the last two hours in the south-west corner of the field dragging two of his calves out of a mud hole from last week's rain. His backside ached like hell from riding that bull earlier. "Damn dumb animals." A note of affection softened his curse.

"Looks like you've had a good day so far," Clive called from behind him.

"Yeah, real good." He tried to wipe some of the mud from his shirt. "I need you to go up to that mud hole and put some wire around it to keep the cows out."

"Sure I'll do it tomorrow. Maybe I should get a bucket and dump it on you. You'd have better luck gettin' clean."

"I best get down to the stream while I can. Livy wouldn't like it if I came into the house lookin' like this." He held his arms out, as he surveyed his mud-covered pants and shirt.

"You still thinkin' on gettin' hitched, hey?" Clive asked, as he wiped down his saddle with an oiled cloth.

"Yeah, I am. Kids need a mother and I'm sick to death of the beans and grits you guys eat down here." He didn't think he needed to tell his foreman about the pancakes they'd had this morning.

He ran his hand through his hair. The mud had dried and it felt like he had all the sand in a Texas desert stuck in it. He shook his head, surprised to see more dirt fall from his head.

"What's she look like? Some big brawny old gal?"

Livy was anything but big and brawny. "Not bad. You'll meet her soon enough."

"Oh, goodie." Clive rubbed his hands together in fake anticipation.

"Hey, maybe that's what you need, old friend."

Clive raised his eyebrows.

"A woman to warm your bed and fix your meals."

Clive had no woman, and never mentioned that he needed one.

"Offer's still good. You can set up house in the west quarter when you find one." He eyed his friend. "But then again, I don't know if you'll find one lookin' like that."

"Well, I won't have to *order* me one that's for sure."

"Get back to work."

"That's what I'm doin', Boss," Clive hollered, as he sauntered out of the barn.

John glanced down at his attire. He was too tired to head to the lake to bathe. His body craved the hot water he'd heat from the stove to soothe his sore muscles. He took one last look at his mud stained denims and headed up to the house.

He could smell pot roast the second he stepped onto the porch. The mouth watering aroma caused his stomach to grumble. After he dunked his hands into the cold water in the rain barrel and washed his face and neck, he dried them on the towel that had been placed there. He glanced down one more time, and shrugged. Nothing could be done about the rest of his attire.

Hungry and sore all over, he opened the back door and tramped inside. John took his hat off and hung it on the peg. "Somethin' sure smells good."

Ben and Emily were already seated at the table, and Livy was standing over them dishing up potatoes. He grinned. Ezekiel had stopped in—he could tell. John was pleased he asked the cook to come and offer some assistance. His stomach rolled when he thought of the salty pancakes they'd had this morning.

He peeked at her out of the corner of his eye. She didn't seem to be angry with him for interfering. In fact, she acted as if he weren't there. She still couldn't be mad about earlier, could she? That had been hours ago. He flexed his jaw. Well, too bad if she was. He was in no mood for a fight, and had no intentions of riling her anymore today.

Damn he was hungry. He pulled back his chair and every muscle in his arms throbbed. The pain reminded him of the warm bath he would soon sink into.

"What happen to you, Pa?" Ben asked, staring at John's muddy shirt.

"Had to pull a few calves out of a mud hole up in the south-west corner of the field."

"Must've been deep." Ben said.

"Sure was, son." He picked up his knife and buttered a piece of bread.

"Smells like it was more than mud too." Livy wrinkled her nose.

He was learning fast that this woman always seemed to have an opinion. He turned and gave her a look.

"Isn't there a stream you could've washed up in?" she asked, as she passed Ben the peas.

This was his house, damn it, and if he wanted to come in here stark naked he would, let alone covered in mud!

"Actually, Miss Green, there is. I chose to bathe in the house tonight, and last time I checked, I owned it."

Her eyes sliced right through him. She didn't say a thing through dinner or later while he was in the sitting room reading a story to the children. She sat in the chair and flipped through her damn cookbook.

John couldn't quite figure her out. What was her problem? Irritated by her cool demeanor, he closed the book he'd been reading.

"Okay, story's over. It's time for bed." He slid Emily and Ben off of his lap, and put the book on the shelf.

"Me want Miss Liby to tuck me in," Emily said.

John stared at Livy. She hadn't moved. Her eyes darted about the room, panic in their depths.

"Um, I....I have dishes to do." She stood and the cookbook fell to the floor in her haste to leave. She scooped it up and fled the room as if a pack of hungry wolves were after her.

He shrugged. She sure seemed nervous and he'd bet ten to one she hadn't been around many children, and hadn't the foggiest idea how to put one to bed. "C'mon Angel, Ben, let's go."

Livy went upstairs after she finished with the dishes, relieved she didn't have to go and help John put the children to bed. She could hear him now, as he talked to Ben and Emily. They were saying their prayers. She frowned. She didn't say prayers anymore. They were never answered anyway.

She sat down on her bed. Why did a man like John believed in God. He had lost his wife, a reason, if any, to be mad at God. Yet he still said prayers with his kids, asking God to bless them. She picked up her satchel and threw it onto the bed. Well, He sure hadn't blessed her. Anger and resentment rolled around inside her ready to explode.

Since arriving yesterday, she hadn't bothered to unpack. She tipped the tattered satchel upside down and emptied it onto her bed. Two dresses fell out. A blue cotton one trimmed with yellow lace, and a dark green dress, her favorite of the two. Scooped around the neck, the green dress hugged her body in all the right places, and pleated below the waist to flow to the ground. She placed them on hangers and hung them in the large armoire in the corner of the room.

She stood back to look at the unused space. The two dresses left ample space for more, which she didn't have. She couldn't do anything about her scant wardrobe, and was used to living without the fancy dresses most women had.

Her brush, some ribbons, and her nightgown lay on the bed. She had gotten the ugly white nightgown from one of the girls in the last saloon she had sung in. She unbuttoned and replaced it with the used nightdress.

Still on the bed, in a rumpled heap, was Emma's blanket. Livy's hands shook as she lifted the ivory cloth to cover her face. She took a deep breath, but her daughter's scent was no longer there. The sorrow nestled deep within her soul strived to be released.

The blanket still covering her face, she sat down on the edge of the bed. Her throat tightened while her body unconsciously rocked back and forth. A haunting tune seeped past her lips and her eyes burned with unshed tears.

Emma.

Livy's arms ached to hold her one more time, to breathe in her milk-and-honey fragrance. Why did *she* have to go? Why didn't God take me instead? She squeezed the blanket until her knuckles turned white. The memories were torture. Like someone held a whip and beat her with it, re-opening the wounds over and over again.

No. She shook her head. She had to stop the memories. She had to make them go away. She could feel her insides turning, and the panic welling up.

She took deep breaths. Straightening her back, refusing to play into her emotions any longer, she placed the only keepsake of her daughter back inside the satchel. Put her shaking hands over her face to rid the lingering memories. She took two more deep breaths. Needing to get out of the room, she went to the door and quietly opened it a crack. All was quiet, so she crept down the stairs and into the kitchen.

The sight before her stopped Livy dead in her tracks. John was bathing in a tub fashioned from a barrel cut in half from top to bottom. His eyes were closed as he relaxed in the tub. His broad shoulders and wide chest hardly fit inside the cramped barrel. The dark, curly hair on his muscled chest glistened in the candlelight, and lay in a *v* shape as it descended down his belly.

"Getting a good look?" he asked, without opening his eyes.

She jumped and spun around, hitting the wall with her nose. Her eyes watered as pain shot up her face. Blood crept down her nostrils and dripped onto her lip.

"Hang on," he said, as he splashed around behind her. "Let me turn the lamp up."

The room grew bright. The aura of the once dim light was gone. Still facing the wall, she held her hand cupped under her chin, holding some of the blood from her nose.

"You can turn around now," he said.

She turned slowly so she didn't get any blood on her nightgown. He stood before her with a white towel wrapped low around his midsection. She couldn't stop her eyes from descending to look at his flat stomach and his protruding pelvic bones. Mortified at how her insides reacted to him, she whirled around again, and slammed her nose into the wall a second time. The pain was unbearable.

"Damn it," She muttered. The blood, unstoppable now, poured like a river through her fingers and onto her nightgown.

"You'd think you saw a damn ghost."

No, only a half-naked man standing in his kitchen.

He gripped her shoulders—the heat from his hands burned through her nightgown branding her—and turned her around to face him. "You're a mess." He led her over to a chair and pushed her into it.

Please don't let his towel come undone. She stared hard at the floor. What was happening to her? She wasn't repulsed, or disgusted by his half-naked body. *How would his strong arms feel wrapped around her?* She closed her eyes, and slowly shook her head. She didn't understand the way her body responded to his near naked one. Her eyes watered from the pressure in her nose, and she was glad her hand covered her pink cheeks.

He glanced at his dirty bath water then went outside to dunk a cloth in the rain trough. He lowered her hand and placed the cool cloth gently on her nose. She pulled back from the pain that seemed to encompass her whole face.

"Easy now," he whispered. His dark hair was wet and draped down his forehead, as droplets of water dripped onto his face. "Have to be more careful."

She didn't need a lecture right now. Her face hurt like hell, and her nose felt as large as a clown's.

"What'd ya go runnin' into that wall for anyway?"

"I didn't do it on purpose." She spoke from behind the cloth.

He glanced down at her nightgown. "Well, looks like that'll have to go in the trash."

"I don't have another one." She inched backward, away from him, and the soapy smell invading her senses.

"We'll just have to fix that."

"How?"

"I'll take you shopping." He thought on it a moment. "Yup, we'll head in to town on Saturday. I need to get a few things anyway, and I figure we should get hitched then too."

She straightened. She didn't want to marry him yet. He thought she was a virgin, and if they were wed, he'd expect her to consummate their marriage. How was she going to explain that one? The awful night had been her first time, and it had been brutal. The bruises between her legs had taken weeks to fade. Since then she had never been with another man, nor had she wanted to.

"You don't have to."

"Yes, I do."

"No really, it's fine."

He took the cloth from her face, and examined her nose. "Nope it's my fault your nightgown is ruined."

"Please, don't bother with a new one."

His finger tenderly traced the length of her red and swelling nose. He was too close, and she inched back.

Could he see how his touch affected her? How her body reluctantly yielded to his slow and gentle caress? Unfamiliar feelings began to stir inside of her. Feelings better left alone. She pulled away from him.

"I will buy you two nightgowns."

"I'll simply wash it in the morning."

"I didn't give you a choice, Livy." He pulled her back toward him, and continued dabbing the blood from her lips and cheeks.

He was careful on her tender skin, and her shoulders sagged, her body relaxed. *Do not let this happen, Livy. You can't trust any man.* But, his smooth fluent motions mesmerized her. Eyes closed, she relished in the slow movements.

"You're so beautiful," he whispered.

His delicate brush of the cloth hypnotized her and she could feel herself falling under his spell. Ignoring all her warnings, she opened her eyes, and found him watching her.

He leaned closer. "Does it still hurt?"

She couldn't speak, so she nodded instead.

He bent and lightly kissed the tip of her nose, his mouth hovering above her own.

Her hand let go of the cloth, and she leaned forward.

He stood, breaking the spell. "There, that should make it feel better."

Her face grew hot, and she tried to swallow past the lump in her throat. What had she been thinking? She wanted him to kiss her, wanted to feel his arms around her. Why? Why now? She vowed to never let another man touch her. Why had she let him? Her eyes simmering with tears, she got up, muttered a polite thank you and ran upstairs.

"Don't you want me to tuck you in?" he called after her, his usual arrogance lacing his words.

She didn't answer him, and sought the solace of her bedroom. Once inside her room she closed the door and pressed her forehead to it. Her body still responding from his touch, she wiped at the tear on her cheek.

John cursed as he dragged the tub outside and emptied it into the yard. He'd almost been asleep when he'd heard her come down the steps. The nightgown she'd worn left little to his imagination. The candle's glow offered a clear view of her body, and he was glad he had been in the tub. Where the hell was her wrap? Didn't most women own a bloody robe? Well, he would fix that on Saturday. He'd make sure she had two of the damn things, just in case. He brought the tub back inside, and hung it on the peg in the storage room.

When she'd hit her face on the wall, he'd been glad for the distraction. He shook his head. She sure was a clumsy thing. Why the hell did he have to help her? He should've told her where the cloth was and let her get it. He ran his hand through his wet hair. She acted as if she'd never seen a man bathe. It wasn't like he stood before her naked, damn it.

She was a frigid little thing that was for sure. When he'd gone to help her, she'd turned so fast she hit her nose again. He cringed. She'll be awfully sore tomorrow, maybe have a black eye too.

She seemed so helpless and scared. The same look he often found on her pretty face. She never spoke of her past, but then again she'd been here all of two days. He hadn't had much time to sit and talk with her, something he'd hoped to do before they got married. He slapped his hand down on the counter. Well, he had till Saturday. She couldn't live here much longer without a ring on her finger. People would talk. Not that he gave a damn. It was Livy he was concerned about. The townspeople could be cruel, especially the women.

He took a deep breath. Her scent still lingered in the room. She smelled of lilacs, and when he'd been cleaning her face, he'd wanted nothing more that to kiss her pink lips. She invaded his mind, and he'd almost forgotten his manners when he bent and brushed his lips across her nose.

When her green eyes met his, he had forgotten all the practical reasons he'd sent for her. He had to get some distance from her. The warm bath, mixed with her translucent nightgown, was spellbinding. Yup, he had to stop these feelings. Becky didn't deserve this. She loved him wholeheartedly, and he couldn't betray her by kissing the first woman that came into his life.

He closed his eyes. A vision of Livy in her nightgown, brown hair flowing past her shoulders, the glow from the lamp cast around her, reminded him of an angel. He opened his eyes. Damn it, he needed sleep. Yup, a good night's sleep was sure to help him forget about Olivia Green. Trouble was, when he woke up, she'd still be there.

CHAPTER SEVEN

Boyd was tired, hungry and pissed off. He had been shoveling shit for the last two hours while Rusty napped under the oak tree near the back of the bunkhouse. *That lazy son of a bitch is going to get it one of these days, and I would love to be the one to give it to him too.* He lifted his arm and smelled his armpit. Damn he stunk. He needed a dunk in the river.

He was almost to the bunkhouse, when he spotted Angel in the kitchen window. He stopped to watch her. His cock twitched, and his eyes took on a lustful glaze. He licked his lips, wanting nothing more than to feast on her unwilling body. His hands fisted into tight balls. His whole body vibrated. He wanted her so bad he could taste it. The back door swung open, and John's son came running toward him. Not wanting to get caught staring at Angel, he pretended to be looking at something up in the sky.

The boy stopped in front of him. "Whatcha lookin' at mister?"

"Now don't ya think that cloud up there looks like a big wagon wheel?" he asked, pointing to no cloud in particular.

Ben stared up at the cloud. "Can you see, mister? That cloud ain't even round."

"I hear you're gettin' a new ma."

He watched the kid's reaction.

"Yeah, I guess so."

"You don't seem too happy about that." He suppressed a grin, as he saw the perfect opportunity with this little brat.

"Well, she ain't that bad. I I..."

"You don't want her here," Boyd finished for him, "she's not your ma."

Ben stared at him.

He ruffled the boy's hair, and led him away from the house and any prying eyes. "I used to have a mother too, but she died."

"She did?" He hung his head. "So did mine."

Boyd ignored him. He didn't care about the kid's dead mother. All he cared about was Angel. "Yeah, she died when I was about your age."

"But you had your Pa, right?"

"Not for long. He married a mean old hag not a year later. She had me doing the laundry, washing dishes, and dusting." He whined. Inside he was rejoicing at his luck on finding this dumb kid to believe his lies and help him capture Angel.

"Those are girly chores," Ben said making a face.

"Yup, they were. And you know what the worst part was?"

He knelt down beside Ben. They were far enough away from the house now that no one would see them.

"What?"

"My Pa didn't have any time for me after he married her."

Ben sat down on the grass. He plucked a blade and stared hard at it.

"I bet your Pa will do the same thing. I know how you can stop that though."

"You do?"

"Yup, but I don't know if you're old enough."

"I'll be eight this spring," Ben told him, sitting up taller.

"Well, I guess I could tell ya, on one condition. You don't tell anybody we talked." He glared at Ben, offering the kid a hint at how it would be if he didn't heed his warning. "No one knows I'm helping you."

"I can do that. I won't tell anyone. I promise."

"Okay, I think the best way to get rid of your new ma, is to scare her off the ranch."

Ben leaned in to hear more.

CHAPTER EIGHT

It was Friday, and Livy had been on the ranch almost a week. She stood inside the front door sweeping the dust out onto the porch. A smile touched her lips. Her time with Ezekiel had been paying off, and she could now make pancakes that weren't salty, but were fluffy and melted in your mouth. Ben's syrup messed face told her he approved, and the empty plates this morning proved John liked them too.

So far she'd been able to avoid much contact with John's daughter, and she thought every day about Emma. Most times it was difficult to get out of bed in the morning, hard to keep living. She craved the busy days, to take her mind off her thoughts of Emma. But when she closed her eyes at night they'd be there, waiting to haunt her until morning.

She gently touched her nose. It was still tender. The bruise, a soft yellow now, had almost disappeared. Broom in hand, she went out onto the porch and was amazed by the vast land before her. This country sure is beautiful, she sighed. The yellow fields glistened in the hot afternoon sun. She watched the tall, skinny stocks dance back and forth in the light breeze.

A rocking chair sat at the end of the porch, and she plopped down onto the hard seat. She placed the broom up against the rail. Her feet moved the chair back and forth at a slow, steady pace. Eyes closed, she inhaled the fresh air. She must be getting used to the awful smell of the cows, for today she didn't notice it. Today, she inhaled good, clean air.

"Howdy, Ma'am."

She opened her eyes and saw a cowboy standing on the other side of the porch below her.

"Can I help you?" she eyed him. He reminded her of John. Tall, muscular and wide. Except, she thought as she still studied him, his expression held no arrogance. In its place was a friendly smile.

"Name's Clive, I'm the foreman on the T-Bar," he said, with a bit of a drawl.

Although she was still unsure of the stranger, she stood and walked to the edge of the porch. "I'm Livy."

He offered her his hand, but she didn't reach out and shake it. Instead she placed her hands behind her back. "My...my hands are dirty," she lied. Whether it was a handshake or a hug, she never let a man touch her. Those simple gestures could lead to so much more.

He raised a blonde eyebrow while smiling at her. "It's nice to meet you."

She didn't return his smile. "Have you worked here long?"

"'Bout three years. Where ya from?"

The question caught her off guard, and it took her a moment to reply. "I'm from down south."

"I've traveled down there some."

Livy thought she was in the clear, until he asked.

"Where did you say down south?"

"Fort McLeod area." Her voice shook, and her arms covered in goose bumps as she fidgeted from one foot to the other. *Please don't let him recognize me from the saloon there*. She saw no need to mention her life before in Great Falls, where the nightmare she'd been living had begun.

"Been there a time or two. Nice place." He stared at her face for a long time. "Well, I'd better get back to work."

She nodded.

Tipping his Stetson, he turned and left, whistling on his way.

She blew out the breath she'd been holding and pushed against the railing. For a moment she thought he'd recognized her. She took another calming breath. It was times like this she was glad she went by her middle name, instead of "Angel the Songbird." As she watched Clive walk back to one of the barns, an uneasy feeling crept up her spine and the hairs on the back of her neck stood.

She spun around to see if someone was behind her on the porch. She was alone. Someone was watching her—she could feel it. She brought her hand up to shade her eyes and stared out into the field.

"Quit being so silly," she scolded, and her body shivered.

Her hands damp, and she flexed her fingers allowing the hot air to dry them. *Clive upset you, that's all it was*. She turned to go back inside the house when she heard John call out to her. She waited to see what he wanted. As he approached, she noticed how his blue shirt covered his muscled arms as if the cotton had been painted on. His hat was pulled low to shade his eyes from the bright August sun, and she couldn't help but wonder what it might feel like to be loved by this man.

"Came to see if you'd like to go for a ride." His gaze followed the length of her body then returned to her face.

She crossed her arms. "Just the two of us?"

"Yup, you and me."

She hesitated. What would happen when they were alone? Would John take advantage of her? She stared down at him. His smile seemed genuine, and so far he hadn't done anything to make her uncomfortable. She frowned. Other than a few nights ago when she'd almost kissed him. But she didn't want to think about that right now, or she'd high-tail it back inside the house to hide in her room.

No, he said they were going for a ride, so that meant she'd have her own horse and he'd be on his. No touching. She took a deep breath. She could do this.

"Okay, I'll come along." She fought off the urge to flee. *No, this is a good opportunity to get away from the house and see some of the ranch.*

"I'll tell Rusty to saddle a horse for you, while you go grab a hat."

"I don't have a riding hat." She reached behind her and grabbed the long braid that hung down her back.

"There's a few hangin' on the peg at the back door, use one of them."

His usual arrogance gone, she found that she was almost excited to spend a few hours alone with the man that, after tomorrow, would be her husband.

"I'll meet you round back," he said, and sauntered away.

John headed over to the tack house. Two of his men were shoving each other, and he could tell a fight was about to start. Rusty was laughing, as one of the hands he didn't recognize gripped him by the collar, his arm back ready to strike.

"Whoa, what the hell is going on here?" he asked. Thinking a moment, he recalled the hand's name, Boyd. The cowboy was quiet, and most times stayed to himself. John had never talked to the man, but as long as he did what he was told and pulled his weight, he didn't much care if he could carry on a conversation or not.

Boyd's chest heaved in and out. "Rusty put mud in my good boots."

John looked over at Rusty, who continued to laugh. The man was a practical joker. He'd moved the outhouse three weeks ago in the middle of the night. John grimaced. Poor old Ken was a mess when he fell into the shit hole. Rusty had never played his tricks on John, and he was thankful. Boyd was choking Rusty now, and John pushed them a part. "Okay, enough. Rusty I need you to saddle a horse for Miss Green. Boyd, go and clean out your boots."

"This ain't over," Boyd said and walked away.

Rusty snickered. "It was a good one, Boss." He plucked a piece of hay and stuck it into his mouth. "Boyd will be cleanin' them boots for a while."

"Yeah, yeah, but you may want to ease up on the jokes Rusty. It's no way to make friends."

"I suppose," he said thoughtfully.

John patted him on the back. "By the way, make sure you saddle the mare in the far stall."

"Sure thing, Boss."

"Lead the horse out front of the barn. I'll grab it in a minute."

The other man nodded, and John went to find Ezekiel. He needed to ask him if he could watch Ben and Emily for a few hours while he took Livy for a ride. He'd meant to go riding alone, but when he'd seen Clive talking with her, he changed his mind, marched over and invited her to come along. He shook his head as he rounded the corner of the cook shack. Ezekiel stood outside, hands deep in suds, as he scrubbed out one of his pots.

The other man smiled when he saw John approach. "Boss."

"Ezekiel, could you watch Emily and Ben for me for the rest of the afternoon? I'm taking Miss Green for a ride." He hoped the cook wasn't so busy that he wouldn't be able to do him the favor.

"That'd be fine." His large dark hands placed the cloth over the metal container he used as a sink, and his full lips tilted into a smirk. "I could use a break anyway."

"Much appreciated."

"Any time, Boss."

He'd come to think of Ezekiel as more than one of his hired hands. He had often relied on him to watch Ben and Emily after their Ma had died, and when Alice couldn't get away. Walking back to get Livy's horse, he watched as a few of his men fixed the gate on a corral.

The mare he had asked Rusty to saddle for Livy was tied to the fence, and chomping on some grass. His own horse, a black stallion named Midnight had meandered close by. He smelled the mare, John was sure.

Grabbing Midnight's reins, he pulled the animal's head close, "Don't even think about it."

Midnight shook his head and grunted, stomping his front hooves on the ground.

"You heard me fella, not today." He held his horse close until he settled down. Still holding Midnight's reins, he went over to grab Livy's horse and lead her to the back of the house.

She was waiting for him on the back step. Her blue dress contrasted with the brown cowboy hat that sat lopsided on top of her head. Her brown hair hung in a long braid, draped over her front shoulder. She was a sight—that was for sure. She stood out like a three-eared rabbit, and not in a bad way.

"Ready?" He offered her his hand. She reached out, and he noticed her hands shaking before she clasped onto the horn of the saddle. He helped her onto the mare. Her body stiffened under his touch, and he knew she was uncomfortable. She wasn't heavy, not that he was surprised. Her waist was so tiny he was sure he could wrap both his hands around it.

"Ever ride before?" he swung up onto his own horse.

"A bit."

"Well, it ain't too hard. Pull on the left rein to go left and the right to go right." He gestured with his own ropes, "If you want to go fast, dig your heels into her side and lay low. But don't forget to hang on."

She bobbed her head.

"Got it?"

"I think so."

"I'll take it nice and slow, till you get the swing of things." He clicked his tongue and the black horse trotted off. The mare followed suit.

They rode for over a half hour at a slow, steady pace. He was determined to let her get the feel of the horse. When he glanced back at her, she sat stiff in the saddle, her body not moving in rhythm with the horse's steps.

"If you don't move with the horse, you'll be sore tomorrow."

He saw that she tried to do as he'd told her. Relaxing a bit, her hips rocked back and forth with the animal's gait. He'd held his own horse back, and could tell Midnight needed to run. Stallions were bred for that, and his was no different. He gave Livy a few more minutes to get her bearings before he called out to her, "You ready for a real ride now?"

"I think so," she said.

He dug his heels into Midnight and let him go. The stallion took off like lightning.

"Yee haw," he yelled. He'd gone a fair distance before he turned and saw her galloping behind him. Back straight again, she bounced up and down as the horse galloped toward him. He chuckled. She'd be sore tomorrow. No horse could match Midnight's speed, so he pulled on the reins to slow him down a bit and let her catch up. A bright smile adorned her pretty face, and he couldn't believe how it transformed her rigid features.

"This is great," she shouted over the clopping of horse's hooves.

He was about to answer her when he saw the look of terror in her eyes. Then she disappeared from his sight. He pulled hard on the reins, and waited for his horse to stop before he scanned the field. The mare was running full tilt for the hill. Livy was not in the saddle.

His stomach in his throat, he frantically searched for her. He blew out a breath when he saw a blue flutter on the ground. He dug his heels into the stallion's sides.

"Yaw, yaw, go boy."

Midnight took off toward her. Before the horse had a chance to stop, John jumped from its back, ran toward her, and slid onto his knees before her. She lay on her side, a crumpled mess. He placed his fingers on her neck and checked for a pulse. "Thank God," he breathed, when he felt it.

He looked her over, glad that no bones were protruding from her frail body. Another wave of relief washed over him. He took his time turning her over. Her right cheek had a nasty scrape, but he couldn't tell how deep it was because of all the dirt and blood that covered it. Both her nostrils bled, and she had cut her forehead above her left eyebrow. He let his hands roam over her body to check if anything was broken.

Coming to, she moaned.

"It's gonna be okay darlin'. I want to make sure nothin's broken." He continued his examination. Lifting her skirt, he felt her left leg first. She called out and then whimpered. He put his hand on her shoulder and lightly rubbed it.

"Okay, honey, I won't touch there anymore." He wasn't sure if the leg—already swollen and bruised—was broken, and he didn't want to touch her again to find out. Instead he went to her other leg and felt from her thigh to her toes. Nothing seemed out of place, and she showed no signs of pain.

He blew out a breath and continued to examine her. Her hips seemed fine, so he moved up to her ribs as she lay beneath him. He gazed down at her tear-streaked face and dirty cheeks. The sight of her tore at his heart.

"Does this hurt?" He touched her shoulders. He moved his hands down the side of each arm.

She slowly shook her head.

"Just the leg then?" he asked, needing to be sure.

She nodded.

She seemed dazed, and he was sure she had a concussion. Worried she could have internal injuries as well, he worked out a plan to get her back to the ranch.

"I'll be right back, lie still." He mounted Midnight and took off toward a stand of trees he'd seen earlier. There he searched for two long sturdy sticks. When he returned, she was passed out again, and he bent to check her pulse. Satisfied she was still alive, he went about making a splint for her leg.

John rummaged through his saddle bags and pulled out an old blanket. He ripped the cloth into short strips, then placed the wood on either side of her leg and tied them together. She moaned and tossed her head from side to side. He tried to be gentle, but knew that with some injuries, it didn't matter how careful you were, they hurt like hell anyway. Once he had her leg wrapped, he woke her.

"Livy." He nudged her. "Livy, I'm gonna lift you onto my horse."

She frowned.

"I know it hurts, darlin',' but I need to get you back to the ranch."

Green eyes stared up at him, and he wished he could do more for her. Wished it was him lying there and not her. With the splints on either side of her injured knee, her leg stuck straight out and he maneuvered his position a few times in order not to hurt her. With his left arm under her butt and the other cradling her back, he lifted her.

She howled in pain.

"Shush, I'm sorry, sweetheart." His lips brushed her temple. "I'll be putting you on Midnight now." He held her higher and gently sat her sideways on the stallion's back.

Her face twisted in pain, and John knew it was his fault she had fallen. He shouldn't have let the stallion run. Why did he take her along? Why did she let go of the reins, especially when he'd told her not to? He shook his head. The blame wasn't hers, it was his, and when she was better, he'd tell her he was sorry. He leapt up with ease behind her and wrapped his long arms around her waist.

"Lean against me," he told her, waiting until she was somewhat comfortable before he continued. "We'll ride nice and slow, so try and relax. It'll take us a while before we get back to the ranch."

She squeezed her eyes shut and bit her lower lip. He was a selfish ass. His stomach rolled. The pain must be unbearable for her. At a loss to help her, he clicked his tongue and the stallion set out in a steady, rhythmic gait.

Livy's leg hurt like hell, and she wished she'd pass out again. The pain was too much. Every step the horse took almost sent her over the edge. She was uncomfortable, but didn't dare move an inch. Her knee felt as if someone dug a knife into it, and left it there, twisting it every few minutes.

Her face felt swollen, the skin tight around her left eye and her mouth. Her head was pounding, and it was a chore to even blink. Just when she'd been able to touch her nose again without sending a jolt of pain up her face, she went and fell off a damn horse. Dizzy and tired, she closed her eyes. Resting her head on John's chest, she hoped the ride back to the ranch would end soon.

John had never been so glad to see the ranch house as he was right now. He glanced down at her, asleep in his arms. She'd been out cold most of the ride.

They would've gotten here sooner if he hadn't stopped to let Midnight have a break. The stallion wasn't used to carrying two for such a long time, and he deserved extra oats for pulling through.

He brought the horse to the front porch and called for Ezekiel. The man appeared through the front door, but his smile disappeared when he saw Livy on top of John's horse.

"Go get Shorty." John told him. He slid off his horse and carried her inside. He took the stairs two at a time, kicked her bedroom door open, and laid her on the bed.

"Is—is she dead Pa?" Ben asked. He stood in the doorway holding his sister's hand, the same wide-eyed expression on both their faces.

John left Livy's side to go talk to his children. "She fell off her horse."

"Is she gonna be all right?" Ben asked, trying to peer around his father to look at Livy.

John's hand came to rest on his shoulder. "I hope so, Son."

Ezekiel and Shorty came bounding up the steps, Clive close behind them. Shorty, named for his height, was the one who fixed up the hands on the ranch. John had seen him do everything from stitches, to setting broken bones, to nursing a cowboy who fell ill with pneumonia. He trusted him.

"What happened, Boss?" Shorty asked, leaning over Livy, his head to her chest. Ezekiel took the children downstairs.

"She fell off the mare while we were at a full run."

John's gut clenched, why did he let the horses run? He asked that question a dozen times on their way back to the ranch, and he still had no answer.

"Where's the mare now?" Clive asked.

"She took off toward the east quarter section, near the line shack." John said.

"I'll go find her." Clive hurried to the door.

John stood on the opposite side of the bed as Shorty. While Livy slept, he watched as Shorty pulled up her skirt to examine her leg. Without being asked, he bent to help untie the strips and remove the wooden splints on either side of her knee. They unwound the ripped fabric, careful not to cause her any more pain. Once they were done, Shorty began his assessment of her leg. Thorough hands moved up and down, steering clear of the swollen knee.

"I'll need you to hold her," he told John.

Livy let out a cry and almost jerked off the bed when Shorty pushed on her knee. John went to her, pressing down gently on her shoulders to keep her from falling off the bed.

"You might've given me a chance to get to her before you started pushin' on her leg."

John glared at his friend.

0

Shorty didn't answer him, and he didn't care—he was busy trying to keep Livy on the bed.

"It's almost over, sweetheart," he assured her, while Shorty pressed and poked at her knee.

John watched as she bit her lower lip and squeezed her eyes shut. Tears flowed down the sides of her face and disappeared into the pillow.

"I'm done for now," Shorty said.

"Well, is it broken?"

Shorty shook his head. "It's dislocated." He glanced down at Livy, passed out again from the pain, her head lulled to the side on the pillow. "I'll have to put it back in place."

"You're sure?"

"Yes. Give her this to bite on." He broke a piece of wood from the splints John had used and handed it to him.

John swallowed and his stomach turned at what lay ahead.

"This is going to hurt like hell," Shorty mumbled.

John opened Livy's mouth, coaxing the stick inside.

Shorty climbed up onto the bed. Placing one knee on either side of Livy's leg, he positioned his hands on her. "Ready?"

"As ready as I'm gonna be." John sprawled across Livy's chest, holding her down once again. Shorty yanked hard on her calf. Her eyes shot open, she tossed her head, bucked beneath him, and screamed as she bit down on the wood in her mouth.

Shorty ran his hand up to her knee, grabbed it, and pulled once more. They heard the loud *pop*, and she went limp under John. He glanced over at Shorty whose nod told him the knee was back in place.

Off of the bed now and looking harried, Shorty's chest rose and fell as he tried to catch his breath. "We need to wrap her knee tight. Do you have an old sheet we can use?"

He went to his room and ripped the sheet from his bed. There were no spares, but he'd sleep without one for her. Back in Livy's room, they tore the sheet into strips and wound it around her knee.

"She may have a concussion. We don't know how hard she hit her head," Shorty told him.

Relieved, John asked his next question, "What about internally?"

"I don't know, but time will tell us that. Watch for fever, unusual bruising, or if she's in any other pain other than her leg."

"What then?"

"Let's hope we don't have to find out." He placed a pillow under her knee. "You're going to have to elevate her leg to bring the swelling down."

"I can do that."

"Give her a teaspoon of this if the pain's too much for her." He pulled out a brown bottle from his bag, and set it on the table beside the bed. "I'll be back to check on her in the morning. Come get me if things get worse."

"Thanks, Shorty."

"Don't thank me yet, Boss." He gave Livy one last look, and left the room.

John dipped a cloth into a basin of cool water and began wiping the blood from her cheek and nose. This was the second time in a week he'd cared for her. The first was when she ran into the wall after seeing him naked in the tub. That was funny, but this was serious.

Once he'd gotten most of the blood off her face, he ripped her tattered, bloodied dress away, leaving nothing but her chemise on. He pulled the sheet over her, leaving her knee exposed, and placed two pillows under it as Shorty instructed. Livy stirred, but did not wake up. He didn't know how long he'd been sitting with her before Ezekiel came in.

"I can sit with her Boss, while you go down and eat."

"Ben and Emily?" He'd forgotten about them until now.

"I've put the young 'uns to bed."

He ran his hand through his hair and sighed. "Thanks."

"No thanks needed. It was my pleasure." He came over to stand beside John. "Now you go get some food in you, while I sit with Miss Livy."

John glanced over at her. "You come get me if she wakes up." He needed to eat if he was going to sit with her all night.

"That I will Boss, that I will." Ezekiel took his seat and turned his attention to Livy.

He checked on Ben and Emily. They were fast asleep. He bent and kissed each one before he headed downstairs. When he entered the kitchen he was surprised to see Clive sitting at the table with a plate of food in front of him.

"How she doin'?" he asked, his mouth full.

"She has a bad sprain."

John grabbed a plate, dished up the chicken pot pie Ezekiel had made, and sat down across from Clive.

"Found the mare."

"That's good."

"Not really. Took us a while to find the saddle. The cinch was cut."

His fork half way to his mouth, he said, "What did you say?"

"I said someone cut the strap on the saddle."

"What?"

"John. Who saddled that horse?"

He dropped his fork and stood up so fast his chair flew back and crashed onto the floor. "Rusty." He was out the door and down the steps in seconds.

"John," Clive yelled after him.

He didn't remember crossing the yard to the bunkhouse. He was in a rage when he threw open the door and shouted for Rusty.

The other man stood up clumsily from his bunk. "Yeah, Boss?"

He headed straight for Rusty, grabbed his shirt and pushed him up against the wall. "You son of a bitch, you've played your last trick."

Eyes filled with fear, Rusty stammered, "I...I don't know what you're talkin' about Boss."

John thrust him against the wall, making it rattle. "I'm talkin' about that horse you saddled today for Miss Green. The cinch on the saddle let loose. She fell and is hurt. She could've died because of you and your damn jokes." His hand came up, clutching Rusty's neck, choking him.

"I...didn't," Rusty tried to say, gasping for air. "I...mean...I...wouldn't... play...a...trick...on...you." His fingers clawed at John's hand around his throat. "I...checked...the....saddle...everything...was...good."

"Don't lie to me." His other hand came back ready to punch him, when someone grabbed John's arm and hauled him back.

"John, calm down. Let him talk." It was Clive. His arm against John's chest, he held him away from a terrified Rusty.

John pushed Clive aside.

"You better not be lyin' or you'll not only have John to deal with, but me too," Clive said.

Rusty rubbed his neck, his voice shaking, "I ain't lyin'. I'd never play a joke on a lady. I checked that saddle. I checked the cinch, honest."

"You're full of shit. You played one of your tricks earlier," John barked.

Rusty's eyes filled up with tears. "I'd never hurt anyone."

The bunkhouse was quiet as all the hands listened. John's chest heaved in and out as he glared at Rusty, every muscle in his body tense. "Pack your things and be gone by morning."

"John, aren't you bein' too harsh?" Clive tried to reason.

"No." His dark gaze studied all of the men in the room. "Let his mistake be a lesson to all of you that I won't stand for screw ups like these on my ranch. Not when my family is concerned and definitely not when someone could've been killed." John pushed past Clive and stormed out of the bunkhouse, slamming the door behind him.

He was furious. He trusted those men, trusted Rusty. He wound up and punched the side of the barn, smashing his fist through the wood, and knocking red paint flakes onto the ground. Pain sliced up his arm, and his hand throbbed.

"Son of a bitch," he yelled, cradling his arm close to his chest.

He thought about what he had done, and he felt like shit. He wanted to believe that Rusty hadn't played another one of his pranks. But he wasn't sure. He shook his head. Hell, he wasn't sure of anything lately.

He thought he saw the truth in his eyes, but having no choice, he had to make an example of him. He had to let his men know that he wouldn't put up with these kinds of mistakes on his ranch.

"Damn it." He brought his arm back to hit the barn again, but thought better of it, and instead squeezed his hand together. He welcomed the pain, and watched the blood drip down his forearm. If Rusty had checked the saddle and it had been fine like he'd said, then what the hell happened? Did someone tamper with it? One thing was sure, he would damn well find out.

CHAPTER NINE

Boyd watched as the boss stormed into the bunkhouse, yelling Rusty's name. Stepping back into the corner, he watched the scene unfold. By the look on John Taylor's face he was out for blood and to Boyd's pleasure, it was Rusty's.

The bunkhouse grew quiet, and all eyes were on the two men. John threw his shoulder into Rusty knocking him into the wall, and he had to restrain from jumping with joy. He never liked Rusty. He always seemed to get the easy jobs around the ranch, while he and some of the others got the harder, longer ones. Most nights when he'd come in sore and hungry after a long day out in the field, Rusty would be licking his fingers having finished his meal, or—even worse—lying fast asleep on his cot.

But as he listened closer, he realized that the boss was accusing Rusty of putting a bad cinch on Angel's mare. He smiled. Rusty had saddled the mare—he had watched him do it. But none of them knew that the boy had frayed the strap so she'd fall. Boyd had planned to wait in the bushes to attack Angel, but was stopped cold when he saw John riding alongside her.

Damn. The boy never said anything about that. Little weasel. He would have a few words with him, next time they crossed paths. He needed to think of another scheme for the kid.

Annoyed that his plan had been cut short, he couldn't get the images of Angel's naked and writhing body out of his head. He kept re-playing their one night together. He desperately needed to touch her. He needed to have her. He was delirious with want, and his cock grew hard while he stood in the shadows of the bunkhouse. Angel didn't know he was on the ranch, and he would use that to his advantage.

Clive was pulling John off of Rusty now, and the boss didn't look too pleased about it. He snickered when he saw Rusty almost cry. What a whinin' fool. A pitiful sight if he had ever seen one. He couldn't even stand up for himself. He could've clapped when the boss fired the baby, all too glad to see him go.

John had left the bunkhouse, but first he warned them all not to make the same mistake as Rusty. He didn't care what Taylor said. The threat did nothing to alter his plan.

He glanced over at Rusty, who was shaking hands with Clive. The men sauntered over to say their goodbyes, and he thought he'd better go too, even if he didn't want to.

Rusty glanced up at him, while he packed his gear. They'd never gotten along. "Come to say goodbye too, Boyd?"

He wanted to spit in his face. "Too bad you were so careless."

"Go to hell, Boyd."

Not before you.

"You know damn well I didn't do nothin' to that saddle," Rusty jammed a pair of denims into his bag.

He scanned the room to make sure no one heard their conversation. "Guess you should've checked the cinch."

"I did check it," he snapped.

"You should always check twice, you never know what could happen around here."

"What are you talking about?" Rusty asked confused.

Boyd gave him a knowing smile and shrugged. "All I'm sayin' is you can't trust everyone around here." He didn't like the way Rusty was eyeing him, and he needed to get away before he said anymore.

"Do you know somethin' Boyd?"

"Nope I don't," he sneered.

Lying on his bed, he listened for Rusty to gather his stuff and leave. He waited until everyone was asleep, and then slipped out of the bunkhouse to follow him.

CHAPTER TEN

Emma lay on the bed kicking her infant feet while she screamed. Angel picked up her daughter and held her cheek to hers. She was hot. Too hot. Her face beet red, and her blonde spiky hair drenched in sweat. Angel paced the floor while she bounced her daughter in her arms.

"Shush baby, it's okay, Mama's here."

Emma screamed louder, her breath leaving a sour smell in the air.

Angel had taken her to see the doctor earlier that day. He'd told her Emma had Scarlet Fever, which explained the rash on her body. He'd also said that there was nothing that could be done, other than to bathe her every few hours and hope the fever broke.

Angel filled the basin with cool water for the fourth time and stripped Emma from her damp nightshirt. She laid her in the large bowl. Her tiny body tightened, and her arms flailed about splashing water all over. Angel's heart ached with every beat it took. She ran the damp cloth over Emma's cheeks and hair once more as she tried to bring the fever down.

She bit her lower lip hard, and wept, "Emma please…please get better."

"Quiet that baby down." Miles banged on the door.

Miles let Angel rent one of the upstairs bedrooms in the Glass Slipper. He allowed Emma there too as long as they were quiet and didn't interrupt the other girls while they were with their clients. The arrangement had worked, until yesterday, when Emma got sick.

"Sorry Miles, Emma's real sick," she called through the door, picking Emma up out of the water and wrapping a thin blanket around her wet body.

"I don't care. Keep her quiet, or you'll both have to find somewhere else to sleep tonight."

She heard him leave, his footsteps heavy on the stairs as he went down them. She paced the length of the room, her daughter wailing in her arms.

"Hush my darling, mama's here."

Emma coughed, and her pudgy hands wiped at her tired eyes. Angel unbuttoned her blouse and tried to feed her, but she turned her head and screamed louder. She hadn't eaten in two days, and Angel worried she'd starve to death. There were no tears on her cheeks, even though she had cried most of the night. A white film coated her lips and tongue. The doctor told her that those were signs of dehydration, and she grew frantic as she tried to push Emma's lips to her breast.

"Eat baby," she begged, but Emma merely whimpered, refusing to suckle.

Angel grasped the cool cloth beside her and placed it on Emma's forehead. Angel tried to quiet her, but her little girl kept right on screaming. Every so often her tiny body would stiffen. She'd hold her breath and then let out a shriek so loud that Angel was terrified.

Sobbing now, Angel let the tears flow freely down her own cheeks. How was she to help her little girl? How could she make her better? She was lost, and didn't know what else to do. Exhausted, her legs no longer able to hold her up, Angel lay on the bed, Emma cradled beside her, mewling, her body listless. Her little girl was burning up. The cloth no longer cold, she removed it from her daughter's face.

"God, please make my baby better," she prayed, kissing the top of Emma's head.

Not knowing what else to do, she hummed a lullaby until they fell asleep.

Angel awoke in the night. Something was wrong. The room was black, the lamp having burned out. She searched the bed for Emma. Her hand rested on her chest. She was cold and still. Angel gave her a little shake. Nothing. Terror seized her, and she hastily lit the lamp beside the bed. When she gazed down at her daughter, a lamenting moan that she did not recognize as her own was followed by a blood curdling scream. Emma was dead.

John was beside her in seconds, as horror erupted on her face.

"No, no, no," she moaned. "Not her, please God, not her."

Livy thrashed on the bed, rolling from side to side. He held her down, afraid she'd hurt herself. She began to cry, and then to sob—a wrenching sound, from deep within her soul.

John had to wipe a tear from his own eye as he watched her body convulse. Her face contorted in misery, and his heart twisted in pain for her. He wondered what had happened in her life to cause her such agony. Without hesitating, he laid down beside her, took her in his arms, and held her until she slept calmly again.

CHAPTER ELEVEN

Livy woke to the sound of rain on her bedroom window. Shivering, she pulled on the blanket, but something heavy lay across her chest. She opened her eyes and was mortified to see John beside her.

His arm draped over her and his hand rested on her breast. She pushed his arm away, the sudden movement sending a jolt of pain up her leg. Biting her lip, she tried to stifle the moan that escaped past her lips as she inched away from him. He stirred beside her, and she slumped onto her pillow, shut her eyes, and pretended to sleep.

"I know you're awake," he said, his voice groggy from sleep. He stretched his long thick arms above his head and yawned, then snuggled back into her.

She stiffened.

"Could you please get out of my bed, Mr. Taylor?" she asked, even though she was unsure if she wanted him to go. Surprisingly, she felt safe and warm with him beside her.

"Just practicing for the real thing." He opened his mouth wide to yawn a second time. Then laying his arm on her stomach, he made small circles with his fingertips.

Her body gave a tiny shiver as her most precious place began to ache. "Stop that." She pushed at his arm. But he didn't move. Instead his circles grew wider and wider, torturing her. Long fingers skimmed the bottom of her breasts sending a shock wave rippling through her body. Her nipples hardened from his touch. Afraid of what might happen next, she bolted up. Groaning, she dived for her knee as it pulsed.

He was bare-chested, wearing only his pants. She couldn't help but gawk at him half naked beside her. His hard chest was carved with tight, bronzed muscles. It wasn't until she stared into his heated eyes that she realized she wasn't wearing her dress from the day before. She wore her chemise, which was thin from wear, and she was sure he could see through it. She yanked on the sheet to cover her chest.

"How did this…?"

"I took your dress off last night," he told her, no hint of an apology on his lips.

"I could've slept in it for goodness sake."

He shook his head while he got up and began buttoning his shirt. He motioned to her swollen leg. "Had to keep an eye on that knee, and I couldn't do it with all that frill and lace you had goin' on with that thing you call a dress."

"Really," she huffed. "I'm sorry you find my attire inappropriate for a *ranch.*"

"Never said that." He went to her dresser, dunked his hands in the basin and splashed water on his face and hair. Instead of reaching for a cloth, he shook his head like a wet dog, splattering water all over the wall. "That felt good." He winked at her.

"Get out." She pointed to the door. In doing so, she pushed the sheet onto her lap.

He laid his hand on his heart. "Why, Miss Green, you've hurt my feelings." His gaze came to rest on her chest. The displaced sheet gave him a clear view of her cleavage, and she scrambled to bring the blanket back up.

"I've taken care of you all night. Even slept beside you, and we're not even married yet." He batted his dark lashes. "I do believe you've compromised me."

She threw her pillow at him. "Get out of my bedroom."

John picked the pillow up off of the floor. He brought it to his face and inhaled loudly. "Mmmm, smells just like you, piss and vinegar."

Her mouth dropped open. "You…you." If her leg hadn't been so sore, she'd have gotten up and given him a swift kick in the ass.

He stalked toward her. His eyes, dark and dangerous, stared straight into her own. Afraid, she sunk back into the bed. "What am I?" he asked. "Gallant? Handsome?" He was an inch from her face now and she could feel his warm breath on her cheek.

She glared at him.

"Do I make you forget yourself when I'm near?"

"You do make me feel something," she told him sweetly.

The corner of his mouth curved up and he gave her a cocky smile. "Oh yeah? What's that, sweetheart?"

She batted her eyes, mimicking his earlier behavior. "Sick."

A scowl formed on his tanned face, and Livy thought she'd pushed him too far when he muttered, "You ungrateful little wench." Then angling his head, he kissed her.

His lips were soft as they moved over hers. His tongue licked at her bottom lip, probing to get inside. She couldn't help the low moan that escaped past her lips, and he deepened the kiss. His hand came to rest on her cheek and his thumb stroked her soft skin. Her arms circled his neck and her lips began to move with his, when he pulled from her.

Breathing hard, he whispered against her moist lips, "You, Miss Green, are a liar."

She was still thinking of their kiss when she heard his rude comment. Stunned, she stared back at him. Anger replaced her shock, and without thinking she slapped him hard across the face. "Get the hell out of my room."

"You know, I don't like liars."

She went to strike him a second time, but he was too fast for her. He held her wrist with his massive hand. "Once was enough," he growled.

"Once is never enough." She yanked her arm from his grasp.

He reached for his hat. "Tsk, tsk."

"Go to hell." Tears threatened to fall.

"Have yourself a good day, Miss Green. I know I will."

Whistling, he strolled away.

She buried her face into her pillow and screamed. Oh how she hated that man. How dare he touch her? How dare he think she encouraged him? And what gave him the right to kiss her like that? She fell back against her pillow, and winced as pain sliced through her knee. She ground her teeth. The next time that mule tried to kiss her, she'd bite his damn tongue off!

John came down the stairs, happy and refreshed. Ezekiel stood at the table dishing up bacon and eggs for Ben and Emily.

"How's Miss Livy?" Ezekiel asked.

"She's fine. Back to her old self," he said.

"That's good to hear. Maybe I'll take her up some breakfast."

"I think she'd like that." He dug into his own bacon and eggs.

Someone knocked on the back door and before anyone could get up to open it, Clive strode in.

"Was wonderin' when you'd get out of bed," he said to John.

"Well, I thought I'd make you work for a change."

Clive dished up a plate and sat down. "Rusty's gone."

"Figured as much." He picked up the coffee Ezekiel had placed in front of him and took a sip.

"I believed him, John."

He'd thought of the man last night, and still felt guilty for having to fire him. "I did too. But you know I had no choice in the matter."

"What happened to your hand?"

John had forgotten all about his hand, and glanced down at the bandage he'd wrapped around it. "Had a run in with the barn last night."

Clive stared at his arm. "If not Rusty, then who would want to hurt Livy?"

"Been askin' myself that same question all night."

"Come up with anything?"

"Nope." He glanced up at Clive. "You?"

"Haven't a clue."

"One thing I can't stop thinkin' about is why someone cut that cinch?"

"Thought of that too and don't rightly know."

"Well, we'll have to keep a close eye out," he said taking a bite of his breakfast. "No one can be trusted, not anymore."

"I agree."

John glanced over at Ben beside him and noticed his plate had been untouched. The bacon and eggs were moved around and mashed together. "Not hungry, Ben?"

"Not really. My stomach hurts." Ben kept his eyes on his plate.

John felt his son's forehead. He wasn't warm. "Well, maybe you should stay in the house today. You can help Miss Livy if she needs anything."

The boy's eyes watered, and his bottom lip shook.

John could see he was about to cry, and nudged his shoulder. "Livy will be all right son. She needs to lie in bed for a few days."

He smiled down at his boy.

Ben gave a quick nod. His head down, he wiped his eyes.

They finished the rest of their meal in silence. He kissed Ben and Emily goodbye. "Remember to watch out for Miss Livy today."

"I'll take good care of her Pa," Ben assured him, "I promise."

"Me too, me too," Emily hopped up and down.

John knelt in front of her. "Yes, you too Angel." He kissed her on the nose before heading outside to work.

Livy could smell her breakfast before Ezekiel came through the door. The steaming plate looked appetizing, and she was famished.

"Mornin', ma'am. Me and the young'uns came to bring you your breakfast."

She hadn't seen Ben and his sister, and peered around the black man to see where they were.

"They went to pick you some flowers," he answered.

Touched by their thoughtfulness, a knot formed in her throat. Ezekiel set the tray on her lap, and she smelled the bacon and eggs. "Mmm, I think you out did yourself Ezekiel," she said.

His hand swatted the air. "Ah, ma'am, don't go sayin' stuff like that."

"It's true, and I can't wait to eat all of it." She smiled up at him, the gesture coming easier to her.

The girl ran into the room. Ben arrived at a much slower pace. Both carried handfuls of daisies, lilacs, and roses.

"Here, Miss Livy," Ben said, extending his hand to pass her the flowers.

"Thank you," she said, smiling at Ben as she took them. "I love flowers."

"We figured so."

"Here, here." Emily held out her hand, petals falling from her bouquet. She took them. "Thank you." She glanced at her for a moment.

"Pa says we should keep you company. I can read ya a story?" Ben piped up.

"That would be lovely."

"Be right back," Ben yelled as he ran out of the room.

"I'll be back in a few hours with your lunch," Ezekiel told her before leaving the room.

John's daughter crawled up beside Livy and plopped right next to her. She didn't want her here, not after the night she had filled with dreams of Emma, deciding to eat her breakfast and ignore her. Ben came back a few minutes later, carrying three books in his hands.

"What did you bring?" she asked him.

"I brought *The Adventures of Tom Sawyer, 20,000 Leagues under the Sea,* and Pa's favorite, the Bible."

She shook her head. "Not the Bible. Pick one of the other ones instead."

"How come not the Bible? Pa says there are plenty of neat stories in here," Ben asked, holding up the heavy book.

"I don't want to hear from the Bible."

"But why?" he asked again.

"Because I don't believe in it, that's why." Her cheeks reddened.

"Oh." Ben placed the book on the table beside her bed and sat staring at the other two, until he decided on Tom Sawyer.

She listened as Ben sounded out the first paragraph before he gave up and with glowing cheeks, asked her to read it out loud instead. For the rest of the morning and well into the afternoon, she read to Ben and his sister the adventures of the legendary Tom Sawyer and Huckleberry Finn. She stopped reading when Ezekiel brought their lunch, and when Shorty came to examine her knee.

She had been able to keep a tolerable distance away from the girl, who now lay fast asleep at the end of the bed. Ben was in the chair beside her in a deep slumber. She placed the book on her lap and yawned.

She took the cloth Ben had gotten for her off of her swollen knee. She stared at her inflamed limb and thought it appeared worse than it felt. Blue and purple, her leg throbbed every so often. The scratch on her face had scabbed, and her nose was still the same—tender to touch. Having banged it three times in the last week didn't help much. She was sure it would be crooked the rest of her life because of it.

The sun shining through her bedroom window warmed her, and she wanted to get out of bed and go outside. But Shorty had said she couldn't try walking until tomorrow. John was making her a pair of crutches to help her get around. She'd have them this evening. She was excited to be able to get out of bed. Livy's stomach fluttered when John's face appeared in her mind.

"Traitor," she said to her midsection.

How was she supposed to keep her distance from him when her body longed for his touch? She knew that sooner or later they would have to consummate their marriage, and the thought frightened her to death.

How am I going to explain why I'm not a virgin? What would his reaction be? She didn't want to know.

She'd keep her distance from him. Since her body couldn't be trusted, it was up to her mind. She snorted, and quickly covered her mouth so she didn't wake the children. She was being ridiculous. John didn't want her. He still loved his wife, and he made it quite clear that no one could, or would, take her place. She let out a long sigh. She didn't deserve a man like John, and she sure didn't deserve his children. Her eyes strayed to the girl. Especially her.

Livy's vision blurred. She blinked to stop the tears from falling. She didn't deserve anyone's love, not after letting her own sweet Emma die. Her heart ached accompanying the dull pain that never seemed to go away. When she'd fallen off the horse, a part of her wished she'd take her last breath and die. And if she believed in God anymore, she would have asked Him to make it so. But He never answered her prayers before, why would He start now?

She laid her head back against the headboard. Her soul longed for comfort. Someone to tell her things will get better. Strong arms to hold her while she sobbed and grieved for Emma. *John.* He couldn't begin to understand how she felt. She didn't know why her mind kept straying to him.

Must be from the kiss this morning.

"Humph." How could a single kiss change the way she felt about him? Could she have feelings for him?

She sat up. *Where did that come from?* She wasn't even thinking about love. She wasn't able to give it and denied her soul the permission to receive it. God had taken that away from her when He'd taken Emma. She was incapable of giving love to anyone ever again. It was never going to happen. The consequences of such an act could only end with her getting hurt, and she'd had enough of that to last a life time.

Her heart sank. The one time in the last year she'd felt safe was when she'd woken in John's arms. Instead of relishing in it, she'd cast him out. Afraid.

Emily started to cry as she woke from her nap. She couldn't console her, instead she pretended to sleep.

You are pathetic. She's a child—a baby.

She wanted to help her, comfort her, and almost had, when Ben woke and went to sit with his sister until she settled down. Eyes still closed, she heard Ben take his sister out of the room.

Livy's hands sought out the blanket on either side of her, and she grasped the quilt in tight fists. She was a horrible person, and right now she didn't even like herself. How did she get to be so cruel, so spiteful? She squeezed her eyes shut and shook her head, disgusted. The child had done nothing to her, and yet she couldn't even wipe a few tears.

Who are you kidding? You can't even look at her. Why? What had that sweet child done to deserve such a thing? Her stomach turned.

Whenever the girl was near her, she turned into an insensitive person. She didn't care whether she'd hurt the child or not. She blamed her for being alive. For being able to skip, run, and laugh. For being flesh and blood. Emma didn't have those things—never would—and she was angry. So angry. She squeezed the blanket harder. Emma didn't deserve to die. She should be alive! She should be alive!

The panic came, like she knew it would, and she welcomed it. Her chest tightened the pain crawled up, slow and heavy. She let the tears fall. Hands still fisted, she allowed the pain to consume her, knowing what would come next. Her lungs burned as her breathing came in short, rapid breaths. Gasping for air, she still refused to stop the panic attack. She let out a loud, sorrowful groan and ground her teeth together.

"Come, damn you. Take me." She willed her body to give up and her heart to stop. Instead, the grief came in waves rolling over her body, crashing onto her, heavy and constricting. She was close to hyperventilating. Her loud gasps echoed throughout the quiet room. Hands shaking, she reached for the glass beside the bed.

She screamed and threw it against the wall, shattering it into pieces. Her face drenched in tears, her soul drained.

"Livy?" John tapped on the door before opening it. He saw the glass on the floor.

"You okay, honey?" He went to sit beside her on the bed. Her rosy cheeks were wet from tears. She looked lost, and he recognized the sorrow in her eyes. He dug into his pocket, pulled out a handkerchief, and wiped the tears from her face.

"Need to talk?"

Her sad eyes stared straight ahead.

He nudged her chin with his thumb in an effort to get her to look at him. "Livy, what's wrong? Is it your leg? Does it hurt?"

She lifted her face to him and shook her head. "No," she whispered.

"Well, if not that, then what darlin'? What's got you breakin' dishes and your face all wet with tears?"

She shrugged.

"I'm here to listen."

Her eyes no longer revealed the sorrow he'd seen earlier. "I guess I hate having to lie in bed all day."

He wasn't buying it. "You can tell me the truth."

"It's nothing that can be fixed," she said.

"You don't know that. Why don't you tell me, and let me be the judge."

"I don't need a judge." She glared at him. "I told you. It can't be fixed. Now leave me be."

But he was having none of it. "Livy, we'll be married soon. We need to trust each other."

She scoffed. "Why do you want to marry me?"

Caught off guard at her question, he stammered, "Well...I need a wife."

"No, you need a housekeeper, and a nanny. You do not need a wife, nor do you want one."

Who was she to tell him what he needed? "No, I need a wife."

"We don't have to marry. I can do all those things without being your wife." She went on as if she hadn't heard him.

"I said I need a wife damn it, and that's what you'll be. Now why don't you stop playin' games with me and tell me what the hell is goin' on," he yelled.

"You still love your wife," she yelled back. "Why do you want a new one?"

He sat back, letting her words sink in. Yes, he still loved Becky with all his heart. And it still hurt to think about her. But he'd been lonesome and he missed the chats they used to have in bed at night. He missed her advice, the way she'd look at him, kiss him, and touch him.

He turned cold eyes toward her. He was angry at her for making him remember, for causing his heart to break a little more. "Yes, I still love my wife. I never offered you love, Livy. I can't, and I won't." His expression was hard, and his dark eyes stared right through her. "Is that what you thought would happen when you came here? Did you think I'd get on my knees and declare my love for you?" He stood by the door, putting an invisible barrier between them.

"No, I didn't expect anything like that."

"Sure." He could see the hurt in her eyes, and he didn't care. It was better for her to know not to have any expectations. "I'll always love her, Livy. I can't love anyone else." He opened the door, and without looking back, he left the room.

CHAPTER TWELVE

Three day's passed since Livy had seen John. Neither made any attempt to be around the other, which was easy since this was the first day she'd been able to leave her room for any length of time without her leg bothering her too much.

She sat on the rocking chair and watched Ben and Emily look for four-leaf clovers. Ben had been offish with her when she'd first gotten here, but after her fall from the horse, he seemed to come around. She often spotted a concerned look on his face, and he'd apologized to her several times, telling her he was sorry that she fell from the horse. She explained that she was riding too fast and it was an accident, but her assurances did nothing to cease his apologies or ease his concern for her leg.

She pushed the chair with her toes, rocking back and forth. As much as she didn't want to admit it, she'd missed John and wondered when, or if, he'd come around.

Alone in her room these last three days, she feared he'd come through the door to tell her he no longer wanted to marry her. Whenever someone knocked, she dreaded the outcome. She had nowhere else to go, and even though she couldn't think of consummating their marriage, she yearned for John's touch. Her heart ached for the little bit of reassurance she had felt when she woke in his arms.

In the evenings she was haunted by visions of Emma. The nightmares never seemed to cease. Not that she expected them to stop, they had terrorized her ever since Emma's death. On most nights she'd try to stay awake, too scared to relive them.

Last night she woke in a panic. Desperate, she searched the dark room for John's shadow, for his wide shoulders to lean her head on. She would've welcomed his comfort and not shied away. The need to be held overwhelmed her. Livy knew she'd find solace in his arms, as she did days before. But it was not to be. The room was empty.

Disappointed, she laid awake thinking of the things he'd said. Ashamed of her behavior, she let the tears fall relentlessly. He didn't care about her, and as the night wore on, she knew he never would.

She rested her head on the back of the chair and let the warm afternoon sun caress her face. She replayed the whole scene in her mind. Heard his angry words, saw his dark eyes as they glared, full of contempt, into hers.

She shivered.

Her intention was never to make him mad, but to get him to leave her alone. She was unsure of his kindness and his concern for her. No one had ever cared about what she thought, or how she felt. And there had been no one around to help her when Emma was sick or, she squeezed her eyes shut, after she died.

Instead of trying to talk to John, she'd done the opposite. She shut him out, made him mad. The whole thing had backfired on her, and she felt horrible.

She rocked the chair back and forth, her sore leg up on a wooden crate in front of her. The swelling had gone down, and after numerous tries she could now walk with the crutches John had made for her.

Shorty told her he didn't need to see her anymore. Her leg was healing fine, and by the end of the week she'd be able to try walking without the crutches. Excited by the prospect, she had been in a good mood ever since. This morning she told Ezekiel she wanted to prepare the evening meal without his help, and asked her friend only for his supervision. Over the course of her recovery she and Ezekiel had become close. She valued him as a good friend.

"Miss Livy. Miss Livy," Ben shouted from the grass below, with his sister jumping up and down beside him.

"Yes, what is it?" she called over the rail.

"We found one." Ben ran up the steps to stand in front of her. Pinched between his thumb and his index finger was a four-leaf clover.

Livy counted the leaves, before she said, "Oh my goodness, you have!" Her excitement, and the smile she gave Ben, surprised her. She instantly covered her mouth.

"Yay, yay," Emily shouted, clapping her hands.

Ben's face lit up while he stared down at his sister. "We actually found one Em."

Her heart lurched at the sound of the familiar name and raced within her chest. *Not now*, she pleaded. *Not when the day had gone so well.* She could feel it come, moving bit by bit up her chest, the demon wanting to be released.

She cleared her throat to try and stop the panic from coming. The hands—evil hands—crept toward her heart and wrapped around it, squeezing. Her face grew hot, her breaths short and quick.

"Miss Livy, are you all right?" Ben asked.

Not wanting to scare him or his sister. "Yes, I…I need a glass of water."

The boy ran inside the house, returned with her water, and handed it to her. She gulped it down in one swallow. Her hands were shaking as she gave it back to him. She closed her eyes while taking a deep breath.

In, out, in, out. The panic began to subside. The demon crawled back into the darkest regions of her soul, waiting to revisit her again later. Her hand at her chest, she took a few more deep breaths to ensure the demon had gone, and then opened her eyes and smiled at Ben.

"Thank you. I'm much better now," she said.

"What was wrong with ya before?" he asked, his blonde head cocked to one side.

Not sure how to answer him, she decided to tell him the truth. What could it hurt? He was a little boy. "I suffer breathing attacks from time to time."

His dirty face scrunched up. "What're breathing attacks?"

"Well, I don't really know if that's what they're called. But I feel panicked when I have one." She placed her hand on her chest. "My heart begins to beat real fast and I can't catch my breath, and then I panic."

"Why do ya get 'em?"

Livy knew why she got them, but she wasn't ready to tell anyone "I don't know. Maybe from lack of sleep?"

"You should see a doctor. I know," his brown eyes lit up, "you should tell Shorty. He can fix up anythin'."

She laughed.

"No, I think I'll be fine."

What was happening to her? In the few days she'd been on the ranch, she had smiled, and now she outright laughed.

He shrugged his shoulders. "Well, if you say so. But maybe you should go to bed early tonight, just in case."

She reached out and without thinking ruffled his hair with her hand. "Maybe I will. Thank you, Doctor Ben." It was getting much easier to talk with Ben, and she found she enjoyed his company.

"No problem."

Emily sang. "Doctor Ben. Doctor Ben."

She smiled at the little girl's song, and allowed her gaze to fall upon the child for a quick moment. Livy was stunned at how beautiful she was. It wasn't until her eyes began to water, that she looked away.

Ben rolled his eyes at his sister's song. "I'm gonna go show Pa our four-leaf clover."

"I'm sure he'd want to see it." She needed a little space from John's daughter.

Ben and his sister jumped off the top step of the porch and raced across the yard in search of their father. Even though she needed to keep her distance from the child, a part of her wished she could go with them. To be accepted, as she knew they would be.

She sighed and gave her head a little shake to get out of her melancholy mood. *What are you thinking? You don't need John.* She sat up straighter. *You don't need anyone.* He'd made his intentions clear, and she'd let a little kiss sway her heart into thinking he'd offer more. She'd let her emotions get involved, even when she'd tried not to. How stupid of her. She had acted like a lovesick school girl. Well, no more.

She was unlovable, untouchable.

There wasn't a strong demand for saloon singers as wives. And definitely not for someone who'd let her baby die. She swallowed past the lump in her throat. If John knew how Emma died, how she couldn't even save her own baby from Scarlet Fever, he'd send her away for sure. She'd have nowhere to go. Maybe that's what she deserved—to be sent away and never have a chance at a real life. She didn't even know what a real life consisted of, or if she would ever have one.

After Emma died, she'd built a wall so high that some days she didn't even think it was possible for her to climb. And even if she could get over it enough to be able to look at John's daughter, how was she to care for someone else's children, especially when she couldn't help her own child?

The questions burned into her head. She fought them, denying all the possibilities of what a life with John could lead to.

Why did she let him steal one kiss? Why did her stomach flutter every time he was near? And why, damn it could she think of nothing else but how his lips felt on hers?

She blew out an exasperated breath.

She'd had enough. She promised to marry John, and she'd keep that promise. But damn it, she didn't have to give body and soul to him. And for the same reasons he couldn't love anyone but his Becky, she couldn't find the strength inside to let anyone close to her again.

Everything she ever cared about, loved and cherished, had died along with Emma. Now she was an empty shell who tried to live through each day without putting a noose around her neck and ending it all.

A tear slipped down her cheek, and she wiped it away with the back of her hand. Her mood no longer sunny, she grabbed her crutches and stood up. There was a rustling from behind her and she fumbled with her crutches, trying to keep her balance as she whirled around to look at the empty yard. Leaning into the wooden sticks perched under each arm, she scanned the area. The hairs on the back of her neck stood up, and her body quivered. Someone was there. She could sense it.

Livy bent over the railing on the porch to peer around the side of the house. She saw a shadow near the corner, but couldn't make out what it was. Resting her hand on the rail, she leaned farther, slipped and lost her balance. She landed hard on her chest. Jaw clenched, she groaned from the pain while she pushed back up.

She tried to find the shadow again, but it was gone. She scanned the yard once more, but no one was there. Feeling an urgent need to get inside, she hopped to the door and went in.

"You look like you've seen a ghost," Ezekiel said as he came out of the kitchen.

She blew at the hair that had fallen in her eyes. "Maybe I have," she said, out of breath and glancing back at the door.

The black man raised a dark eyebrow at her. "I beg your pardon, ma'am?"

She didn't want to tell him about the shadow she'd seen, or that every time she's alone outside she senses someone watching her. "I'm kidding, Ezekiel."

Ezekiel slapped his hands on his knees and laughed. "You had me. I thought you was seein' things."

"The only thing I'm seeing is a nice cold glass of lemonade."

"Well, come on into the kitchen, and I'll fix ya up one."

She hobbled behind him and sat down at the table. The cozy room smelled of the chicken she'd put in the oven this morning, and her stomach growled.

Ezekiel was busy cutting up lemons to squeeze into the pitcher of water on the counter.

"Ezekiel," she asked, "how many men work on the ranch?"

His long fingers pinched the lemon, and she watched as the juice dripped into the water. "Well, there used to be twenty-five. But now that Rusty's gone there's twenty-four."

"Rusty's gone?" She remembered him from the day she'd watched the bull riding.

"The boss fired him after," he hesitated, "after you fell off that horse."

She leaned forward in her chair. "Why?"

His brown eyes searched the floor. "I don't think I should say."

"Well, if it concerns me, don't you think I have a right to know?"

Ezekiel shook his head. "Ain't my place to tell ya. If you want to know, you best ask the boss."

"Ask the boss?" she echoed. *What is going on? Why won't Ezekiel tell me why Rusty was fired? Does it have anything to do with the odd feeling someone is watching me?*

"Yes'm."

Unable to get anymore out of Ezekiel, she grew angry. Oh, she'd ask John all right. *Mr, we need to trust each other.* She grabbed her crutches and headed for the door.

"Now where you off to?" Ezekiel called after her.

"To find your *boss*, and ask him what the hell is going on." She stormed out onto the back deck.

She wished she could move faster, but with her leg, one boot and these damnable crutches, she was forced to go at a snail's pace. She stopped twice to catch her breath before she got to the tack barn. She hopped inside and paused in the doorway to let her eyes adjust to the dimly lit area.

The sun peeked through the uneven boards of the barn, and tiny specs of dust danced in the bright rays. Her boot sunk into the soft dirt, and she held her stocking foot high, so she wouldn't get it dirty. Straw and feed littered the floor of each stall.

She soon realized she was alone in the barn. She inhaled the leather from the saddles mingled with the sweet scent of the straw. Boards creaked and whined from somewhere nearby, and she stepped toward the door. The air felt heavy.

She made a beeline for the barn door and almost toppled over when pigeons flew out from the loft. She was rearranging the crutches under her arms when she heard a crunching sound near one of the empty stalls in the back. She squinted, hoping to get a better look.

Dark shadows lurked in the corner.

Deciding not to wait and see what was there, she high-tailed it to the back door. The bright sun almost blinded her, and she held up her hand to shade her eyes. She stared over her shoulder into the dark barn, jumping when she saw someone run out the front door.

Curiosity getting the better of her, she tried to see who it was and where he was going. Was it someone she hadn't met yet? Maybe she startled him as much as he did her. Whoever he was, he had disappeared behind one of the other buildings. With no chance to see his face, she turned back to find John.

She noticed a few cowboys sitting on the fence at the far corral. Taking one more look around for John, she took a deep breath and limped toward them to ask where their boss was.

Halfway there she heard a loud bawl from behind her. She turned, and nearly lost her balance on the crutches. The bull John had ridden stood twenty feet from her, out of its pen. She watched the black monster paw at the ground, head down, ready to charge—at *her*.

She searched her surroundings for somewhere to go. The fences on either side of her were too far away to get to with her crutches. She tried to scream, to alert the cowboys on the fence, but nothing came from her mouth.

With wide eyes, she stared back at the bull. He snuffed while he raised his head. She was sure he could smell her fear. The massive beast stomped his hoof once more and then charged straight toward her. She froze and squeezed her eyes shut.

John was rounding the corner of the tack house on Midnight, when he saw Livy standing in the middle of two corrals, a panicked look on her face. He followed her frightful gaze, and his stomach pitched when he saw the bull heading toward her.

"Yaw," he yelled, kicking Midnight hard in his sides. Afraid he might not make it to her in time, he kicked again. "Come on. Yaw."

He was hunched low in the saddle as Midnight cleared the fence and raced alongside the bull to the gap between Livy and the beast. Once they were ahead of him, he bent down and scooped her up. Midnight's back legs cleared the gap as the bull crashed into the falling crutches. He held her tight under his arm, and kept Midnight a safe distance from the loose bull. Until the crazed beast stopped chasing them, turned around and meandered back to its pen.

He tugged on the reins to slow down his horse. Once the animal was at a trot, he dragged her up to sit in front of him. He could feel her heart beating against his arm as he held her tight to his chest, and he loosened his grip so she could breathe. His own heart raced from the burst of adrenaline he'd had.

He rode Midnight over to the pen where the bull was lounging inside the open gate. He slid off his horse and closed the gate. While he was there, he decided to inspect the wooden closure. The rope had frayed, leaving nothing to hold the fence closed. All the animal had to do was lean on it, and the gate would've opened.

He tipped his hat back and glanced up at her. She was still trying to catch her breath. He shook his head. What the hell had she been doing out here? He secured the gate the best he could, and walked over to retrieve her crutches a few feet away. He picked them up and inspected them. One was broken. The wood split right down the middle. He tossed the wrecked crutch back onto the ground, and headed over to Livy with the other one still in his hand.

"I hope you're able to get along with one crutch," he said holding up the prop. "The other one's broke."

She didn't say anything, instead took the wooden stick when he handed it to her and clutched it in her hands. His eyes narrowed. He had a few things to say to her, but that would have to wait. Back on Midnight, he made his way over to where some of his men were taking a break on one of the fences.

"You boys didn't happen to notice that the bull got loose?" he asked them, pointing at the bull now safe inside his pen.

The three men scrambled off the fence, each one shaking their head. "No, Boss."

"Well, go on and fix that gate," he ordered.

Heads down, the cowboys hurried to do what they'd been told.

John pivoted toward her. "What the hell were you doing out here?"

She didn't answer, but swiveled in her seat to stare down at him, a dazed look on her pale face.

"Well?" he demanded.

She cleared her throat, and he watched as the shock faded from her pretty face. "I was looking for you."

"Well you found me." He was vibrating with anger, and had to restrain from paddling her backside. She could've been killed. "Why didn't you run?"

"How was I supposed to run with my leg?" she said, as if he should've known.

"Fear would make anyone run," he shouted at her. "You're damn lucky I was there."

"Oh, well let me thank you for that. Thank you so very, very much!"

He shook his head, confused. Why was she being so damn hard to get along with? She should be grateful to him for saving her life. "What's got your feathers all ruffled?"

"Why did you fire Rusty?"

He got back on Midnight and headed toward the house. "I had my reasons."

"What reasons?" she persisted, trying to swivel in her seat and look at him.

"They don't concern you."

"Oh, yes they do. You fired Rusty because I fell from that horse and I want to know why."

He was in no mood for her attitude, but if she wanted a fight, he'd give her one. "This is my ranch and if I fire someone I don't owe you or anyone else a damn explanation."

"I'm so sick of hearing that. Why won't you tell me?"

He hadn't seen her since the night she'd questioned him about why he wanted to marry her. He didn't trust his lips when he was alone with her not to lose control and kiss her senseless. He had to restrain his desires, had to concentrate on figuring out why someone wanted to hurt her. "Look Livy, you'll find out when I'm damn good and ready to tell you."

"I am not a child, Mr. Taylor."

"Then quit acting like one." He lifted her from his horse, and all but dropped her onto the front porch. Guilt washed over him as he watched her fumble to catch her footing.

She cradled her one crutch under her arm, and when she met his stare her eyes shot fire. "You, John Taylor are an arrogant...stubborn...bossy...jackass." Turning on her good heel, she hopped into the house almost ripping the door off its hinges as she entered.

He tipped his hat back and blew out a long whistle. No one had ever talked to him like that. Not even Becky when she'd been madder than hell at him. He shook his head. She sure was a prickly one. He sat there a moment longer, still stunned.

Well, at least her leg was healing, but he couldn't say the same for her head. She'd gone completely loco. Why the hell would she care if Rusty was fired? He clicked his tongue and rode Midnight back to the barn. *Unless,* he scratched the stubble on his jaw, *she knows something I don't.* His mind raced with all sorts of possibilities. After all, how well did he know her?

He flexed his jaw. If he found out the little vixen was keeping something from him, she'd be on the next stage out of here—wife-to-be or not. He dismounted and led Midnight into the stall. He had a feeling there was something amiss, but he'd be damned if he could figure it out. She was hiding something from him. He was sure of it.

He took the bucket from a nail on the wall, pulled out a brush, and began grooming his horse. The smooth even strokes calmed him, and his mind was soon invaded with pictures of Livy. Her soft lips, round bottom, and flashing green eyes. He sure did like that kiss they'd shared—had thought about it several times these last few days—and couldn't help but wonder if she did the same.

He hadn't been able to go to her room, and see how she was after he'd yelled at her. The daily reports he received from Ezekiel, Shorty, and the kids were all he needed.

But at night, when she was asleep, he'd sit with her for a while and watch her chest rise and fall in peaceful slumber. He had been there when her sleep was interrupted by nightmares too. He'd watched in dismay as her pretty face changed from calm and serene to frightened and panicked.

She woke from one last night. He wanted nothing more than to go to her, to hold her, but something held him back. Instead, he'd stayed hidden in the dark corner until her eyes closed and she'd fallen back to sleep. When he was sure she wouldn't wake, he tiptoed to her side, and peered down at her. He saw that her lashes were wet with tears. Too much for him to take, he'd left the room.

He knew she suffered from something. He had heard her across the hall every night since she'd been here. He wished she'd trust him enough to tell him what it was.

He took off his hat and ran his forearm across his forehead. These long days were getting to him, and his shoulders ached like hell. The pressure in his lower back reminded him that he wasn't getting any younger and, much to his annoyance, there wasn't a damn thing he could do about it. That was why he'd sent for her in the first place.

He didn't want to admit it at the time, but he'd needed her, and still did. He needed the reassurance that if something ever happened to him, Ben and Emily would be taken care of and, most importantly, loved.

He had no choice but to use her for his own benefit. And if he had to be honest, he hadn't thought about her feelings when he'd sent for her. His kids were more important. He never lied about his expectations. He'd told her what he wanted from her—a wife and a mother. His conscience criticized him. He might've forgotten to mention to Livy when he'd written that there would be no love between them.

At the time, he didn't think it was important. Besides, what more could a woman want? She'd have a home on one of the largest ranches this side of the Rockies. Children to care for, and a husband who...

He frowned. *Who what? What do I think of her? Do I even care for her...a little?* Ah, hell. It didn't matter. What mattered was that she fit in and made a pleasant family atmosphere. And so far, that hadn't happened.

Damned if he could figure her out. She was nice to look at, and she kept the house clean. Her cooking left something to be desired, but he hoped Ezekiel would be able to fix that. She seemed to do well around the children—what he'd seen of her anyway.

She often wore a scowl on her face, turning her pretty features hard and unreadable. Come to think of it, he'd only ever seen her smile a few times in her two weeks here. He didn't even know if she liked it here. He laughed miserably. He sure didn't know much about her, given the fact that the woman was soon to be his wife.

He put Midnight's brush and hoof pick away then made his way out into the warm afternoon sun. A wagon pulled up to the house, and he recognized Alice and Hank.

"Thought we'd come by for a visit," Hank said with a smile on his weathered face.

He liked the elderly couple. They reminded him of his own mother and father. He missed them, and often wondered what they'd think of the small farm they'd left him now crawling with cattle and five times its original size.

"Nice of you to stop by." John helped Alice down from her seat.

"How are things going with Miss Green?" she asked, her light blues eyes showing a hint of mirth.

"She had a little accident a few days back, but she's fine now. Why don't we go on in and have a cold drink."

"That would be lovely."

Livy was in the sitting room when he came in. The surviving crutch was tucked under one arm while she stretched for a book high on the shelf. When she noticed them standing there, her eyes lit up and she limped toward them.

"Alice, have you come for a visit?" Livy's thin lips opened to display a brilliant smile. Hank extended his hand, and she shook it. "It's a pleasure to meet you, Sir."

"We've come to see how you're getting along," Alice said, glancing sympathetically at Livy's injured leg.

"Oh, I'm fine. Had a little accident is all. I'll be as good as new in no time."

He stood back staring at Livy, dumbfounded by her ability to be so kind. Not twenty minutes ago she tore a strip off of him for firing Rusty.

"Yup, Livy's a tough one that's for sure," he said, winking at her. He watched as her spine went rigid, a sign that she was still mad at him.

"Ezekiel made some lemonade earlier. Let's go into the kitchen and have a glass," she said.

John stepped back to let the elderly couple pass, then reluctantly followed behind. The kitchen was clean, and he could see that someone had tidied the counter. Ezekiel wasn't there, and John assumed he was at the cook shack preparing supper for the hands.

He inhaled. Something sure smelled good. He lifted the lids and peeked inside the pots. Potatoes and carrots were cooking on top of the stove. He opened the oven door and peered inside. Surprised to see a chicken nestled in a black roaster, its skin sizzling he glanced up at Livy. "You made this?"

"Ezekiel helped," she said, handing Alice and Hank each a glass of lemonade before giving him one.

"Well, I can see you're coming along," Alice smiled.

"Mr. Taylor thought it would help to have Ezekiel show me a few things." Livy said and sat down at the table across from John.

He smiled at her. "Well, I'm sure by the end of the week Livy won't need Ezekiel's help anymore." John was surprised to see her cheeks go red. "You should taste her pancakes, they're mighty good too."

"I can teach you how to make the best apple pie in the west," Alice offered.

Livy's eyes lit up. "That would be wonderful."

"You folks are welcome to stay for supper," John said, grateful that Livy seemed to open up when Alice was around.

"We'd like that. It will give me some time to pick out a few of your calves to buy," Hank said.

Livy smiled.

John couldn't help but smile too.

They finished their drinks, and the men headed outside. Alice and Livy sent Ben and Emily off to pick apples, and while they were waiting, Alice showed her how to make the crust for the pie. It seemed an easy task to Livy, but she wrote the recipe down anyway.

"The thing with the crust," Alice explained, "is to handle it as little as possible, so the crust is flaky, not tough."

When the children came back, they proudly lugged a bucket filled with shiny red apples into the kitchen. She gave an apple to Ben, and forcing herself to pay attention to the girl, handed Emily one as well. The women went about peeling and slicing the apples, filling the two pie shells they had prepared. Alice put the pies in the oven while she continued preparing supper.

The kitchen was hot, so Alice suggested they eat their meal outside at the table on the back porch. A red and white checkered table cloth and some matching blue plates made the rustic table look inviting.

While Livy sat beside John, eating the bountiful feast, she was astonished at how good it all tasted. Everyone congratulated her on what a fine meal she had made, and she couldn't keep from smiling. She'd done it. She made a real supper, and there wasn't too much salt.

CHAPTER THIRTEEN

Livy cleared the table after Alice and Hank left. The calm that had settled over the ranch distracted her from the task. She pressed her waist against the table's edge. The sun, descending behind the rolling hills, highlighted the green and gold fields with an orange glow. She lifted her face toward the sun and let the heat soak through her, warming her insides.

The cattle had stopped lowing, and the squawking of the chickens had ceased. A light breeze grazed her face, and she watched the trees sway back and forth, lost in their rhythmic dance. The river gurgled as it rushed by, and above her, chickadees and house wrens chirped loudly from the trees. She had begun to enjoy life on the ranch, and she could now take solace in the little wonders that surrounded her. She relished these peaceful moments. But a shadow still loomed over her, reminding her of the burden she carried.

"It has a tendency to put one to sleep," John said from behind her.

She flinched at the sound of his voice. She placed her hands on the wooden table and quieted the rattling dishes.

"Sorry, I seem to have startled you."

He had crept up on her again, and she was sure she looked like an idiot leaning up against the table in a daze. Her face was warm, and she knew she was blushing. Thankful her back was to him, she cleared her throat before she spoke. "It is calming."

He came around the table to face her, and smiled. His hat was off and his hair, black and wavy, fell on either side of his face to hang at his chin. He was a handsome man, and she couldn't stop from staring.

"I've gone to sleep many nights out in the field listening to the sounds of God's creations," he said, picking up a bowl.

Her heart dropped, and she could feel her body grow rigid at the mention of God. Her face became tight and stiff.

"Why the frown?" His finger nudged her chin.

She squeezed the edge of the table. "You talk about Him as if He did something for you."

"Him?" John's eyebrow rose.

"God." She all but shouted the word.

He stared at her for a long moment, and she thought he wasn't going to answer her. Any talk about God usually got her in a huff anyway. Busy with clearing the table, she thought the conversation was over, when he spoke in a matter-of-fact tone.

"He did do something for me. He gave me all of this." John spread his arms out, as if to embrace the vista before them that made up his ranch.

She took in the land before her, the barns, the corrals, and the trees surrounding them. "Humph, He didn't give you this. You worked for it." She pointed her finger at him. "You did this."

"No. He helped me."

"I don't see how." She grabbed the rest of the forks and spoons off the table and placed them on her plate with a loud clatter.

"Well, He let it rain so I could grow food for my family and my livestock."

"That was Mother Nature."

He rolled his eyes. "No such thing exists. That was God." He crossed his arms. "He gave me Ben and Emily."

She laughed. It was a bitter and harsh sound.

"If you believe that, then you have to believe He took your wife from you too."

He put down the bowl he held and went to stand in front of her. "No."

"You make no sense. If you believe in God and think He gave you all of this, then He's to blame for your wife dying!"

"No, He isn't."

"Yes, He is."

John blew out an exasperated breath and ran his fingers through his hair. "Look Livy, God doesn't take your loved ones from you."

"Oh yes he does, Mr. Taylor."

He placed his hands on her shoulders and turned her toward him. "God loves us and would never hurt us."

She stepped back, putting some distance between them and his touch. "Really, then how come people die?"

"I can't answer that. But I do know that if it wasn't for Him, I wouldn't be able to get out of bed each day and do what I do. I couldn't make it through if I didn't have Him to lean on or talk to. He gives me hope."

"You are wrong. When you do something bad, He punishes you by taking away the ones you love." Her voice shook.

John stared at her. The silence overwhelming, she went for her crutch.

"Who did you lose, Livy?" he whispered.

She took a step back. The stabbing pain in her chest came suddenly. The weight so heavy and painful she held her breath as she tugged at the suppressed emotions now starting to surface.

"No one," her voice was barely a whisper. She turned from him, grabbed her crutch and limped into the house. She was standing with both hands pressed into the counter when she heard him come up behind her.

"Did someone you love die, Livy?"

She didn't turn from the sink, didn't want to. How many times had she seen the pity and the sadness on the faces of those who did not understand? How many times had she heard 'I'm sorry' when they didn't even know what happened, or what she'd done.

"I don't want to talk about it."

He placed the bowl in the sink and stood beside her. "Well, I do."

Angry at his persistence, she glared up at him. "I don't care what you want."

"Sometimes it helps to talk these things out."

"Why?" She grabbed the bucket of lukewarm water beside her, and dumped it into the sink before adding some soap. "Is it going to bring them back, Mr. Taylor?"

"No, but it does offer some comfort."

"I can't see how." She tossed the rest of the plates into the soapy water.

"Maybe I can help, even if I listen."

"So, now you want to help me?" She scrubbed the dishes as if they had glue on them. "Don't flatter yourself, Mr. Taylor. I do not need your help."

"I think you need my help. In fact, I think you *want* my help."

She slammed the plate she'd been washing onto the counter. The force sent suds flying through the air. Hands wet, she gave him a little shove.

"No," her voice cracked, "I don't want, nor do I need your help." She pushed at him again, as the barrier around her soul started to crumble. "You don't even know me. You know nothing about me. You have no idea how I feel, or what I feel." Her arms flailed wildly. "You sit here, in your nice house, with your healthy children and you presume to tell me I need to talk to someone, least of all you? I need no one!" she screamed, her chest starting to constrict. "No one." Tears fell down her cheeks.

"I...need...no...one." She tried to push past him, but he wouldn't let her by.

"Livy, please tell me what's wrong." His strong hands held her arms.

"Why do you want to help me?" She exploded, and her puny fists pounded into his chest. "Why me, why me? You can't make it better. No one can." Despair filled her, and she started to sob. Her hands crashed into him again and again and again. The fury that simmered inside of her for so long erupted, bursting out of her to drip onto the floor in a puddle of misery and hopelessness.

John's arms came around her, holding her close.

"I...can't...breathe," she cried, her chest tight. "I...can't...breathe."

John rocked her back and forth, whispering soothing words into her ear. But she heard nothing except the sounds of her own demon screaming to be released.

"It hurts...too much." Bitter sobs wracked her body. The control she'd fought so hard to maintain had started to crack and break. Unable to hold on any longer, she shattered. Pieces of shame, guilt, and agony spewed out of her, and her body trembled. Emma. She saw her lying still and cold...her baby.

Livy's knees gave out. "Emma," she wailed. "Emma."

He caught her before she fell to the floor. He carried her to the sitting room, sat down in his reading chair and cradled her on his lap. He smoothed back the wet tendrils of hair that had fallen into her eyes and felt helpless as he listened to her cry.

"Livy, who's Emma?" John felt her stiffen in his arms, and her desolate sobs faded to silence. "Livy?"

She got up from his lap, and stumbled to get her balance. Her pale face wet from crying, she stared at the floor. "I need to be alone," she whispered, and limped from the room.

He heard her go up the stairs. *Who was Emma? Was it her sister? Her mother? A close friend?* He couldn't get the images of her out of his head—her sorrowful eyes, the agony and pain. How was he going to help her if she refused to talk to him?

For the little bit of time she had let him console her, he felt as if they had finally connected. When he thought she'd open up to him, let him in, she shut him out so fast he hadn't had time to stop her before she left. He knew if she didn't let it out soon, it would eat at her soul and tear her into pieces.

He ran his hand through his hair, and blew out an exhausted breath. Grief had no mercy. He knew this from his own experience. Her suffering tore at his soul, and he had hoped to take some of it away tonight. But now he had no choice. He'd have to wait for it to happen again, and he knew without a doubt that it would. That's how it worked. The sorrow came in waves until you dealt with it. He rubbed his tired eyes. And even then, it could still rear its head when you least expect it, to rip you apart all over again.

CHAPTER FOURTEEN

A loud knock at the front door woke John. He sat up and stretched his stiff muscles. Damn he was tired. He yawned as he got out of the chair. Clive stood outside on the porch, his hand up ready to strike the door again when John opened it.

"Why the hell are you bangin' on my door for in the middle of the damn night?" John yelled. He couldn't help being annoyed. He'd had a terrible night, staying up late thinking about Livy.

Clive pushed past him to enter the house.

"Well?" His neck was stiff and sore, and every time he moved it a piercing pain shot straight for his head, a sign that a headache was about to start. *Great, just what I need.*

"I need to talk to you, and you're not gonna like it," Clive said, while taking off his brown Stetson and scrunching it between his hands.

He watched his friend pace the length of his sitting room. "Well, what the hell is it?"

"I sent a few of the boys up to the east pasture today to start bringing in some of the herd."

Clive's pacing was making him dizzy, so he decided to sit down. The sofa was soft and plush, and he realized had he slept here instead of in the chair, he wouldn't be so sore now.

"They came back a half hour ago," Clive paused to look at the floor, "and they had Rusty with them."

He shot off the couch. "Why'd they bring him back here? He has no business on the T-Bar—

"John, he's dead."

"What did you say?"

Clive wiped his face. "I said he's dead. Rusty's dead."

He could see that Clive was shaken, and asked—calmly this time—"Was it an accident?"

"The boys said he had the lead from his horse wrapped around his neck." Clive drew in a ragged breath. "He'd been dragged a while."

"Was it an accident, or not?"

"Don't think so." He pushed his hands deep inside his pants pockets making his broad shoulders pull in toward his chest. "Way I figure it, Rusty knew how to handle a horse. There's no way he'd let the rope get tangled around him."

"Why would anyone want to kill Rusty?"

"Don't know that either. But whoever did it never left any trace that they were there. They tried real hard to make it look like an accident." His hands gripped his hat so hard it lost its shape.

"Get one of the boys to ride into town for the sheriff. If you don't think it was an accident, we aren't taking any chances."

"I'll ask Gill when we're done."

"Do you think this has anything to do with Livy falling off her horse the other day?"

Clive gave John a look. "Seems too coincidental if you ask me."

He nodded in agreement. "We'll bury Rusty tomorrow. I'm sure the news has already spread to the rest of the men. Tell them that after Rusty's funeral I'll be talking with them."

"I'll let them know right now. See if any of 'em act suspicious."

"Let me know what you find." He followed his friend to the door. "And watch your back."

"You watch that family of yours." Clive motioned upstairs. "I'll see you in a couple of hours."

He bolted the door after Clive left. They had never locked the doors on the ranch. But after tonight, things were about to change. At least until they found out who killed Rusty. He passed through the dark hallway and into the kitchen. He saw a shadow go by the window. Assuming it was Clive, he smiled at his foreman's diligence in making sure all was well. The handle on the back door turned.

"Miss me already?" He called out. But instead of seeing Clive entering the kitchen, he heard loud footsteps as someone ran away.

He pulled his rifle off the shelf by the back door and clutched the cold metal barrel in his hands. Grabbing the stock with his right hand, he cocked the gun. The click echoed throughout the silent kitchen.

He yanked the door open. Without making a sound, he stepped outside. He couldn't see a damn thing and he swung his rifle from side to side waiting for his eyes to adjust to the darkness. He'd grown immune to the sounds on the ranch, and instead listened for anything out of the ordinary.

Moving silently, he inspected the yard. Tall grey shadows stood in front of him, and he recognized them as the barns. To his left sat the garden, scanning it, he heard the trees rustling overhead. All seemed normal, but his gut told him otherwise. Whoever had tried to come into his house couldn't have gotten far.

Cautiously, he dropped each foot, barley touching the steps. He winced as the wooden boards creaked under his weight, and made a mental note to fix the step the first chance he got. The rifle tight under his chin, he was ready to fire if given the need.

He made his way around the house staying close to the wall. *Where the hell did he go?* He swung around when he heard a scuffle over by the tack barn. Listening, he heard voices and ran in their direction.

Two of his men were rolling on the ground, fists flying. He propped his gun up against the barn and hauled the two men apart. "What the hell is going on?" he yelled, holding their shirts to keep them from running off.

"I was out havin' a smoke when I saw Danny here, tryin' to go into your house, and then run away. I chased him down and…well, you know the rest." Boyd huffed.

John released him, and turned his attention to the other man. He had to squint so he could see his face. The moon, offering little light, outlined them in a dark green. John recognized the boy as Danny, the young cowboy he hired to help in the fields for the harvest.

He pulled him close and asked, "This true?"

"No Sir," Danny answered, his head shook back and forth so fast that John could feel the air it radiated. The kid stunk. He smelled like he'd been shoveling manure, or bathing in it. John scrunched his nose, and tried hard not to push him away.

"Don't lie boy." Boyd gave him a shove.

Clive showed up, and John was glad his friend was there offering his silent support in case things went wrong.

"You better start talkin', son," John said, relieved that he could let him go. The smell was getting to him, and his eyes began to water.

"I was up by the house," Danny admitted. He glanced over at Boyd, who glared at him in return. Then he turned back to John and Clive, "But I never went onto your porch…and…and I never tried to open your door, Mr. Taylor."

John didn't know if he should believe him or not. But he didn't want to make the same mistake he had with Rusty. He glanced at Clive. "You believe him?"

Clive was silent, and John knew his friend was pondering what he'd said.

The boy took this as his opportunity to plead with the other man. "Mr. Clive I...I didn't do what Boyd said I'd done. I didn't try to go into Mr. Taylor's house."

"But you said that you were by his house," Clive verified.

"Yes, Sir." His expression reminded John of Ben whenever he was in trouble and begging not to be disciplined.

"What were you doing up there?" Clive asked.

"I couldn't sleep after the boys came in and said they'd found Rusty, so I went for a walk." His voice was close to a whine and John was beginning to feel sorry for him. "I was wanderin' is all. Never meant no harm."

"I believe him," Clive said to John.

That was all he needed to let the boy stay. Unsure, John was glad his friend had made the decision for him. He stared at Boyd. "You go on back to the bunkhouse. We'll take it from here."

"You gonna keep him on?" Boyd sneered. His rotten breath smelled of stale liquor, and John didn't like it.

The way Boyd said the words hit him in all the wrong places. "Yeah, I'm gonna keep him on. I'm the owner of the T-Bar, and I do whatever the hell I want," John growled.

"Whatever you say, Boss." Boyd spat on the grass and walked away.

John felt as though he were missing something when he watched Boyd leave. But instead of investigating it further, he brushed it off to lack of sleep and the eventful evening he'd had. He turned back to Danny. "You are on shaky ground with me. If anything like this happens again, you'll be gone."

"Yes, Sir."

"Now git." John swatted at the air. "And take a bath."

"Yes, Sir."

He waited until the boy was out of earshot before he addressed Clive. "What do you make of all that?"

"Well, like I said before, I think he's tellin' us the truth." Clive dug his hands inside his pockets. "But I'm not too sure about the other one. Somethin' ain't right there, and I don't know what it is."

"Yeah, I get the same feeling." Both headed toward the bunkhouse. "Did you talk to the men?" John asked.

"Yup, I did."

"Good. We'll keep a close eye on the other one."

"Figured as much," Clive said, and they parted ways.

John left the barn and wandered around a few of the corrals checking on the cattle and making sure no one else was lurking about. Restless, he picked up the pitch fork and threw some hay into Midnight's pen. His horse snorted and danced around the perimeter of the fence. He dug his hand into the bucket on the ground and grabbed a fistful of oats. He rested his arm on the railing as Midnight nuzzled his snout into John's palm and gently took the food.

"Good boy," he crooned, rubbing his shiny black coat.

On his way back to the house, he watched the rising sun change the field's hues from navy blue to a light grey. Dawn used to be his favorite time of day. He imagined the sun to be God's finger as it painted the earth, His canvas. He swore that each time he and Becky would watch the sun rise, the colors He'd painted were always different, but the masterpiece was awe-inspiring all the same.

His shoulders sagged, and his hand went inside his pocket to finger the locket there. He hadn't sat and watched the sun rise since Becky died. It wasn't the same without her there beside him.

Sighing, he climbed the steps. He stopped to gaze out at his land. He blinked back tears. He tried to stay and watch, but the scene was too much for him. He turned away, leaving the memory behind.

CHAPTER FIFTEEN

Livy woke early. She hadn't slept well. She squeezed her eyes shut and held the pillow over her face. She had almost told John about Emma. She had almost lost control. The images of her breakdown re-played in her mind, and she tossed the heavy covers off the bed and forced her legs to stand.

She'd have to go downstairs sooner or later. She groaned at the prospect. She'd prefer later—much later. She splashed cold water from the basin onto her face and put on her light green dress. She glanced around the room looking for her crutch. *Where did I leave the blasted thing?* She searched her room again, but the crutch wasn't there.

She tried not to think of last night, of John's strong arms around her, holding her tight. She shook her head and hoped the crutch would turn up somewhere.

She opened the door, and smelled the coffee. Hopping to the stairs, she stood there for a few moments wondering how she was going to get down them. She took a deep breath and braced her arm on the rail. She pressed her shoulder into the wall and hopped down one step. It was one step, and she was still on her feet, not sprawled out on the floor. Even though she'd have reached the bottom a lot quicker, that was not the way she wanted to arrive there.

She took another deep breath—the coffee was calling to her—and she hopped down the next step and the next, until she was on the main floor. She hobbled into the kitchen, her good leg tired from limping down the stairs. She was relieved when she spotted her crutch propped up against one of the chairs at the kitchen table. John was seated in the chair next to it.

"Oh." She stumbled backwards, grasping the wall to catch her balance. She wasn't prepared for a conversation with him. What was she going to say? With her bottom lip tucked between her teeth, she chewed nervously. She figured she'd have more time to be composed, rehearse something to say that had nothing to do with last night.

"Help yourself to a cup of coffee. I just made it," he told her without turning around.

She gripped her crutch, relieved to take some of the weight off of her good leg, and hobbled over to the wooden counter, to pour a cup. "Why aren't you out in the fields?" she asked, her back to him. It was much easier if she didn't have to face him.

"Well, there was some trouble last night."

"What kind of trouble?"

She forgot all about her meltdown last night and faced him. His hands massaged his face, and she noticed for the first time how tired and rundown he looked. If she didn't watch it, she'd soon be telling him to go take a nap.

"Rusty was found dead up in the east pasture last night," he said.

"What happened to him?"

"Lead to his horse was wrapped around his neck." His eyes were focused on the table.

She pressed against the counter and stared at him. Used to seeing him as a force to be reckoned with, she thought he looked worn out and defeated inside his blue checkered shirt.

"What a terrible accident," she mumbled.

He shook his head. "It was no accident, Livy."

She put her crutch under her arm balanced her coffee in her other hand and limped over to the table. Afraid to ask, but pushing the words out any way, she said, "What do you mean it wasn't an accident?"

He brought his head up to look at her. His sad brown eyes were framed with dark circles. "Someone killed him."

The coffee scalded her throat when she swallowed, and she couldn't stop from coughing.

"I expect the sheriff here any minute." John's hands were clasped together on top of the table. "Clive sent one of the boys out to get him last night."

"Why would anyone want to kill Rusty?" She wasn't blind to the violence that happened in the world—she had experienced it firsthand—but she didn't think it would happen out here, in the middle of nowhere.

"Don't know."

"Do you know who did it?"

"No."

He sighed and dropped forward to rest his head in his hands.

The kitchen seemed to close in on her, and she could feel panic begin. "Are any of us in danger?"

He was silent a moment. "Someone tried to come into the house last night."

Her eyes grew wide.

"You need to stick close to the house for a while."

"What about the children?" She was surprised by her own words and that she'd thought of the children first. *Could I be capable of caring for them?* The thought overwhelmed her, and her panic intensified. *Breathe, in, out.*

She coughed, her chest growing heavy and her breathing shallow. Someone had tried to come into the house. *Were any of them safe? What if someone hurt the children?* Her stomach dropped. *What about Emma? Am I betraying her if I care for another child?* No one was to ever take her place, ever. No one was to make her feel these things again.

"Are you okay?" John asked.

She glanced up at him, and knew by the look on his face that she hadn't hidden the attack very well. Only able to nod, she reached with shaky hands for her coffee, her throat closing.

"You don't look okay."

She tried to smile.

"Do you need something? Can I get you anything?"

She shook her head. She didn't want him concerned, didn't want him to help her. She opened her mouth to tell him so, but nothing came out except short puffs of air.

The uneven grooves from the wooden table irritated her wrists, annoying her arms as they shook.

"Here, I'll get you a cool cloth. Your face is beet red." He stood.

"It's okay, Pa." Ben came into the kitchen. His navy blue pajamas were wrinkled from sleep. "She's havin' a breathin' attack." The child pushed a chair up to the counter. His skinny arms jacked the pump handle up and down. Gurgling, the metal pipe ejected water into the glass he held. Jumping down from his chair, Ben handed the glass to Livy.

"She needs a glass of water is all."

Livy took the cup from Ben's hands. Close to hyperventilating, she chugged the water. It felt cool in her throat, and she could feel it flow all the way down to her stomach as she battled the war going on inside of her.

"It's okay, Miss Livy. Take deep breaths," Ben told her, as he patted her shoulder.

She listened to the boy, inhaling through her nose and exhaling out her mouth, her eyes on Ben the whole time.

John hadn't said a word up until now. "How did you know what to do, Son?"

Ben didn't look at his father, instead he stared at her. "Cause it's happened before."

Her breathing slowed to normal, and she was finally able to speak. "Thank you," she whispered to Ben. Not ready to look up at John, she averted her eyes.

"What's a breathing attack?" John asked.

Her stomach churned at his question. She wiped at the perspiration on her forehead.

"It's when your heart beats real fast and you can't catch your breath," Ben said. "Right, Miss Livy?"

She took two more cleansing breaths. Her back straight, she sat stiffly in her chair.

"Why do you get them?" John asked, his brown eyes searching her face.

"I...I...well," she stuttered. *What am I supposed to tell him? I can't tell him the truth. Not yet. Not ever.*

"Have you always had them? Are you ill? Do you need medication?"

So many questions and none pertained to why she suffered with them.

He leaned over the table toward her.

Lie. Tell him you've always had them and they are incurable.

"I... I have—"

A loud knock at the front door saved her from answering him.

"We'll finish this conversation later," he said, pointing his long finger down at her.

Livy bobbed her head like a child who had been scolded. Her loose hair hung heavy down her back, and she stretched back fingering the brown locks. After John left, she placed her head on the table. She was thankful for the interruption. He had a way of getting under her skin and causing her to lose control. The events of last night came rushing back to her and she proceeded to bang her head on the table.

"What are ya doin', Miss Livy?" Ben asked.

She'd forgotten about the boy and brought her head up to look at him. "Oh, I'm trying to cause amnesia that's all."

"Amneeza?" the boy repeated.

Livy laughed at his effort to say the hard word.

"It's actually pronounced am-nees-ee-uh."

"What's that?"

"It's when someone can't remember anything. You have to hit your head real hard for it to work though."

"Why would you wanna do that?"

Because I don't want to have to deal with your father. Because I've told so many lies I can't keep track anymore. "I don't," she reassured him. "I was only kidding."

"Oh."

She knew he didn't understand why she'd kid about hitting her head, and she decided not to discuss it further. "Would you like me to make you some breakfast?"

Ben's little face perked up. "Yes ma'am!"

John opened the front door, not at all surprised to see Sheriff Bootly standing on the other side, cowboy hat in hand. He never really liked the lawman. Boots was a drunk, and he smelled like the pigs on the Jefferson's farm, foul and rotten. The NWMP had let him stay on as Sheriff in Calgary, giving him the occasional job to keep him busy. But everyone knew they were the ones who ran the town and kept the order.

He realized that the familiar smell of stale liquor was absent from Boot's breath this morning. He examined the law man, and noticed the greasy strings of hair on the top of Boots head had been combed, and his clothes weren't wrinkled and stained.

Curious, John asked, "All dressed up for me, Boots?"

"I sure could use a coffee, Taylor," he said, peering around John.

Realization dawned as to why the sheriff appeared so clean today. He must have heard about Livy. He shook his head as a possessiveness he'd never felt before stole over him. The sheriff didn't have a snowball's chance in Hell with her. She was his.

"Come on in." Stepping to the side, he allowed the large man entry.

Boots patted his hair and wore a toothy grin on his fat face as he strolled past John. They entered the kitchen as Livy was preparing Ben and Emily's breakfast.

She put a smile on her pretty face. "Good morning. You must be the sheriff."

Boots' eyes looked as if they were about to pop out of his head when he glanced at Livy, and John had to restrain from punching them back in.

"Howdy, ma'am." Boots stuck out a meaty hand and shook Livy's.

"Are you hungry, Sheriff?" she asked.

Boots rubbed his round belly where the too small shirt threatened to burst. "Why thank you ma'am, I reckon I am." He pulled out a chair while she poured him a cup of hot coffee.

John watched as the other man ogled Livy. He went and placed his arm around her tiny waist, and planted a light kiss on her cheek. "I'll take a coffee too," he whispered in her ear.

"If you would take a seat, Mr. Taylor," she whispered back, her voice tense, "I would kindly fill your cup."

He winked at her, and took a seat across from Boots.

"So what seems to be the problem, Taylor?" Boots asked in between long glances at Livy.

Yup, Boots fancied her. Damn his luck. He'd had a hell of a time reaching her, now he had to compete with the sheriff. Irritated with the other man, and his obvious attraction to Livy, John answered in a gruff tone, "Rusty, one of my hands, was found dead last night."

Ben dropped his fork onto his dish, making a loud clanking sound.

"I reckon it was no accident if I was called," Boots said.

"Nope. It wasn't."

"Any ideas on who might've done it?"

"Don't know that either." John glanced over at Livy. He knew she was listening as she fried up the eggs. "But someone tried to break into the house last night."

Ben dropped his fork again, and Livy handed him a clean one.

Boots turned from Ben to address John. "Think it might be the same person?"

Damn, the lawman was actually doing his job. Boots usually didn't take these things too serious, and he had him figured for a coward.

"One of my hands said he saw someone sneaking around, in fact he swears it was Danny, a boy I hired a month ago."

Livy placed their plates on the table, and Boots wasted no time digging in.

"This sure is good, ma'am," he told her.

She smiled at the compliment, and dropped two more pancakes onto Ben's plate. Ben stuffed his face. He was eager, John thought, to go outside and play.

"Well, the way I figure it Taylor, is you got untrustworthy men workin' for you." Boots said, a piece of egg stuck to his chin.

"I'm aware of that Boots."

"I'll do some digging around, if you don't mind. See what I can find."

"I'd appreciate that. Thanks, Boots."

The sheriff gave a brief nod before he got up and left the kitchen.

Ben shot up out of his chair once he was done, thanked Livy, and ran out the door. Emily followed going outside to swing on the wooden seat John had hung for them last week.

Livy grabbed his empty plate, and John inhaled her, the scent of lilacs filling his nostrils.

"How do you get that smell?" he asked her.

She peered over at him, a confused look on her face. "What smell?"

He grabbed her arm, and pulled her close to nuzzle at her neck. "Lilacs," he whispered.

She pushed away from him, and with shaking hands, smoothed her skirt. "It's soap."

He watched her. She was beautiful. Her hair was woven into a long braid that allowed little wisps to escape and caress her face. "I like it. It reminds me of a spring morning."

"It's only soap, Mr. Taylor," she said, brushing him off and taking a step back.

She was scared of him. He could tell. She stood wringing her hands together. "Are you afraid of me?"

"No, I'm not afraid of you." Her eyes darted about the room.

He stood.

"I'd never hurt you, Livy."

"I know that."

But the quiver in her voice told him otherwise, and he took another step toward her. "Why don't you call me *John?*"

Her cheeks grew rosy, and he couldn't control his hands as they crawled up either side of her waist. "I won't hurt you," he whispered.

She tried to push him away, but he pulled her closer instead. "Please Mr...uh, John let me go."

Unable to walk away from her, he brought his head down and brushed his lips across hers. "I know you like me, Livy."

She didn't answer, and he took his cue, deepening the kiss. Her lips, firm at first, softened and move with his. He felt her arms wrap around his neck, and he pushed his tongue into her mouth. She tasted of honey and coffee, and he was crazy with want.

He grew hard as they bumped into the counter behind them. His hands caressed her ribs, inching upwards to fondle her breasts. She inhaled a sharp breath, but never stopped kissing him. Her fingers in his hair, massaging his scalp, she held him to her. He groaned and began unbuttoning her dress. He slipped his hand inside to cup one naked mound. She sighed into his mouth, and he thought he would come undone right there.

The back door opened, ending their kiss. Still holding Livy, he saw Clive standing halfway in the door, a dumbfounded look on his face.

"Damn it, Clive, don't you knock?" he yelled.

She pushed past him and ran out of the room, clutching her dress closed. With no time to stop her, John had no choice but to watch her go.

"You sure know how to make an entrance," he snapped at his friend.

Clive didn't answer right away. He stood stock-still at the door.

"Well? Don't just stand there gawking. What the hell do you want?"

"Sorry, John," he said his face a light shade of pink. "The funeral is about to start, thought you might want to be there."

He ran his hand through his tousled hair. "Yeah, I'm comin'." Grabbing his hat off the table, he glanced in the direction Livy had run, and went outside with Clive.

CHAPTER SIXTEEN

Livy watched the funeral from her bedroom window, her skin still tingling from John's caresses. When Clive caught them this morning, she'd fled the kitchen with her dress half undone.

She squeezed her eyes shut and groaned loudly.

She must've looked like a floozy. How could she have let that happen? What had she been thinking? And why had he kissed her at all? Especially after he'd told her he would never have feelings for her.

Oh, what was the matter with her? She didn't even like him. He riled her with his bossiness and his holier-than-thou attitude, snapping at her one minute, and then kissing her the next. He'd hypnotized her with his silly words about how beautiful she was, or how she smelled of lilacs.

She wrapped her arms around her middle. She didn't understand him. She pressed her forehead against the cool plate glass window, but it did nothing to ease the fire in her cheeks. Every time John came near her, touched her, she'd melt like snow in the spring time. And when he kissed her— *I have no control.*

She touched her fingers to her lips and could still feel his mouth on hers. She was positive that he wanted her as much as she wanted him. But he was a man, and she knew all too well that a man's wants were different than those of a woman.

She shuddered at the memory of Boyd on top of her. *No. Do not think of him. You will never get that night back.* The night that sick bastard stole more than her pride. After the bruises healed and the aching in her most private places had gone, she vowed never to be with another man again.

Her dreams of getting married and starting a family had been ruined. He had taken so much from her, and she'd been determined not to think of that night again. Once Emma had been born, she had almost erased it from her mind completely. Boyd would never be a part of her life again. But it was clear she would never forget.

She had lived with a hidden fear of all men until she'd come to the ranch. John changed all that. When she thought of him, her skin didn't crawl and she never became nauseated. He helped her forget about the awful night, the rough hands on her skin, bruising her. John had never hurt her, and she knew somehow that he never would. She was beginning to care for him, her feelings growing stronger and stronger every time they were together.

She glanced below her at the men gathered around for the funeral. Mother Nature knew they were mourning. Thick gray clouds littered the sky and covered the sun. Without the sun's light, the fields were drab, drained of their many colors. Before her was a mixture of blues and grays, the fields held a mirror reflecting the sky.

How John was going to figure out who had killed Rusty? Any one of those men down there could've done it as far as she was concerned. They all seemed alike to her. Her green eyes scanned the men, stopping at one in particular. He was the only one who hadn't removed his hat. Squinting, she tried to see his face, but his hat obscured her view. All she saw was his jaw and that—could it be?—he was smiling. She tilted her head to get a better look. Surely he couldn't be. Why would he?

There was something about him that was familiar to her. The way he stood, leaning over to one side, his hand in his jeans pocket like he didn't want to be there. Who could she possibly know way out here? She'd seen so many men working in the saloons that they all seemed to blur into one face. *That was it. He was a mixture of them all, nothing else.* Clive was saying a few words from the Bible, and her eyes sought out John.

He wasn't hard to find. Tall and strong, he stood separate from everyone else. Her chest grew tight and her heart raced. She was about to let the curtain fall when he stared up at her bedroom window. Their eyes met. He held her gaze, penetrating and raw. Each drawn to the other, she couldn't move as he held her prisoner. She was mesmerized by his handsome features. When he smiled up at her, she took a step back, dropping the curtain, and breaking the spell.

She fanned her face. *What is he doing to me?* Frightened of her own thoughts, she rushed from the room.

John had seen Livy watching the funeral from her bedroom window. Drawn to her, he'd glanced up and found her staring at him. Not able to take his eyes from hers, he stared back. Her beauty captivated him. Her long brown hair, showing strands of red woven through, reminded him of something out of a fairytale book he'd read to Emily. A princess who lived in a tower, her long flowing hair hung down for a prince to climb.

Livy's creamy white skin, dotted with a few freckles, was soft and supple. John's fingers itched as he remembered caressing her. She was something to be desired—that was for sure—and he was finding that he desired her more and more each day. They had never really talked, so he couldn't say he knew her all that well, but there was something there that drew him to her.

He pulled his eyes from the window and scanned the yard, stopping when he saw Becky's grave—a wooden cross hammered into the dirt. A lump formed in his throat, and John's chest weighted with guilt. He'd forgotten about Becky.

Resentment settled itself low in his belly. He couldn't, shouldn't be thinking such thoughts about Livy. He owed Becky more than that. Livy was a mail order bride. Ordered for one purpose, and he'd do right to remember that, instead of listening to his lower half. He ran his hands through his hair. Damn his head ached.

He needed to put some space between them. He glanced over at Boots. He couldn't act like a jealous husband every time someone looked at her the wrong way. She wasn't his. Besides, he didn't love her, never would. It was best for both of them if he steered clear of her.

"John," Clive said.

"Yeah?"

Clive stared back at him, then raised an eyebrow.

"What did you need?" John asked, trying to keep the harsh tone from his voice.

"I thought you might want to say a few words to the men, seein' as how they're all here."

John cleared his throat. In a firm voice that relayed his authority, he said, "You all know how Rusty died." He eyed his men, some of them nodding, others straight-faced and somber. "I believe one of you is to blame. There is a lockdown on the ranch. No one is to leave without telling me or Clive first. And no one is to go in or around my home." He gave each one a menacing look. "If any of you disobey, you will be fired on the spot, no questions asked. Is this clear?"

All nodded in agreement.

"Good. There will be light chores today, out of respect for Rusty."

The men began to disperse, and he called them back. "Oh, one more thing, all alcohol will be turned into Clive. Until this matter is resolved, there is no drinking on the T-Bar."

The men reacted by cursing and kicking at the ground.

Ignoring their protests, John walked away.

He needed to go for a ride. He needed to get some privacy, and try to sort things out. He headed straight to where Midnight lounged, chewing on some grass. He grabbed his saddle off of the fence and threw it over top of the horse. Latching the cinch underneath, he gave it one final tug before he leapt onto the well-muscled animal. Kicking his heels, the horse took off.

He let his horse run for a few minutes, until he pulled on the reins bringing the animal to a steady trot. He was anxious. The back of his throat felt thick, and his muscles tense. His mind raced with thoughts of Livy, and Becky, and the problems on the ranch. He led Midnight to the creek, dismounted, and sat down under an oak tree. The long thick branches, speckled with bright green leaves, offered shade on a hot day. But since the sun was hidden behind the clouds, it didn't much matter today.

He leaned against the thick trunk, and felt the corded wood press into his back. Taking off his hat, he ran his hand through his hair. How the hell was he going to figure out who had been causing all the trouble on the T-Bar? Who killed Rusty? Who wanted to hurt Livy? His mind raced with all sorts of possibilities, but none seemed right. He was missing something. He knew it.

"Damn it."

How was he going to go through with marrying Livy, when he felt as if he were betraying Becky?

Livy was nothing like his wife. She couldn't cook for one thing, and her temper often caught him off guard and fueled his own anger. Becky never challenged him in all the years they were married. But in the last few weeks, Livy had balked him on almost everything. She fought with him about firing Rusty. She gave him the silent treatment when he came into the house smelling like one of his cows.

He shook his head. She sure did make things interesting.

Life with Becky was far from boring, he blew out a breath, but life so far with Livy had been one problem after the next. She challenged him, riled him, but also made him feel things he never felt when he had been married.

He couldn't deny that he'd lusted for her. She was beautiful. And he knew he could have her if he wanted, and almost had. Thinking back to this morning when Clive had interrupted them—at the time he'd been madder than hell at his foreman for opening the kitchen door when he had—now he was grateful that things hadn't gone any further. He couldn't offer Livy what she deserved. He wasn't free to love her. His heart belonged to Becky. Besides, the hurt that comes from losing someone you love was something he wasn't willing to go through again.

He plucked a blade of grass and placed it in his mouth. Chewing on the green string, he let his mind wander to the trouble on the T-Bar. He knew having Livy on the ranch without a ring on her finger was sure to stir up trouble. But until he figured out who the hell was behind all the mishaps on the ranch, he wasn't going to town—wedding or not.

"Damn. Where the hell do I start?" He couldn't figure out why the culprit was doing it. "It doesn't make sense," he whispered. The questions burned into his mind. He couldn't sleep. He couldn't eat. Damn it he couldn't think. He and Clive had gone over all the men and possible reasons for their actions, but still came up with nothing.

He thought of Rusty, and his stomach turned. It was his fault the man had died. If he hadn't fired him, the man might still be alive. At the funeral, he couldn't help but notice that Boyd didn't remove his hat as the others had. He found it strange, not to mention disrespectful. There was something about the man that didn't sit well with him, and he vowed to keep an eye on him.

He picked up a rock, and flung it sideways into the water, watching as it skipped halfway across the creek, and then sunk to the bottom. He closed his eyes, and placing his hat low over his forehead, he tried to picture Becky. But instead, another woman's face appeared in his mind.

CHAPTER SEVENTEEN

Boyd couldn't believe his luck. A lockdown, and no damn liquor allowed. *No bloody way I'm handin' over my bottle.* He'd hidden it well, and no one was taking his nightly drinking away from him. *Damn that John Taylor with his stupid rules.* Taylor was a bloody pain in the ass, and he was bent on getting rid of him too. He spat on the ground. He'd take care of that little bit of business after he had Angel.

It was time to make a move. He was gettin' tired of all the sneaking around, tired of his plans falling short, and damn tired of merely watching Angel Green. He rounded the bunkhouse and saw Ben sitting on a stump, head in his hands, crying. He was in no mood for a whining kid.

"Hey," he gave him a little shove, "what're you cryin' for?"

The kid shrugged, his face wet with tears. "Livy almost died from fallin' off that horse."

"Yeah, but she didn't." He sat down beside him. "She hasn't left, has she?" He knew Angel hadn't left, but couldn't let the kid know that.

Ben shook his head.

"Well," he smiled, "we'll have to think of another plan."

Ben shook his head again. "No way, mister," He wiped his face with his hand, "I'm not gonna hurt Miss Livy no more."

Boyd's face turned red with anger. "You're not too bright, are ya kid? You see, you cut that cinch. You got Rusty fired. All of that is your fault."

"I never wanted to hurt her. You know that." Ben pleaded.

"Do you think your Pa is gonna believe that?" He was getting sick of the kid.

"Rusty got killed last night, and my Pa thinks someone on the ranch did it." He snickered.

"Well, your Pa is right, kid." He spat on the ground, and then sank forward so only Ben could hear him. "I killed Rusty."

Ben gasped and stood up, but he grabbed his arm jerking him close. "He couldn't keep a secret, and I don't like it when my friends can't keep secrets."

Ben's eyes began to tear, and his bottom lip quivered.

He squeezed Ben's arm hard enough to bruise it. "So you see kid, either you do as I say, and keep our secret, or I'll kill you, and your sister, and your damn Pa."

"I…I…don't want to hurt Miss Livy. I don't want her gone anymore. You don't have to help me."

He laughed.

"Do you think I give a damn about what you want, kid?" His lip curled. "You better keep quiet until I tell ya so, or," He sliced his index finger along his throat. "Understand!?"

Ben swallowed. "Ye…yes, sir."

"Good." He pushed him off of the stump. "Now get out of here, before someone sees us talkin'."

Ben took off toward the river.

He frowned. His hatred for Angel was spreading to anyone associated with her, and he needed to end this once and for all. He stared at the house and saw John leaving. Closing one eye, he held up his fingers like a gun, aiming them at the man. "Bang, you're dead, Taylor." How he'd love to blow his head off. Who would the little bitch run to then? He could take Angel and John's damn ranch. He could have it all.

Certain his boss had slept with Angel, he felt a tinge of jealousy at what the other man could have and he couldn't. He didn't doubt she'd spread her legs willingly, unlike when he'd had her. His cock grew stiff at the thought of her thrashing beneath him, her loud cries while she pleaded for him to stop.

He'd seen her a few times, hopping around on those crutches of hers, and fantasized about how she'd react if he was to walk up to her. The fear he'd see in her green eyes turned him on. She wouldn't know what to do. If he couldn't figure out another way to get her alone, he may have to take her right out in the open for all to see. *And that would be fun.*

Mmmm. Licking his lips, he could still taste her. He wanted to touch her, feel her squirm, and wrestle him as he took her. The fun he would have tormenting her. Then slowly he'd kill her, laughing while she screamed for John Taylor.

CHAPTER EIGHTEEN

John, back from his ride, rounded the corner of the house and heard a woman humming. Curious, he crept up onto the back porch to look into the kitchen window. He took a step back when he saw Livy. Her voice was beautiful, hitting each note. Leaning up against the side of the house to hear more, he was intrigued, and wondered why she had hidden this talent from him.

But as the tune floated past her lips, he noticed something else. The melody was laced with a hint of mourning, and he couldn't help but feel sad as he listened to her. The song she hummed was a lullaby. He recognized it as one Becky had often sung to Ben when he was a baby. Wondering why she hummed it so forlornly, he opened the back door to find out.

"You have a beautiful voice," he said, standing inside the kitchen.

She gasped, and swung around to face him, her thumb stuck in her mouth.

When he saw blood running down her hand, he grabbed a towel and pulled her thumb from her mouth to apply pressure on the wound.

"What happened?" he asked.

"I…I…you scared me, and I cut myself."

"A little bit more pressure and then I'll have a look at it," he said.

"No, I'm fine. I can bandage it myself," she told him, trying to pull her hand away.

Refusing to let go of her, he removed the towel to examine the thumb. "It probably feels a lot worse than it looks," The knife had sliced the middle of her thumb, but as far as he could tell, it wasn't deep enough to warrant stitches. "You'll be fine. I'll wash it up and let the air get at it to dry it out."

"No." She pulled her hand away. "You go about whatever you were doing. I can clean it," she said.

He clasped her hand and pulled it back to him. He guided her over to the wash basin. A bucket of clean water sat next to it so he dumped it over her hand. She hissed from the pain as the water turned a light shade of pink.

"I wasn't doing anything except listening to you sing," he told her, feeling her tense under his touch.

She stared at her hand.

"You have a lovely voice. Do you sing often?"

She didn't answer him.

"Livy?" He tipped his head so he could look at her, "Where did you learn that lullaby?"

Her face red and she averted her eyes. "I...my..." she bit her lower lip, and shrugged.

Taking the opportunity to talk with her, to find out more about her, he asked, "Was it your mother who sang it to you?"

She wrenched her hand from his, splashing water all over him. But he wouldn't let go. He pulled her back toward him, and stared into her terrified green eyes.

"Is that who you were crying over the other night? Was it Emma?" he asked, watching as her face twisted with misery.

She didn't answer, instead closed her eyes as the tears slipped past her thick lashes.

"Livy?"

"Yes," she whispered.

He pulled her into his embrace, and kissed the top of her head. "I'm sorry, sweetheart. Were the two of you close?"

She cried softly, burying her head deeper into his chest.

He wanted know more. He wanted to take away the hurt that he'd seen on her face so many times before. "How did she die?"

She didn't answer him. She clutched his shirt and cried into his chest.

"Ah, darlin'," he whispered, rubbing her back. He could feel her pain as her tears soaked through his shirt. "Is that why you have those breathing attacks Ben was talkin' about?"

She moaned, but still didn't answer him.

"Do you want to talk about it?"

She shook her head.

He figured she'd talk when she was ready. He wouldn't push her. "If you ever need to, I'll be here." He smiled down at her, glad she had opened up to him.

Sniffling now, she lifted her head to look up at him. The agony he saw in her eyes, the fear in her face, pulled something loose within him, and he wanted to take all her pain away.

Holding her face between his hands, he wiped her tears with his thumbs. He brushed his nose against hers, then touched his lips to hers in a velvety kiss.

She kissed him back, her lips melting to his.

"I better go and get some work done," he whispered against her mouth, "Will you be all right?"

She nodded and he bent down to kiss her forehead one more time before he left.

Livy thought she was going to vomit. She lied to John. She told him Emma was her mother. How could she have done that? It was not her intention to tell another lie. Groaning, she covered her face with her hands. She was horrible person. She shouldn't have said anything.

And of all the people to say Emma was, she told him it was her mother. She didn't even know her mother that well, and couldn't say whether she even liked the woman or not. Her mother had lived her whole life inside a saloon, drinking and carousing. And she had grown up watching her mother hang off of the men who drank there.

While her mother was with her clients, she crouched in a dark, musty corner framed by a dressing screen. It wasn't what she called a great life. She recalled a time when she needed her mother. She was thirteen, and had woken up with blood between her legs. Afraid that she may be dying, she went to search for her mother. Livy found her, drunk at the bar with the other women like her. She tried to get her attention, as her mother was sprawled across a cowboy's lap. The filthy man was groping her, and Livy's stomach turned at the things her mother was letting the man do to her.

When her mother realized she had been standing there, and not in her room where she was supposed to be, she slapped Livy hard across the face. That was enough to send Livy fleeing back to her corner while clutching her throbbing cheek.

The next day, with money she stole from her mother, she went to the doctor. The kind man brought his wife in to talk to Livy about what was happening to her and what to do when her monthly came. She also told her what to expect if her monthly's stopped. Livy knew she felt sorry for her. A woman now, with an uncaring, drunken harlot for a mother.

Did she love her mother? She didn't know. They barely spoke, and when her mother wasn't working she was passed out from all the liquor she'd consumed. The woman never taught her anything, other than to depend on yourself for what you want. She wasn't shown how to behave toward others, how to dress, or talk properly.

And if it wasn't for Sam the bartender, she still wouldn't know. He used to bring in his daughter's old dresses for her to wear, instead of the rags her mother had let her run around in. Sam would sit with her for hours, teaching her how to read and write. He told her that if you can't read you may as well be blind. But even with the old man's kindness, she would've traded that life for one that was normal, like the one John led with his children.

She was fifteen when her mother died of pneumonia. Scared, and with nowhere to go, she remembered begging the woman not to die. Not to leave her. Her mother was all she'd ever known, all she had. But her pleas were not heard, and her mother died a few hours later.

Still living at the saloon, she began singing for its patrons instead of selling her body as her mother had. When Emma was born, she sold her mother's jewelry, and with the few dollars Sam had given her, she left town.

She tried finding a respectable job, but with Emma to care for, and no one willing to give her a chance, she was forced back into the saloon to sing for her money. She strived to be everything her mother was not. She wanted nothing more than to give Emma the things she never had.

She blew out a frustrated breath as she paced the floor admitting she cared for John. *Why did I have to lie to him?* Even as she asked the question, she knew the answer. She was ashamed and humiliated. John was a proud man. She knew that much about him.

Would he be any different than those who had ridiculed her? Those who refused to walk on the same side of the street as her? If she told him the truth about Emma, and the circumstances that led up to her birth, would he understand? Would he profess his undying love? Would he tell her it didn't matter what had happened before, he knew her now and wanted to be with her? The answer was simple. No. He'd be angry that she'd lied to him, and tell her to leave.

She didn't want to leave the ranch. She felt wanted and needed here. To have to go would mean returning to her old life. Something she vowed never to do again. Tears poured from her eyes. How was she ever going to make this right? How was she going to come clean with all the lies?

"Miss Livy?" Ben asked.

Looking up at the child, she saw the concern on his small face.

"Are you okay?"

She wiped her face, and forced her lips to smile at the boy. "I'm fine." She didn't see Emily until she peeked around her brother. Her cheeks, muddy from playing outside, were streaked with tears. Concerned, Livy went to her. "What's wrong?" she asked, kneeling down in front of her and Ben.

"Em fell off the swing," he told her.

"Oh." She sat there a moment, frozen with fear. *What should I do?* Her hand trembled as she reached out and took the little girl's hand in her own. Soft and pudgy, the child's hand clasped onto hers. Livy cleared away the lump in her throat as she tugged on Emily's hand, pulling her closer.

"I want Pa," Emily cried.

"Let's have a look, shall we?" She led Emily to the table, and sat her down on a chair where she examined her scraped knees. "A little soap and water and they'll be as good as new."

She cautiously eyed the girl. Livy smiled. Soft blue eyes held hers, and she felt like a weight had been lifted from her shoulders. Still unsure around the child, at least now she was able to look at her and not see Emma's face. Blinking back more tears, she went to the bucket of water on the counter. It was empty. John had dumped it on her finger earlier.

"Ben, could you please sit with your sister while I pump some more water into the bucket."

Ben sat next to Emily and took her hand in his.

"Thank you," she said while dunking a cloth into the water. She wrung it out, and went to Emily. "Okay, let's get you all fixed up." She knelt in front of her. Careful not to hurt her, Livy dabbed at the dry blood on her tiny knees.

Sniffling, and biting her bottom lip, Emily sat still as Livy cleaned her wounds.

"There. You're as good as new," she said.

But instead of getting off the chair, the child sat there and shook her head. Confused, Livy looked at Ben, who was watching them.

"I think she wants you to kiss it better like Pa always does," he said.

Livy hesitated. She didn't know if she could do it. Her heart raced inside her chest. Her hands now clammy and shaking, she tried to swallow. *She is not Emma. She is only a child, John's child.* Taking a deep breath and closing her eyes, she bent and kissed the little girl's knee. Surprised that the show of affection wasn't at all difficult, nor was it followed by a breathing attack. Helping Emily down off the chair, she was overcome with emotion when the child wrapped her pudgy arms around her neck and hugged her.

"C'mon, Em," Ben said, pulling on his sister's arm. "Let's go find clovers."

Still on her knees, Livy watched as they ran outside. Her insides raw, she wrapped her arms around her middle, and rocked back and forth on her heels, trying to hold back all the emotions that had begun to surface. She let the tears fall, washing her, cleansing her. The girl, Emily, had hugged her. She could still feel the warmth of her arms as they clasped around her. The tears that fell from her eyes could not be stopped, and she realized what a fool she had been to deny the child as long as she had.

Emily had nothing to do with Emma. She was innocent. Sobbing now, she thought of her baby. She was gone and would never come back to her. She'd never hug her, or kiss her again, and she mourned for her, longed for her.

Livy thought she'd never be able to care for another person after Emma had died, but coming here had changed all that. She cared for John, and Ben, and now found that she cared for his daughter as well. Overwhelmed, she let her heart open to these feelings. She let the grief and agony dwindle and seep from her. Drip from her, as the tears fell. She'd always love her daughter, always miss her. She knew that the guilt would never leave her. But something had happened here today, and she accepted it.

Her heart ached, and her chest was tight. Gasping she fought the panic as it came, refusing to give in to it anymore. Still rocking back and forth, she released the demon that had held her captive for the last year. She expelled the anguish, misery, and torment she had been suffering. Letting it all out, she cried, and cried, and cried.

CHAPTER NINETEEN

John came into the kitchen for breakfast. He was excited to see Livy, especially after she'd told him about her mother. He smiled. It was like unwrapping a present. The more paper he took off, the closer he got to knowing who she was, the real prize. Under her tough exterior was a kind, soft-hearted woman, and he was happy he'd picked her to be his wife. Even if he never loved her, he did admit to caring for her, and that was damn well better than nothing at all.

When he came into the kitchen, he was surprised to see Boots sitting at his table with a plate of steaming flapjacks in front of him. The lawman was too busy eyeballing Livy to look up when he entered the room.

He shook his head. "Boots, I didn't figure I'd see you for a few days," he said, as he bent and kissed Emily's head. "Mornin' pumpkin."

His daughter smiled up at him, her face messy with syrup.

"Well Taylor, I'm just doin' my job," Boots said, still staring at Livy.

"Yeah, I can see that," he mumbled, pulling back a chair to take a seat.

Livy walked toward him holding a vase full of wild flowers that she placed on the table.

"Where did you get those?" he asked, staring at the white daisies, honeysuckle, and pink roses that filled the kitchen with a sweet fragrance.

"Boots brought them. Aren't they lovely?" she hummed, her voice cheery.

He eyed the sheriff who was smiling up at Livy like a love sick-school boy. "Yeah, lovely."

"After the nice breakfast Miss Livy fed me yesterday, I felt the need to repay her." The man shrugged as he continued, "These flowers are a small token."

"Well, I love flowers." Livy said to the children. "Isn't that right?"

"Yup, she sure does," Ben piped up, "Em and me picked her flowers when she hurt her leg and she sure liked 'em."

"Yes, I did." She ruffled Ben's hair.

John didn't like them. But nobody seemed to give a damn about what he thought. His mood turned sour as he watched Livy fuss over the flowers on the table. Ah hell, he'd never made her smile like that. What if he wanted to give her flowers? The damn lawman beat him to it. John glared at him across the table. What the hell was Boots giving Livy flowers for anyway?

"Have you found anything out yet?" he asked gruffly.

"Nope, need a few more days."

"How many is a few?"

"Three or four." Boots stuffed his fat face full of pancakes.

"Last I checked a few meant two."

Boots shrugged.

If he didn't take his eyes off of Livy soon, John was going to come across the table at him. "Well maybe you should be workin' instead of eatin'."

"John," Livy said to him before turning her attention back to Boots. "You're always welcome, Sheriff."

"Why, thank you, ma'am," Boots grinned up at her.

The two of them seemed to be in a world of their own. He had seen enough. Pushing his plate away, he got up. "I have work to do." Not bothering to say goodbye, he slammed the door on his way out.

Still hungry, John decided to walk over to the cook shack to eat with the hands. He knew if he stayed in the kitchen any longer, Boots would be clutching a broken nose. The air was crisp, and he breathed it in. Soon it would be fall. He stared at the trees surrounding the cook shack. The leaves were a vibrant green now, but in a few weeks they would turn rust and gold and fall to the ground as the giant elms went to sleep for the winter. He loved fall as a child, because that meant winter was on its way.

Smiling, he remembered building a snow man every year with his Pa, and dressing it in an old scarf and a beat up Stetson. They'd hunt for hours to find two eyes and a nose for their frozen friend, often ending their day with a snowball fight. The tradition carried on to his children. Ben and Emily loved winter as much as he did.

In the colder months, he seemed to have more time to spend with his children. He wasn't stuck in the fields for days, or busy preparing for a cattle drive.

The cook shack was littered with tables when he entered. He was soon comforted by the loud chatter of his men as they ate their breakfast. Heading straight for Ezekiel, who stood behind a long table, John grabbed a plate and waited for the cook to serve him.

"Boss?" Ezekiel asked, "Everthin' okay?"

"Yup," John answered, already regretting leaving his earlier meal when he glanced down at the runny oatmeal on his plate. Taking a seat next to Clive, he ignored the look his foreman gave him.

"She burnt the food again?" Clive asked.

"Nope, don't like the company that it came with."

"Miss Green's?"

"Sheriff Bootly's."

"He's here again? I thought he'd be back in a few days."

"So did I."

"Did he find anything out?"

"Nope." John wasn't in the mood to talk about the sheriff.

"Well, then why is he here?"

"He brought Livy flowers."

Clive laughed.

"What's so funny?"

"Oh, I get it."

He glanced up at his friend. "Get what?"

"You're jealous," he said, over a mouthful of food.

"You're crazy."

"It's as plain as day."

"I am not jealous."

"Boots is sweet on Miss Livy," he pointed the shiny spoon at him, "and you don't like it."

"You have no idea what you're talkin' about."

"Sure Boss, I have no clue."

"Why the hell would I be jealous?" He raked his own spoon through the white oatmeal on his plate. The texture made his stomach turn.

"Oh, I don't know. Could it be the fact that your soon-to-be-wife is quite pretty?" Clive teased.

"You're a damn fool."

"I don't think so, John."

"You don't know what you're talkin' about."

"She is quite fetching. Any man with eyes can see that."

"Well, I didn't ask you." He dropped his spoon in his oatmeal splattering the white goo all over his shirt. "Damn it." He picked the oatmeal off of his chest and sleeve.

"You didn't have to. I can see it on your face."

He glared at his friend.

"You have feelings for her," Clive confirmed.

He narrowed his eyes at the other man.

Clive smiled.

"So what if I do? She is going to be my wife." He clenched his jaw.

"Yup, she is."

"I should like her."

"Never said you only liked her."

"So now you're a damn fortune teller?" he growled, getting angrier by the minute at his foreman's insinuations.

"Don't have to be. I see the way you look at her."

"Is that so?" He leaned in, pretending to be enthralled with what Clive was saying. "Do tell more."

"Make fun all you want, but you'll admit it soon enough."

"Don't hold your breath."

"Stop holding yours, John." Clive picked up his plate and stood. "Let nature take its course."

He watched Clive leave the bunkhouse. He followed his friend out the door. He wasn't ready to end their conversation. "What makes you the expert?" he called after him. "You've never even been married."

Clive stopped half way to the corrals and spun around to face him. "I was married once," he said, his voice low.

Stunned that he never knew, that his foreman had never told him, John stood frozen. "When?"

"In Montana, before I came back here to work for you."

"What happened?" His anger gone, he moved closer to his friend. The cattle in the nearby pen stood staring at them as if eavesdropping on their conversation.

Clive shrugged.

"She left."

"Why?"

"Didn't like bein' married to a farmer." He picked up a bucket, dipped it into a barrel of feed, and dumped it into the pen for the cows.

I'm a damn idiot. The worst kind of friend. "How come you never told me?"

The metal tin still in his hand, Clive's eyes turned sad and withdrawn. "You had just lost Becky, and I couldn't even talk about it without breaking down."

"Do you still love her?"

Clive was silent for a moment before he dropped the bucket back into feed barrel. He took off his hat and ran his arm across his forehead.

"Not a day goes by that I don't think about her, if that answers your question."

"Why didn't you go after her?"

His lips formed a thin line and opened a little. "I did. A few months later. I begged her. Pleaded with her. Made a damn fool of myself too when I found out she was engaged to another man."

"What?"

"Yeah. She came from a wealthy family," he said shrugging. "Her parents never liked me, and once she came back they were quick on marrying her off to one of the richest men in the city."

"Didn't she love you?" John asked, still shocked that he hadn't known any of this.

"Said she did, but the money was more important to her I guess." Clive kicked at the dirt on the ground.

"I'm sorry, Clive." And he meant it. The man was his best friend, had always been there for him, and he hated to see the anguish in his eyes.

"It's over and done with John."

He was silent.

"I can't change the past."

"Isn't that the truth," he agreed, patting his friend on the back.

"Aren't we two of the sorriest fools around?" Clive said.

"That we are, old friend. That we are."

After Livy had cleaned up the dishes from dinner, she went into the sitting room where John was about to read to the children. Taking a seat on the sofa next to Ben, she listened to John's deep voice as he began the story of David and Goliath. Reluctant to stay—she hadn't much faith in the bible—she couldn't find it in her heart to get up and leave when Ben snuggled up close to her.

The story was quite fascinating. She couldn't help but be enthralled by the enormous giant and little David, wondering the whole time if the boy was going to die. She and the children went into fits of laughter when John used different voices for every character, making Goliath sound like a loud, mean man and David a soft, timid boy. He was quite the storyteller, and when he glanced up at her and smiled, she felt her heart expand with joy.

The kerosene lamp cast shadows dancing on the walls around the cramped room. She was content, and hadn't felt this way since Emma had been born. Placing her arm around Ben, she hugged him close to her, relishing in the comfort the child offered. Soon he was snoring, fast asleep nestled into her.

He closed the Bible, and whispered, "I think it's time for these two to go to bed." Emily was fast asleep in his arms as well.

"Yes, I think so."

Cradling Emily, John eased up and out of his chair.

"I'll be right back to get Ben," he said.

She no longer needed the crutch, but since she was still healing she couldn't risk carrying Ben upstairs. Pulling the boy into her, she inhaled, taking pleasure in the few moments she had alone with him. He came back to gather Ben from Livy's arms. As he leaned in close to her, their eyes met. He inched closer as if to kiss her, and she couldn't help but lean forward.

"Miss Livy?" The child murmured.

She lowered her eyes from John's gaze. "I'm here Ben," she said softly, as she rubbed his back.

"Can you tuck me in with Pa?" he asked half asleep.

Touched that he had wanted her to help put him to bed, she couldn't say no. "If that's all right with your Pa."

John's eyes were soft as they peered into hers. "I think that'd be fine." He smiled.

"I'll turn down the lamp and be right up," she whispered.

Because of her leg, it seemed like it took forever for her to climb the stairs. Almost out of breath when she arrived at Ben's room, she could hear him snoring softly, snuggled deep inside his covers.

John held his finger up to his mouth. "Shush."

She crept over to Ben's bed to wish him goodnight. Rolling over, his eyes closed, Ben mumbled, "Night...Mama."

Her hand went to her chest and her eyes misted with tears. She bent and kissed him on his forehead. "Goodnight, Ben," she whispered back.

John was still standing in the doorway when she passed by him to leave. His dark eyes void of any emotion, stared past her.

She tipped her head as she passed him. "Goodnight, John."

"Goodnight, Livy," he said, his voice barley louder than a whisper.

She went straight to her room and closed the door. Leaning against the wall, she took a deep breath. She had never heard those words before, had never felt the overwhelming joy she felt now hearing them for the first time. Unsure if Ben had called *her* Mama, or if he'd been dreaming of his mother, she realized that she didn't care.

She had dreamed of Emma calling her Mama, but her child hadn't grown old enough to talk, taken away from her before she could hear those precious words. But she wasn't angry that they had come from someone else. From a little boy who missed his mother very much. A little boy she had come to care deeply for, and who without any other reason but pure innocence, had said the word she would hold dear to her heart.

Ben and Emily had somehow nestled themselves deep into the corners of her soul, forcing her to love again, care again—something she thought would never happen. They were a gift. She could see that now. A second chance she was lucky to have. The thought of caring for another person, much less two, frightened her to no end. But without them she'd be lost.

Vowing not to waste another minute feeling sorry, or dwelling on the things she couldn't change, Livy instead decided to act like the mother the two little darlings deserved.

John lay in his bed, thinking of Ben. He knew his son missed his wife something fierce and longed for a mother's touch. But he had no idea that Ben would take to Livy as quickly as he had. This caught him off guard, and brought to surface feelings he hadn't realized were still there. He had been so consumed with the guilt of betraying Becky that he hadn't even thought about his children, or how they would react when he brought another woman into the house to take their mother's place.

He blew out an exasperated breath. *What did you think would happen?* She was offish and cold at first, but over the last few weeks she had come around, opening up to him about her breathing attacks and her mother. He had come to care for her, so why wouldn't his own children?

When she bent and kissed Ben's forehead, he was so overcome with emotion he almost broke down right there. Seeing his son cling to another woman hadn't affected him the way he thought it would. Instead of feeling guilty, he was relieved. He wanted this after all. Someone to watch over his children if something happened to him. Someone to love them and care for them. And Livy had filled that position, proving to him that she cared for his kids almost as much as he did.

Rolling over on his bed, he stared out the window. There were no clouds in the sky, and the stars sparkled against the black night, winking at him. His thoughts strayed to Livy. Her smile, the way her eyebrows scrunched up when she was confused, and her beautiful shamrock colored eyes full of sorrow and pain as they stared up at him. Yes, he cared for her. He guessed he always had. He'd been jealous this morning when the sheriff brought her flowers. He wanted to be the one who made her face light up with joy.

Can I be happy again? Am I able to live the rest of my day's content with Livy in my life? He ran his hand through his hair. "*I don't know.*"

CHAPTER TWENTY

Humming cheerfully, Livy dusted the furniture in the sitting room. The damp cloth skimmed the edges of John's books, wiping them clean. Breakfast with John and the children had been wonderful. Ben and Emily giggled at the silly faces their Pa made at them across the table, and she participated in their cheer, laughing along with them. They were becoming a family, and John even bent to give her a quick kiss on the cheek before he headed out to work.

Her life had begun to change. She no longer walked around angry and depressed, lost in her own misery, snapping at or casting judgment on those around her. She felt content—safe. And she found each day easier than the one before it.

Although still waking with dreams of Emma, her guilt over the death of her daughter would forever torment her, she had accepted the truth that Emma was gone. She missed her baby and always would. The pain in her heart was a dull ache that never went away, but John's family had somehow made her days peaceful, comfortable.

Her breathing attacks had almost stopped, and she thanked Ben and Emily for that. They kept her so busy that whenever Emma's face appeared in her mind, and a breathing attack was about to start, she would be whisked away to help them with a game, or to push Emily on the swing, and she'd forget all about her short breaths and tight chest.

Ben and Emily had been helping her heal, and she was grateful to the pair. As the days passed, the three of them grew closer, and she wanted to be a part of their lives. She wanted to help Ben with his reading, and to sing with Emily. She wanted to laugh with them and to cry with them. For it to be her arms they'd run to when they were scared or hurt.

"Miss Liby?" Emily called from the kitchen.

"I'm in here, Emily."

Every time she saw the little girl, she was taken aback by how pretty she was. Her round face and chubby cheeks reminded Livy of a cherub she'd seen in a book, and she understood why John called her his angel.

"I'm wet," Emily said. She was standing in the doorway leading into the sitting room. Her pinafore was soaked through and dripping onto the floor.

"Oh my," Livy said, rushing over to her. "What happened?"

"I fwell."

She is so sweet and innocent. And I can hold her tight any time I want to.

She giggled at the adorable picture before her. Covering her mouth quickly so she didn't hurt Emily's feelings, she said "Come on sweetheart, let's go get you changed."

She held Emily's hand, and took her upstairs. Emily stripped off her wet clothes, and Livy helped her into a clean, dry dress. Rubbing her eyes and letting out a long yawn, Emily reached for her blanket on her bed.

"I think it's time for a nap." Livy said as she smiled down at her.

Emily crawled onto her bed. She snuggled into her blanket, stuck her thumb in her mouth and sucked quietly. Her eyes fluttered. Livy sat with her, and ran her fingers through Emily's blonde hair. She hummed a lullaby until Emily's eyes closed and her chest rose and fell with deep, even breaths. Not wanting to leave, she settled next to Emily. With her arm around the child, she closed her eyes and drifted off.

"Miss Livy?" Ben shook her.

She opened her eyes and found Ben nudging her gently. Sitting up, and afraid she'd slept too late to get supper ready, she asked, "What is it, Ben?"

Whispering so he didn't wake his sister, he said, "Pa's lookin' for ya."

She stretched her arms above her head and yawned. Slowly, so she didn't wake Emily, she got off the bed and followed Ben out of the room.

"Where is your father?" she asked.

His eyes downcast, he shrugged his thin shoulders. "Last time I saw him he was in the tack house."

Her knee still sore, she limped down the stairs. She found that if she didn't stretch every few hours, the tender limb would stiffen up. She slowly paced the length of the kitchen, in long strides, stretching her leg. Ben stood off to the side, and Livy noticed that he didn't seem like his old self. Instead of being hyper and jumping around, the youngster was subdued.

"Are you okay, Ben?"

His eyes began to tear, and he quickly wiped at them. "I'm okay."

She knelt before him. "Are you sure, sweetheart?"

He nodded.

"You can tell me anything and I'd do my best to help you."

"I'm just hungry."

"There's nothing else bothering you?"

"No."

"Okay, I'll make you a sandwich for lunch, and then I'll go find your father." She ruffled his hair.

"I don't think it was important. You could probably talk to him at dinner." Ben's voice seemed strained.

"No, I'll go find him in a bit. I'm sure he can wait until I make you a sandwich."

After making Ben a third sandwich, he'd said the first two hadn't filled him up, she headed outside in search of John.

The bright afternoon sun blinded her, so she grabbed a wide-brimmed hat off of the swing. She could hear the cows bawling in the fields. The sound that once annoyed her was now comforting, and it reassured her that she wasn't alone. She went through the door of the tack barn and called John's name. She made her way toward the other end of the barn, while running her hand along the shelves. Hearing someone behind her, and thinking it was John, she turned.

"There you are," she said, but was caught off guard when a hand, rough and hard, clamped around her mouth. Her heart beat wildly inside her chest. She tried to turn and see who had grabbed her. Whoever it was, he was pulling her into the corner of the barn, away from the door. Her arms were held tightly to her sides. She screamed into the hand around her mouth.

"Did you miss me, Angel?"

Livy's eyes grew wide when she recognized Boyd's voice whispering in her ear. *No, no, no!* She shook her head. *It can't be. How did he find me? Where did he come from?*

"I sure missed you." His hot breath on her cheek reeked of stale liquor and cigarettes.

Her stomach revolted at the awful smell, and she gagged into his hand. Memories came rushing back. Horrible memories of the last time her took her.

He threw her to the ground.

She scrambled to get up—to get away—but he slapped her hard across the face, dazing her. Frantically she looked around. He had taken her to one of the stalls in the back of the barn. She watched petrified, as he closed the gate and leered down at her. He laughed, a menacing, evil sound that made her skin crawl, and she recognized the desire in his crazed eyes.

She screamed John's name, but he was too fast for her. He covered her mouth with his hand, and got on top of her. She wiggled beneath him. Her hands grasping at anything nearby, pulling up the hay and dirt around her, as she fought for her life.

Boyd's body was grinding up against hers. His weight pushed her further into the ground, and she could feel the needles of straw as they stabbed through her dress and nicked her skin. She rolled from side to side allowing her to get one hand free and she scratched his ugly face. His skin hung from her fingernails as blood dripped from his cheek.

"You little bitch," he snarled, and slapped her so hard he cut her lip. Boyd's face came within an inch of her own. His foul scent invading her nostrils made her kick harder.

He licked the blood from her face.

Please, God make it stop. Make him stop.

He kissed her, and rammed his tongue into her mouth. His right hand pulled her skirt up over her knees, while the left one fondled her breasts. She kicked, and tried to roll away from him. But his tongue still invaded her mouth. She bit down hard, until she tasted his blood.

"I'm gonna take you whether you're willing or not," he sneered, spitting the blood from his mouth onto the hay beside her.

"Get off of me," she shrieked. *Last time he beat me bloody raw. Last time I wanted to die. God, please let me die now. Please don't let me live through this again.*

He ripped her petticoat, and tossed it aside. "You are a sight, and now you're mine."

His fingers cruelly mauled at the cleft between her legs.

"No, no," she pleaded, "Stop."

Fighting him harder and flinging her head from side to side, she saw Ben standing inside the barn, his eyes big and full of tears. She couldn't risk calling out to him, afraid that Boyd might kill him. "God please…" she cried, tears streaming down her face. When she looked again, Ben was gone.

"Stop movin'," he yelled.

"You'll…have…to…kill…me…first," she gasped, while straining to get free.

He was rubbing his crotch against her, and she could feel him, hard and poking her stomach. She tried to twist her body away from him. Viciously he ran his tongue along the tops of her breast, licking them. He bit them several times, drawing blood.

She cried out from the pain.

He moaned into her skin.

How could this be happening again? How could he be here? How?

She gasped for air.

"I have waited way too long for you," he said, sitting up on his knees and unbuttoning his pants.

Taking the opportunity, she kicked him off of her and scrambled away. Her torn dress hung open, revealing her breasts. She screamed for John. Boyd clawed at her, his nails slicing into her back. He grabbed her hair, swung her around, and smacked her face with the back of his hand. The blow to her cheek had her seeing stars, and Livy's eye's rolled back as she fell to the ground.

Ben ran from the barn and straight into Clive. He clung shaking and stuttering onto Clive's leg. "Livy…Livy…" He pointed toward the tack house.

Clive bent to help him up. Dusting him off he asked, "What is it Ben? What's wrong?"

He scanned the yard, looking for John.

"Livy…he…he…" Ben moaned, tears running down his cheeks.

"Slow down, little fella, Now, what's wrong with Livy?"

"She's…hurt…bad…man…" Distraught, Ben pointed again to the tack house.

Clive didn't need him to say anymore. He ran toward the barn and burst through the doors. He stopped to let his eyes adjust to the dim light. When he heard rustling in the far corner, he went to investigate. Boyd was on top of Livy, his pants down, her dress pulled up exposing her most precious parts. Growling, Clive lunged at the man and pulled him off of Livy. His fist smashed into Boyd's face, and blood spewed from his nose.

"You son of a bitch," Clive snarled.

But Boyd wasn't going down without a fight. He threw his body into Clive, knocking him to the ground, and the two of them rolled through the straw.

A loud scream made Clive look up, taking his attention off of the fight. Ben stood a few feet away. Boyd sucker punched Clive, got up and belted his pants. He ran out of the barn, pushing Ben to the ground on his way. He grabbed the closest horse and rode off.

Unable to go after him, Clive called to Ben, "Go get your Pa." He pushed up off the ground, and went to see if Livy was all right.

Kneeling beside her, he checked for a pulse. Her pretty face was bloody, and her left eye, with a purple bruise forming around it, was beginning to swell shut. Clive grabbed the horse blanket hanging on the nearest stall gate and went back to where she lay unconscious. He wrapped the blanket around her, picked her up, and headed for the house.

John had been working out back mending one of the broken fences, when Ben came running toward him. When he saw Ben was crying, he dropped his hammer and darted toward his son. "What's wrong Ben? Is it Emily?" he asked, picking him up, and wiping his son's tears with his shirt sleeve.

Shaking his head, he whimpered, "Miss Livy."

"Livy? Something's happened to Livy?" With Ben in his arms, he took off toward the house. When he came around the cook shack, he saw Clive coming out of the tack house carrying her wrapped in an old horse blanket. John's pace quickened when he saw his friend's bloody nose and scraped cheek.

"What the hell happened?" he yelled, glancing down at Livy, her face hidden inside the blanket.

Clive didn't answer him. He kept rushing toward the house.

John followed as Clive kicked open the back door and climbed the stairs two at a time. He laid her gently on the bed. As the blanket fell from her face, John inhaled a sharp breath. He put Ben down. Kneeling in front of him, John said in a low voice, "Go and find Emily, and stay in the house, Livy will be all right."

"Okay, Pa." The boy fled from the room.

"What happened?" John asked Clive.

His friend rubbed his hands over his face before answering, "I ran into Ben and he told me Livy was in trouble. When I went into the tack house, Boyd was on top of her." Clive glanced over at John, remorse shadowing his face. "He was trying to rape her, John," he whispered.

"What!" he shouted, not wanting to believe what his friend had said.

Clive shook his head and spoke more clearly. "I got there in time. But she's pretty beat up."

"Where is the son of a bitch?" he growled, heading for the door. He was going to kill him.

"He got away."

"Get Shorty and send him up here. Then gather some of the men. Search until you find the bastard." His hands balled into tight fists at his side.

"Sure thing, John." Clive gave Livy one last look, then left the room.

"Damn it."

John clenched his jaw. Why hadn't he watched Boyd closer? Why didn't he see him for the sick bastard he was? *How could I be so blind?* He went over to the bed. She was still unconscious. Her face was a bloody mess, her bottom lip cut, and her neck was scratched up.

He pulled back the blanket Clive had wrapped her in, and almost retched at the picture before him. The front of her dress was ripped, and her petticoat torn. Her breasts were marked with red welts, cut and bleeding. Some of them, starting to bruise, were light blue around the edges. She was covered with nasty looking scrapes. He tenderly put back the pieces of her dress so they covered her.

He rubbed his face, stopped to cover his mouth and, biting the inside of his hand, he groaned loudly. What had Boyd done to her? She looked broken. He stared down at her, and his vision blurred.

He heard Shorty come up the stairs, and quickly wiped his eyes. Coughing, he covered Livy with the blanket as Shorty entered the room. His face was somber as he glanced over at John.

"We'll fix her up, Boss," he said.

John couldn't utter a word even if he wanted to, his throat was thick with emotion, and so he nodded instead.

Shorty put his bag down lightly on the bed, and went to wash his hands in the basin. When he returned, John was composed and ready to help. Shorty took a bottle of whiskey from his bag, poured some onto two clean, white cloths, and handed one to John. "Dab at the scratches. We don't want her to get an infection."

He took the cloth and began blotting the scratches on her neck and face, while Shorty did the ones on her arms and hands. Livy moaned, but didn't wake up. After they were done, Shorty checked her over from head to toe. He felt for broken bones, checked her pulse, and listened to her breathing.

"I've done about all I can," he said, placing the bottle of whiskey and some more clean cloths on the table beside the bed.

"Thanks, Shorty."

Alone with Livy, John gently ran the cloth over a scratch on her arm. Satisfied that he had thoroughly cleaned all of her cuts, he took off her dress and covered her with a clean blanket. She started to stir. Kneeling beside the bed, he held her hand and waited for her to open her eyes. He winced as her face twisted in pain and one eyelid fluttered open. The other, slightly swollen, opened halfway.

"What," she tried to speak.

"Shush, darlin'," he whispered.

"How?"

"Livy, do you remember what happened?"

He watched as she lifted a shaky hand to her face, and grazed her black eye and bruised cheek. She chewed on her bottom lip, and her eyes filled with tears. Her head shook back and forth slowly while she moaned and squeezed her eyes shut. He couldn't stand to see her like this. He nuzzled his face into her neck and whispered into her ear, "Livy you're safe now, I'm here and I'm not goin' anywhere."

The sounds that erupted from her tore at every part of him, and he felt as if he were going to fall apart right there. He'd kill Boyd for doing this to her. As her cries faded to a light whimper, he brushed back the loose hair that had fallen in her face. He traced kisses, first to her swollen eye, then to the other, placing his mouth lightly there as well. Next he went to her nose, until he came to her cut lip. He let his lips touch hers.

"I'm so sorry, Livy," he whispered against her mouth. This was his fault. He had his suspicions about Boyd but never acted on them, and now she was lying here beaten and bruised. The inner torment she must feel was sure to remain long after the cuts and bruises healed. How would she survive after this?

He sat with her until she fell asleep before heading down stairs to see if Clive had come back. The need to punch something—anything—overwhelmed him, but he savored the thought of getting his hands on Boyd and beating the life out of him.

"Papa," Ben said, sitting at the kitchen table with Emily and Ezekiel, "is Miss Livy okay?"

He hadn't even thought about Ben, what he must've seen. Pulling back a chair, he sat in front of them. "Yeah, son, she'll be fine."

"The bad man. Is he gone?" Ben stammered.

"He's gone," John confirmed. Emily slid off of her chair and came over to him. He lifted her onto his lap.

"No more bad man?" she said.

"Don't worry, pumpkin. You're safe." He kissed the top of her head. "You're both safe."

"I brought up the rest of the soup I made the men for dinner. It's on the stove if you're hungry, Boss," Ezekiel said quietly.

John thanked him, but declined anything to eat. Instead he took Ben and Emily into the sitting room. He sat down on the sofa and hugged his children. The room was quiet except for the ticking of the clock above the fireplace. John stayed where he was, waiting for Clive to come back with Boyd.

CHAPTER TWENTY-ONE

Livy opened her eyes after John left. She needed to be alone, needed to work things out in her head. She couldn't stand to see the pity in his eyes every time he stared at her bruised face and mutilated body. She peered out her window, but against the black sky all she could see was her reflection in the glass. She lifted a trembling hand to her face and ran her fingers along the jagged cut on her lip.

How did Boyd find me? Did he know about Emma? Is that why he'd come? Her chest seized at the thought. *What do I tell John? How can I ever explain things to him now?*

Her loose hair hung knotted and messy around her shoulders, and she appeared as bad as she felt. Her body ached. Her soul was defeated. She wanted to die. She turned from the window, unable to look at her beaten face any longer. She laid her head back on the pillow, but could still feel Boyd on her, could smell his foul odor.

Draped in the blanket John had covered her in, she inched out of the bed. She took short steps. Her body throbbed with every move. She went to the basin of water on her dresser. Dropping the blanket onto the floor, she shuddered as she stood naked. With shaky hands she dipped the wash cloth in the tepid water and grabbed the bar of soap. She scrubbed at her face, hard and fast, breaking open the wounds, and allowing them to bleed. Moving down to her neck, her breasts and her stomach, she scoured her skin until it was raw.

Her breaths shallow and quick, she fell to her knees, rubbing the cloth between her legs, burning her skin, as she tried to erase all traces of Boyd from her. Her body tense and cramped, she shivered as she wrapped the blanket securely around her.

Then she curled into a ball on the floor and wept.

CHAPTER TWENTY-TWO

It was dark outside when John heard the horses come in. Ben and Emily were asleep beside him on the sofa. Outside, the men were getting off of their horses, and looked tired and worn. He scanned the men anxiously for Clive. When he saw his friend, he stepped off of the porch and rushed over to him.

Her life had begun to change. She no longer walked around angry and depressed, lost in her own misery, snapping at or casting judgment on those around her. She felt content—safe. And she found each day easier than the one before it.

"Where's Boyd?" he asked, not waiting for Clive to get off of his horse.

"We couldn't find him." He averted his eyes.

John threw his hands up in the air. "What do you mean you couldn't find him?"

Clive dismounted and stood in front of him. "Sorry, John. We searched for hours."

"That's not good enough," he shouted, "get back on your horses, and keep looking."

"John," Clive said, placing a hand on his shoulder. "The men are tired, and they need to rest."

He pushed Clive's hand off of him, and faced his foreman. "I don't give a damn. Get back on your horses."

"We'll look again in the morning. The men need to eat."

John shoved him.

"I give the orders around here, not you."

"I know how you're feelin,' John."

"You have no idea."

"Livy is my friend."

He grabbed Clive's shirt, and yanked him close. "You should've killed him when you had the chance."

"You're acting crazy," Clive yelled back and shoved John off of him.

"You had him, and you let him go."

"Yeah, I did, and I feel like shit for lettin' that happen."

"You should, damn it." He glared at Clive. "Look what he did to her. You saw what he did to her." Enraged and wild-eyed, John grabbed Clive jerking him close, his arm pulled back ready to strike him.

"Don't do this, John."

"That son of a bitch."

"It wasn't me. I didn't do those things to Livy."

He listened to reason. Clive was right. It wasn't his fault. He thrust his friend away from him, turned around and smashed his fist into the side of the tack house.

The men were still gathered around and Clive told them to head to the bunkhouse and get some grub. He came back over to John. "We'll find him," he said, as he leaned against the barn.

Bringing his hand back again, John threw his fist into the wall another time. He didn't care if he broke the damn thing or not. He wanted to beat the wall until there was nothing left. He wanted to smash his fist into Boyd's face. The bastard should be feeling the same pain as Livy. He inhaled a ragged breath, and pressed his forehead against the barn. His hands—still fisted—lay at his sides.

"John—"

"I should've been there. I should've known it was him all along."

"None of us knew."

"I knew." He pushed his head into the barn. The uneven wood scratched his forehead. "We had our suspicions."

"Yeah, we did. But how were we to know he'd do this?"

John faced his friend. "Did you see her? Did you see her body, what he did to her?"

"Yeah," he whispered, "I saw."

The darkness couldn't conceal the agony in his voice. "She's a mess. She's a bloody, broken damn mess." He couldn't stop the tears as they bled from his eyes.

"But she's alive, John."

"I can't even look at her without feeling like I'm going to be sick."

"I know." Clive stared at the ground.

"What do I tell her when she asks me why this happened? How do I answer when she asks why I didn't protect her?"

"I don't know, I don't know."

Banging his head against the wall, *Livy didn't deserve this. She should feel safe on my ranch.* "How am I supposed to help her, when I can't even be in the same room as her without feeling like I'm going to explode?" Every piece of him ached for her. *Please, God heal Livy. Please, let her be okay.*

"You have no choice."

He knew what his friend said was true. He'd help Livy because he cared for her. And even though it broke him apart to see her like this, he'd bottle up all his emotions, so he could sit next to her bed and help her mend. He wouldn't let her see the pain in his eyes, wouldn't let her know how looking at her tortured him.

"How are the kids?" Clive asked, pulling John back to their conversation.

He ran his hand, sore and pounding, through his hair. "They're asleep in the sitting room, too scared to go upstairs to bed."

"Ben was pretty shaken."

"Yeah, I know. He's taken a real liking to Livy."

"I've noticed."

"I hope she doesn't want to leave after all this. Especially when she finds out I had my suspicions about Boyd."

"She cares for you, John. Livy won't blame you for this."

"I hope you're right. But I still have to tell her." He closed his eyes, dreading the conversation he'd have to have with her.

"It'll all work out, you'll see."

"First we have to find Boyd."

"We'll go back out at dawn."

The moon sat alone in the dark sky, and John could relate. Even though Clive stood next to him, he felt isolated, as his conscience battled back and forth at what he was going to do. No stars shone tonight, leaving the grey sentry to stand guard on its own. "I'm comin' this time," John said, dragging his eyes from the sky.

"Thought as much."

John faced his friend. "I'm sorry, Clive. You know...about earlier."

Clive smiled at him. Without uttering a word, he threw his arm around John and the two of them strolled back to the house.

They had been searching for hours, and still hadn't found Boyd. John had picked up his trail past the corrals before they'd left yesterday morning, but it disappeared once they got to the rocky terrain of the mountains.

"Damn it," he shouted.

Clive rode up beside him. "Think he's hidin' up there somewhere?"

He searched the rocky landscape for any sign that Boyd was near. "Don't know."

"He could be long gone by now."

"I was thinkin' the same thing," John said, angry that the bastard had gotten this far.

His men looked ragged and sleep-deprived. In the two days they had been searching, he had been relentless, never stopping. He'd finally let the men rest for a few hours last night before they continued to search for Boyd. When they reached the fork in the river, he had separated the men into two groups, telling half to go left, while he and Clive and a few others headed right.

He didn't know if Boyd was smart enough to backtrack and leave them following a cold trail. The bastard had a full day on them, and John was growing more nervous the longer he was away from the ranch.

A cool wind blew down from the mountains and the dark clouds over top of them were ominous. He inhaled and could smell rain. He pulled the collar up on his coat and turned his horse to face his men.

"Let's head back. It's too risky to go further." The rocky landscape wasn't any place for a horse, and he knew that by taking his men up there, he'd be endangering them all—a risk too great to take. "Go and find the others," he told Clive, "then head back to the ranch."

Clive gave him a quick nod before he kicked his horse and took off with the rest of the men following him.

Disappointed that the search had come to an end, he dug his heels into Midnight's sides and cantered away. He had left Ezekiel at the house, armed with a shotgun and strict instructions not to let anyone in or near the place. Ben and Emily had been told to stay inside with the cook, and Livy hadn't come out of her room. He doubted she would, for a while anyway.

His gut clenched at the thought of telling her about Boyd and how he'd become suspicious of him the previous week. Would she be able to forgive him for putting her and his children in danger?

He hoped she'd understand and not want to leave the ranch. How would he explain her leaving to Ben and Emily? They'd be crushed, and it would be his fault.

Leaning over his saddle, he urged his horse to go faster. The winds picked up, almost blowing his hat from his head, and his duster flapped open. The thunder's loud crash echoed over the prairies, followed by the crackle of lightning behind him. Trying to outrun the storm, he kicked Midnight to go faster.

The sky opened up dumping its heavy load onto the fields. The rain came down in sheets, pelting him, and making it hard for him to see. Looking for shelter, he spotted a nest of trees about twenty yards away. The yellow and green fields became a blur as he headed toward the dense forest, frustrated that he'd have to wait out the storm before he could get home.

Livy sat up in her bed. Three days had passed since her run in with Boyd, and she was tired of staying in her room. John checked on her before he left to search for Boyd, but when she heard him come up the stairs, she pretended to sleep. She was too afraid he'd want to talk about what had happened. She'd have to tell him about Boyd, and that included Emma. She shuddered. What would he say? Would he understand? She didn't know, and that scared her more than anything.

She went to her armoire and took out the only dress she had left. Sliding the heavy material over her body, she flinched as it rubbed against her bruises. She brushed out the knots in her hair, her scalp still tender from when Boyd had grabbed her there. The brush ran along the brown tresses until they crackled and shone. Deciding to leave it down, she tossed it behind her back and gazed in the mirror.

The swelling had gone down around her eye. A light shadow of blues and greens were smudged there, marring her fine features and making her look deformed. Her lips had healed, and the bruise on her cheek was outlined with yellow.

She looked like hell. She knew she couldn't hide in her room any longer. For the last two days she replayed the horrible incident over and over again, leaving her exhausted. She was tired of seeing Boyd's face every time she closed her eyes, tired of the way her skin crawled whenever she thought of what he'd done. She didn't want to remember. She didn't want to talk about it. All she wanted to do was go on as if it had never happened.

She thought of Emma and how she'd been conceived. Her arms ached and she yearned to hold her baby close one more time. It was the one thing that would heal her, mending the pieces that lay jagged and broken inside of her.

She took a deep breath and headed for the door. Her knee still throbbed from time to time, today being one of those times. She grasped the railing, limped down the stairs, and eased into the kitchen. The house was quiet. Desperate for a hot cup of tea she pumped some water into the kettle and placed it on the stove to heat.

"Miss Livy?" Ezekiel stood behind her, shotgun in hand.

She turned and smiled at her friend. "Hello Ezekiel."

"Ma'am, you sure you should be up?" His brown eyes were full of pity.

She didn't want to see the sadness in his dark depths. "I'm okay. I'm making a cup of tea. Would you like one?"

Ezekiel sat down at the table, and rested the long gun against his leg. "Thank you, ma'am."

The kettle whistled. She took a cloth from the counter, lifted the hot pot from the stove, and poured the steaming water into two cups. She brought him his cup and sat down across from him, her hands instinctively wrapping around the warm mug.

"How are the children?"

Ben came rushing into the kitchen and ran straight into her arms, hugging her tight and crying.

"Ben, honey, it's okay," she tried to reassure him, rubbing his back as he shook with sobs.

"I'm sorry, Miss Livy," he cried. "I'm real sorry."

She ignored the sharp pain in her side as she pulled him onto her lap and rocked him in her arms until his crying ceased. Lifting his chin, she wiped the tears from his chubby cheeks.

"There, there, everything will be all right, Ben."

"But you're hurt."

"I am fine. See?"

She smiled down at him.

Ben wouldn't leave her lap, and she was in no hurry to have him gone. She rocked back and forth until his eyes closed and he fell asleep.

"Ezekiel, where is Emily?"

"The two of them were takin' a nap in the sitting room," he said. "He must've woken when you came downstairs."

Livy could tell she made him uncomfortable. Ezekiel's dark eyes stared at his cup, and his leg shook under the table. She laid her hand across his. "Ezekiel, I am okay."

"I'm sorry that happened to you," he whispered.

"I haven't died," she said, squeezing his hand. "I'll be fine." She wouldn't tell him about Emma or how she knew Boyd. Those things needed to be said to John, and she knew she'd have to tell him when he got back. As much as she dreaded the outcome, she would be relieved to finally speak the truth, to come clean with all of it.

Ezekiel took a sip of his tea and smiled. Livy shuffled Ben on her lap. Ignoring the pain in her sides, she reached behind her to open the drawer and pull out a deck of cards. "How about a game?" she said, placing the cards in front of him.

"Well, now that's a grand idea." Ezekiel grabbed the tattered deck, shuffling them noisily in his hands.

For the rest of the hour she held Ben while she and Ezekiel played gin and chatted about the children and the ranch. She relished the easy flow of conversation between two friends, and more importantly the laughter they shared.

When John entered the house he was shocked to see Livy sitting at the kitchen table helping Ben sound out words from a book. Emily was perched on a chair beside her, her blonde head resting on Livy's shoulder. Livy smiled up at John, who stood speechless at the door. How could she be sitting here after what had happened? If it wasn't for her black eye and bruised cheek, John would've thought it was a normal day.

The three of them sat nestled together. He removed his hat, and hung it on the peg by the door. He wandered around the kitchen for a while, unsure of what to say, or do. He wasn't expecting to see her up, and wasn't sure what to say to her.

"Would you like a cup of coffee?" Livy asked her voice light and soft.

Not wanting her to get up, John held out his hands. "I can get it," he said, quickly moving to the pot on the stove before she could get out of her chair.

He held the mug in his hand as he sat down across from her, listening while she slowly repeated each word for Ben. When he sounded out a word on his own, Livy congratulated him with a hug and a smile that stretched from ear to ear. Ben beamed with pride.

She was amazing. He gazed at her. He couldn't think of anyone that was even comparable to Livy. John admired her for the courage she was showing. Hell, most women would've still been in shock. He shook his head. Not Livy, she was here at his kitchen table cuddling his children.

"I'm hungwey," Emily said.

She finished the book with Ben, and went to the stove to begin making dinner.

"Are you sure you're up to that, Livy?" John asked.

Her long brown hair was loose from its usual braid, and hung to her waist. "I'm fine, and the children are hungry."

He couldn't argue with her. "What can I do to help?"

Her green eyes scanned the room. "Well, you can cut up those carrots and potatoes Ezekiel brought in for me." She pointed to the stack on the counter.

Remembering that he had asked the man to stand guard, John asked, "Where is Ezekiel?"

"He's out on the front porch—keeping watch," she answered.

Satisfied that the man hadn't deserted Livy and the kids, John went over to the counter beside her and began peeling the vegetables. Livy bent over the cookstove to check on the ham roasting inside. When she grabbed her side and inhaled a sharp breath, John was quick to place his hands on her and help her stand up.

"Are you okay?"

"I'm fine."

"You're sure?" he asked, his hands still around her.

"I'm fine, John."

He eyed her.

She lifted her head and smiled.

Reluctant to let her go, John let his hands remain where they were. He was surprised when she didn't back away, but instead relaxed against him. His arms closed around her, and John pulled her close. "I'm glad you're okay, darlin'," he whispered into her hair.

It felt good to hold her, and John hoped she could feel his remorse for the things she'd gone through. Damn, he didn't want to let her go. He placed a light kiss on the top of her head. They stayed that way for some time, each taking solace in the other.

"I'm hungry," Ben groaned, interrupting them.

"We're gettin' at it," John said, releasing Livy.

They finished supper preparations a short time later with the vegetables boiling on the stove.

"Would you like to help me set the table?" Livy asked Emily.

Jumping off of her chair, Emily ran to where Livy stood waiting, and held out her hands. Livy laid four forks in them. John stood back and watched—the scene pulled at his heart—as the table was dressed for dinner. His daughter and son treated Livy like their mother. This is what he'd wanted. This is what he'd strived for.

Overwhelmed with emotions, he went outside to dismiss Ezekiel and to tell him he'd keep watch for the rest of the night. Then he went back inside and settled down to a quiet dinner with his family.

Clive showed up in the middle of their supper, and Livy dished him up a plate, smiling and carrying on as if nothing had happened. Nobody mentioned the unpleasant incident that occurred a few days before. Instead they made small talk about the weather or when they'd be mating the heifers with the bull.

This relieved John. He had waited all day to talk to Livy—to tell her about Boyd—and he didn't want it brought up until they were alone. He tried to go into her room several times and tell her, but she was always asleep. He made excuses. He didn't want to wake her. He should wait until she felt better. But he couldn't put off telling her much longer.

Clive thanked Livy for the fine meal and left shortly after dinner. John noticed Emily's head lull to one side and her eyes begin to droop. Ben yawned loudly, and rested his chin on his hand, while the other hand rubbed his eyes. He decided to put the children to bed. He knew they were still scared, so he let them sleep in his room for the night while he slept on the sofa to keep watch.

Livy hadn't joined them, but gave the children hugs and kisses before they went upstairs.

After reading to Ben and Emily until they fell asleep, he came back downstairs. He was surprised that Livy wasn't in the kitchen. He wandered into the sitting room and found her standing in front of his bookshelf, fingering through a book. He recognized the one she held as *Romeo and Juliet.*

"Have you read William Shakespeare before?" he asked, startling her.

She fumbled with the book, trying not to drop it. "No, I haven't."

"It's a good one. You'd like it."

"I'm not sure I'd understand it." She gazed at one of the pages. "I'm not familiar with this language."

"Yeah, it's a difficult one."

She placed the book back on the shelf.

He went over to where she stood. Scanning the shelf, he pulled out another book and handed it to her. "I think you'd enjoy this one more."

"*Pride and Prejudice?*" Livy read the title aloud.

"You've probably never heard of it. Jane Austen is an English writer. Becky's cousin sent it to her as a wedding gift from London."

"Have you read it?" she asked flipping through the pages.

"Becky read it to me." Although he enjoyed her presence and the light conversation that passed between them, he knew he had to tell her about Boyd. "Livy, can we talk?"

She glanced up from the book, and her green eyes searched his. "About what?"

He coughed to clear his throat.

"I need to tell you somethin'." He coughed again. "I need to get somethin' off my chest about the other day."

She placed the book down on the table beside her and sat down on the sofa.

He took a seat next to her. "I know this must be painful for you, to have to talk about the other day, but…"

Her hands knotted together.

He placed a hand on hers.

"You sure you feel okay?" he asked. He didn't want to put any more stress on her than she already had.

"Yes," she said quietly, and he knew he could listen to her talk all day. The soprano tone had become music to his ears.

Her hair was loose, flowing free to lie across her back, and He longed to run his fingers through the rich mass. "I had my suspicions about the man who attacked you, and…and I had been keeping an eye on him before you were attacked." He exhaled.

She didn't say a word, didn't move. She stared straight ahead.

"I...I thought he might be to blame for Rusty's death." His forehead moist with sweat, and his hands cold and clammy, he forced the words to come and told her the rest. Bringing her hand to his chest he said, "It's my fault this happened to you."

She shook her head.

He squeezed her hand lightly. "I can't begin to tell you how sorry I am, sweetheart." He watched as her eyes closed and a single tear slipped past them to rest on her cheek.

"John."

"Livy, I'm sorry. I'm so damn sorry." He kissed her hand and waited for her to say something.

"John," she whispered again turning toward him. "This is not your fault." She wiped the tear from her cheek and John's gut lurched at the bruises he saw around her wrist.

When she looked at him, her expression held no malice, no blame, and he felt the burden he'd carried being lifted.

"If I would've acted on my gut feeling you'd have been safe."

"I trust you, John. I know you'd never let anyone hurt me."

"Ahh, darlin'." Laying his arm across her shoulders he pulled her close and rested his chin on the top of her head. She felt so good, tucked into him, and he couldn't imagine being anywhere else but here with her.

"There are things you should know about the other day too," she said. "But before I tell you, I need you to know...I need to..."

"You can tell me anything, Livy."

She maneuvered to look at him. "I care for you John."

He smiled down at her, mesmerized by the rich color of her shamrock eyes. "I care for you too, Livy."

Overwhelmed with affection, he brought his lips down to meet hers. Supple and warm, John's mouth moved slowly over Livy's, drawing out every ounce of regret, anger, and fear inside of him, making it fade and disappear.

"John," she mumbled against his mouth. "I have to tell you something."

He didn't want their kiss to end, and he shook his head. It wasn't until he felt her relax in his arms, that he deepened their embrace, letting her tongue dance with his to a melody that played from their souls. Soft and sensual, their passion surrounded them, radiating and warm, as they clung to one another. He wanted her, but he refused to go any further and ended the kiss. He lay back on the sofa, bringing her with him. She nestled in the crook of his arm, as his fingers penciled circles on her back. He reveled in the comfort her presence gave him.

"John?" she whispered her head on his chest.

"Shush, darlin', we'll talk later. Tonight I want you in my arms."

CHAPTER TWENTY-THREE

Livy woke in John's arms. Her muscles cramped and stiff from sleeping on the sofa, but she didn't care. The aches and pains were a small sacrifice to be close to him. John's chest rose and fell as he slept, and she delighted in the way his arm was draped across her waist, protecting her.

Pushing aside thoughts of Boyd, she snuggled deeper into John's embrace. She loved him, and couldn't imagine her life without him or his children. She needed to tell him the truth about Emma. She didn't want any more lies between them. Livy's chest was heavy, making it hard for her to breathe, the burden of her past weighing her down, and she felt her courage fading. She didn't want to keep the charade going any longer. She needed to start fresh.

She tried to stop him from apologizing last night. She tried to tell him about Boyd, but her requests to talk fell on deaf ears, as he wanted to hold her. She felt safe and loved for the first time in her life, and didn't want to lose their night together, instead she chose to bask in his strong embrace.

Guilt-ridden for letting it wait until morning, letting him think it was his fault that Boyd had attacked her, she knew the time to open up to him was now. John had told her he cared for her, and to Livy that was close enough to love. He would understand. He would wrap his arms around her and tell her it didn't matter, it wouldn't change the way he felt for her. He'd be there for her. He'd wipe her tears.

John rolled toward her.

"Awake already?" he whispered, his voice hoarse from sleep.

She smiled.

The room had brightened as the sun shone through the front window. "I haven't slept that soundly in a long time."

He kissed her forehead.

She closed her eyes. She could stay like this, him holding her, forever. This is where she belonged. She was thankful that John and his family had rescued her from a life full of misery and guilt.

He must have noticed the change in her, because he pulled back. "Livy?" he asked, "Is somethin' wrong, Sweetheart?"

She had to tell him about her past, had to clear her conscience. *What would he say? How would he respond to my words?* Livy's heart hammered in her chest with hope. She didn't want to move from his embrace, but she needed to sit up and look at him. She patted at her messed hair.

"I need to tell you something," she said, her voice shaking.

Stretching his arms above his head, he sat up beside her and gave her a wink. "Okay darlin'. I'm listenin'." His black wavy hair hung at his jaw, and she had to stop from running her fingers through it.

John's dark eyes gazed into hers, and she wanted nothing more than to lie back down beside him. *No, I have to do this. I have to tell him now.* She clasped her hands together and took a deep breath.

"I...I had a child before I came here." She took another breath before she went on, "Her name was Emma." She couldn't look at him, afraid of what she'd see when he stared back at her. Afraid she would cower and not finish. "Before I came here, I sang in saloons. My...my mother worked in them, selling her body."

He was silent. His jaw was covered in black whiskers and she longed to press her cheek up against the rough surface.

"I never did that. Instead, I sang for my money. But...but one night a man broke into my room."

She squeezed her eyes shut, and forced the tears not to fall. "He...he didn't care that I wasn't like the other women, and forced himself on me anyway, leaving me with child."

He still hadn't uttered a word. She glanced over at him. In his dark eyes, she thought she glimpsed concern, and grasping onto the notion that he cared for her, she continued. "It...it." *Say the words. Say his name.* "It was Boyd," she whispered.

He shot up off the couch, running his hand through his hair, and rasped, "Boyd gave you a child?"

Feeling the distance he'd put between them like a cold winter day, she shuddered.

"Yes," she whispered lowering her head.

"Where is your daughter now?" He asked, looking at her, his eyes narrow slits.

Livy's own eyes blurred preventing her from seeing the disgust on his face. "She...she died last year."

He was silent. She waited for him to say something—anything. She needed him to tell her he loved her, to hold her, to make it all go away. But as he slowly turned his back to her, she knew what was coming. She squeezed her eyes shut.

"Boyd gave you a child?" he repeated.

She didn't answer him. There was no need to.

"You lied to me?" he whispered.

She bit her lip.

Pacing the floor, he came back to stand in front of her. "You lied to me," he said again, his voice barely louder than a whisper, his chest protruded and his shoulders straight.

Ashamed, she pushed her shoulders back into the sofa.

"You told me Emma was your mother. You made me think this was my fault." He motioned toward her bruised body. "Why, Livy?"

She couldn't find her voice, and shook her head.

"Answer me, damn it," he growled, "Why Livy?"

Her heart aching, she whispered back, "I...I was scared that you wouldn't want me if you knew the truth." She loved John with her whole heart, but as she sat there, she could feel him draw away any feelings he might've had for her.

"You're damn right I wouldn't want you," he yelled.

She flinched.

"You're a liar. A fake."

"I'm sorry, John," she mouthed the words, unable to speak past the lump in her throat.

"You're sorry?"

Too afraid to speak, she felt the tears seep from her eyes.

"You brought Boyd here. You put my children in danger. Everything we talked about, everything you said to me, the whole damn time you've been here has been a lie!"

She stood from the sofa and went to him.

"No."

He took a step away from her, his eyes clouded. "I don't even know you."

"John please, let me explain," she begged. She needed to tell him about her daughter, about how she died and how his family had saved her.

"Explain? You were a whore," he yelled, "the same as your mother."

The insult cut into her. Not expecting him to say such harsh words, she wrapped her arms around her middle.

"That's not true," she cried. "Please, please don't say that."

"It is true," he bellowed. "You made me fall for you, care for you."

"No, no," she whispered, trying to reach out to him, needing to touch him. But he stepped away from her, and she felt helpless.

"It all makes sense now." He crossed his arms. "You knew what you were doing all along. This was your plan."

Shocked at his accusations and blinded by her tears, she shook her head. *No, no, no.*

"Well congratulations Livy, you won." He slammed his chest with his fist. "I'm the fool."

She couldn't stand this any longer. She'd been ashamed all her life, disgusted with how she'd lived. "Yes, I lied," she shouted back at him. "And I'm sorry for that, but I didn't bring Boyd here. I would never do that to Ben and Emily."

He came close to her, his nose an inch from her own. "Don't talk about my children. You have no right to talk about them." His chest heaved as he stared down at her. "You're nothin' but a liar, and you've weaseled your way into their hearts."

"No," she said adamantly, "I love Ben and Emily."

"You don't even know what love is. How could you?"

"I loved my daughter!" Livy screamed at him. Losing all self control, she brought her hand up, and slapped John hard across the face. The crisp sound echoed throughout the room. "How dare you. My daughter was a gift. She was my life. She meant everything to me, and when she died a piece of me died with her."

Her fists pounded into his chest.

John grabbed her arms to stop her from hitting him. Their chests rose and fell, both ready to explode, when Clive pushed them apart. His forehead was creased and his mouth hung down at the corners.

"What the hell do you want?" John yelled at him, letting go of Livy.

Clive had been staring at Livy, and she knew he recognized her. "You used to sing at the Rusty Slipper in Fort McLeod," he said.

John threw his arms up. "Oh, so you knew Livy before? Thanks for keeping that information to yourself, Clive."

Clive turned to John and then back to Livy, his eyes full of sorrow. "I knew her as 'Angel the Songbird'."

"Oh, well, pardon me." John placed his hand on his chest. "Apparently I'm the only one who was kept in the dark."

Clive glared at him.

"So tell me friend, did you have her too?" he growled.

"What the hell is the matter with you John?" Clive shouted, "She sang there—she wasn't like the other women."

"And I'm supposed to believe you when you've known all along who she was?"

"I didn't know, not until she told you she was a singer did I put two and two together."

"Well, bravo." He clapped his hands while rolling his eyes.

"Please, stop, John," Livy pleaded.

He twisted to face her. "You will address me as Mr. Taylor."

She stepped back as if he'd struck her. "Please, if you'd only let me explain."

"No," he shouted. "I want you gone."

"John," Clive yelled, trying to calm him down.

His hands in his hair, he pulled at the long strands as his face twisted with rage. "I have to get the hell out of here." He spoke to Clive. "I'll be up in the east field until tomorrow."

Clive was silent.

He looked at Livy, disgust in his eyes. "Take her into town and buy her fare to wherever the hell she wants to go." He headed for the door.

"Please, John," Livy ran toward him. "Don't do this."

"Say your goodbyes to Ben and Emily." He kept walking, refusing to even look at her.

Livy grabbed his arm. She couldn't lose him, couldn't imagine her life without him. She grasped at anything to keep him here with her.

John took her hand and threw it away from him. His lip curled. "Be gone when I get back."

He slammed the front door as he left.

Clive raced after him. "John! Wait."

Hand clenched, John swung around and punched Clive. All the anger, hurt and resentment he was feeling he packed into that one hit. His friend had lied to him. He knew all about Livy and didn't tell him.

His chest expanding he yelled, "Stay the hell away from me."

"Think about what you're doing."

He was furious. His lips formed into a thin line, and his fists were knotted at his sides. He ignored Clive's plea. "I'll tell Ezekiel he needs to come up to the house in the morning to watch Ben and Emily while you take Livy back." His blood boiling, he left Clive standing there, speechless.

Livy stood in the middle of the room after John left. His cold words still lingered, beating her up inside and leaving bruises that would remain with her forever. In a daze, she backed up and lowered onto the sofa. Her dress was wrinkled, and her hair was a mess, but she didn't care—she had lost the only man she'd ever love.

She hung her head. *He was gone. He didn't believe me.* Last night had filled her with false hopes. She now knew that he didn't love her in return and probably never had. Instead he was disgusted with her, ashamed to have her in his house, near his children.

And it's all my fault. I lied to him. I lied to Ben and Emily. I did this. I fabricated a life that never existed.

Her stomach knotted, and she wrapped her arms around her middle. Slowly, wretchedly, she rocked back and forth.

The front door opened and Clive strode into the room and removed his hat. "I'm sorry, Livy," he said quietly.

She couldn't have him think this was his fault. "No, Clive. I'm the one who's sorry," she whispered.

He sat beside her, and she could see the red welt on his right cheek to match the bruise on his left. "I'll be taking you into town in the morning."

She didn't say anything, too afraid she'd break down.

"Is there anything I can do for you?" he asked, regret written all over his face.

She shook her head.

Clive placed his hand on hers in a friendly gesture. "John didn't mean the things he said."

"I lied to him, Clive."

"I know that, but I believe you had your reasons."

"It doesn't matter," she said, "I deceived them all."

"Do you love him, Livy?"

Yes, I loved him. But she was unable to say the words as tears slid down her face.

"Have you told him?"

"He doesn't love me, so it wouldn't matter." Her life was over. Any chance at happiness had been ripped from her, taken so abruptly that she hadn't had a chance to fight for it. Clive was silent, and she knew he didn't know what else to say to her.

"Clive, thank you for all you've done, but I'd like to be left alone for now."

"I'll be back tonight after supper to keep watch." He placed a light kiss on her forehead and left.

Livy's heart ached with every beat it took, and she couldn't hold back the tears as they fell from her eyes and soaked her face. The agonizing realization of what she'd lost came crashing down on top of her. Guilt blanketed her soul and cast her into an abyss of loneliness and despair. Her hands shook from the shock of it all. She hadn't a clue as to where she would go when she left here. Nor did she care. Everything was lost to her now. She hadn't felt this much anguish since the night Emma died.

She dreaded having to say goodbye to Ben and Emily. The two reasons she'd started to heal in the first place. Her face in her hands, she sobbed for the daughter she never knew, the life she'd come so close to having, and the love she had lost.

"Miss Livy?" Ben stood at the door holding his sister's hand. Both were in their pajamas.

They were so precious, so fragile, and she owed them nothing but the truth as well. She opened her arms, and the children ran toward her. Livy hugged them tight and kissed the tops of their heads.

"Come," she said sniffling, "sit up here with me." Waiting for them to sit on either side of her, she took a deep breath. "I need to tell you a few things."

"Like what?" Ben asked as he stared up at her, his brown eyes honest and pure. She felt horrible for lying to him.

"Well, I…I have to go away tomorrow."

"When ya comin' back?"

Ben's innocence tugged at her heart, and she tried hard not to sob as she wiped at the tears on her face. "I'm not, Ben."

His dark eyes, so much like his father's, filled with tears. "But I said I was sorry for all the bad stuff that's happened to you."

Livy's heart lurched. "Ben, those things weren't your fault." She pulled him into her.

"Yes they were, Miss Livy," Ben started to cry. "I cut the cinch on your horse. I wanted you to leave. I felt so bad afterwards. I told the bad man I didn't want to hurt you and I had changed my mind, but he said if I didn't tell you to go to the barn, and that pa was lookin' for you, he'd kill us all."

She couldn't believe what she was hearing. Anger pulsed through her veins at what Boyd had done. Poor Ben! Boyd had used him to get to her. She nudged Ben's chin. "You listen to me. That man is awful, and it wasn't your fault what happened to me."

"I'm sorry, so sorry you got hurt," he bawled.

"Benjamin Taylor, it would've taken a lot worse things to get rid of me, you hear?"

"Then how come you have to leave?"

Livy sighed.

"I've said some things I shouldn't have."

"Like what?"

"I lied to all of you about who I am," she whispered, barely able to speak. She wanted to tell them, but at the same time she wanted to hold onto this moment forever.

"You stay, Miss Liby," Emily whimpered beside her.

"I can't, Emily." *Oh, how I wish I could.*

"What'd ya lie about?" Ben asked.

"Did you know I used to have a little girl?"

They shook their heads.

"Her name was Emma," she took a deep breath before continuing, "and January 25th—a month after Christmas—would've been her third birthday."

"How come you didn't bring her with ya?" Ben asked.

A stabbing pain in her chest, Livy remembered her daughter. "Because Ben, she died a year ago."

"How'd she die?"

She had never talked to anyone about Emma. She buried her daughter's memory deep down inside for only her to remember and call upon when she needed to. But because she loved Ben and Emily so much did she open her heart and let them know her little girl as she did.

"She had Scarlet Fever."

"How old was she?"

"A year and a little bit," she said, seeing Emma's face.

"What'd she look like?"

"She had the bluest eyes." Livy gazed down at Emily. "Like yours, Emily, and little bits of blonde hair on the top of her head." She ran her fingers through Emily's hair.

"She must've been pretty like you," Ben said.

"She was beautiful," she whispered.

"Do ya miss her?"

"I do," she choked out. "I think of her every minute of every day."

"I miss my Mama too, sometimes."

She rubbed his back, and whispered, "I'm sure you do, Ben."

"Pa says she's in heaven and looks down on us, makin' sure we're all safe." His brows furrowed. "But when I'm out in the field playin' and I look up, I can't see her."

Livy had never thought about how much Ben must miss his mother. She wished she could spend more time with them. She refused to talk of God before, thinking he'd ignored her pleas to save Emma, but as she glanced down at Ben, saw the sadness in his eyes, she couldn't let him think the same thing.

"I don't think we're supposed to see heaven," she told him, "but it doesn't mean it's not there."

Ben nodded, and two fat tears slipped from his eyes.

"Sometimes I think I feel Emma, as if she were right here in my arms." She motioned with her hands. "And when I realize that she's not, I get scared thinking she's all alone without me."

Ben placed his hand in hers. "Don't worry, Miss Livy. Emma's in heaven with our mama and she'll take good care of her for ya."

Tears fell from Livy's eyes. "Thank…you…Ben."

They stayed on the sofa, talking some more about Emma, the ranch and all the things they'd done together while Livy had been with them. She made them breakfast—they laughed about her first day's salty pancakes—and lunch. Afterwards she read to them two books Ben had chosen. The sun, disappearing behind the mountains turned the sky black and she brought the children upstairs to tuck them in one last time.

"Do you really have to go in the morning?" Ben asked, sitting up in his bed. Emily, wanting to sleep with her brother, perched next to him, her blanket snuggled close beside her.

"I'm afraid so, Ben."

Ben reached under his pillow, pulled out a tiny brown box, and handed it to Livy. "This is so you won't forget about me and Em," he said.

She took the box from him and placed it in her pocket. "I will never forget you or Emily," she whispered, hugging them both close. "I love you both very much. Don't ever forget that."

Ben smiled up at her, and wiped the tears on his face. "Can you sing us one of the songs you used to sing to Emma?"

Nudging them over, she crawled in between them on the bed. Ben and Emily cuddled into her. She closed her eyes, savoring her last night with them, as she let the familiar tune float past her lips, singing them to sleep.

CHAPTER TWENTY-FOUR

Boyd crouched behind a bush, hatred leaking from every pore in his body, as he watched the Taylor house. Angel had once again gotten away from him. That bastard Clive interrupted him before he made her his for the second time. The fields were black, and he was sure no one had seen him sneak into the yard.

Careful to hide the light from his cigarette as he took a drag, He ducked down, covering the orange glow. His eyes narrowed as he stared at the large white house a few yards in front of him. He despised John Taylor. The tall rancher had everything. A fancy house, a lot of money and Angel. His arrogance irritated Boyd. The way John walked and talked, as if he were someone to fear. Ha! Taylor didn't scare him. And after tonight, he'd never have to think about the damn rancher again.

Boyd's blood boiled as his thoughts went to Angel. The little bitch thinking she could make a home with Taylor and his family. She didn't belong in there with them. She was a whore, a tramp, and he had proved it, taking her once already.

He remembered the other day when he'd touched her, when he'd almost had her as she wrestled beneath him. Damn, he was so close. Now he'd kill her. He had enough of her games. Anger coursed through his veins, mingling with his sick blood. He dug into his pocket and pulled out a clump of Angel's hair. While she'd been fighting him, some of her hair got tangled in one of his buttons. Later that night, he took pleasure in unwinding the brown wisps.

Bringing the hair up to his nostrils, he inhaled, smelling her. Then running his tongue along the strands, he placed them in his mouth. His hands clenched at his sides, while he sucked on her hair.

He laughed. *Tonight I'll finally get my revenge.*

All of the windows in the house were black. Everyone was asleep. Hunkering down, he ran toward the bales of straw beside the tack house. He lifted one and carried the yellow bundle to the back porch, where he set it down quietly. He dug into his pocket and pulled out his matches. Lighting one, he watched through glazed eyes as the stick came to life with an eerie hiss. He threw it on the straw, smiling as it went up in flames and set the back of the house on fire.

He scrambled onto his horse. Then he laughed as the entire back of the Taylor house was devoured by red and orange flames.

Chapter Twenty-Five

Livy, still in her day dress, sat up in bed with Ben and Emily asleep beside her. She couldn't breathe. The bedroom was cloudy as a light haze hung in the air from the smoke creeping under the door. Choking on the smoggy air that pushed its way into her lungs, she tried to call the children's names, as she shook their sleeping bodies. Ben was the first to wake up, and she could tell he'd inhaled some of the smoke already. As he tried to cough, his chest sounded tight and pressed.

She needed to get them out of the house. Fast. She went to Emily and shook her again, but the girl didn't move. *Oh, no!* She laid her head on Emily's chest, she couldn't hear anything. She gave her a little shake. Nothing. *Oh God, please.* She placed her ear to Emily's chest again elated when she heard her heart beating. She picked Emily up, and went to Ben, who was sitting on the edge of the bed and coughing loudly.

"Come on, Ben," she said, reaching for his hand. She bent and picked him up, her knee almost giving out from the weight as she carried the two to the door. The knob was warm under her palm as she turned it. She opened the door and burst into the hallway.

Coughing, she tried to see through the dense fog in front of her. Dizzy and gasping, she slumped against the wall.

She could barely breathe!

She held Emily close, snuggling her face tight to her body so she couldn't inhale anymore of the black smoke. "Ben, put your head into my neck," she said.

Coughing, her eyes burning, she thrust away from the wall, and made her way down the hall toward the stairs. With every step she took, her knee felt as if it would snap, and her face grew hotter and hotter.

She couldn't see anything through the thick smoke that made her eyes water. She yelled at Ben to hang onto her neck and fumbled for the railing. She screamed as hot flames shot out, scorching her fingers. In front of her, bright red flames danced and sizzled, as the fire climbed the stairs, roaring at her to get out of the way.

How are we going to get out of here? Livy's chest tightened, and she hacked, trying to catch her breath.

Her throat gritty as she inhaled another mouthful of soot, coughing, she choked on the black air while she held her breath and ran to her bedroom, closing the door behind her. She laid the children on the floor in front of the window. She wedged her fingers under the wooden frame, and opened it, welcoming the fresh night air as it entered the smoke filled room. Emily's face was smeared with ashes, and her eyes were still closed. *Please, God let her be okay. Let us all be okay.*

"Help!" she screamed her throat sore. She glanced down at the children. If they inhaled anymore smoke, they'd suffocate and die. *Oh God. Please help us. Send someone to help us.* Frantic, she shouted out the window again.

"Livy," Clive yelled from below. Men were running around the corner and shouting as they threw buckets of water onto the house.

"We can't get out. The stairs are blocked!"

"I know. I tried to come up. You're gonna have to drop the kids out the window. I'll catch them."

Livy glanced behind her at the closed door, the smoke easily came through. She knew she had no choice, and without a second thought, she picked up Emily. Kissing her on the forehead, she sat Emily in the window sill. Her little legs dangled down the side of the house.

"Are you ready?" she called to Clive.

"I'm ready." Clive held his arms out. "Drop her, Livy."

She lifted the child out the window, squeezed her eyes shut and let Emily fall from her arms. She couldn't help the scream that came from her lips as she watched the child fall through the air. Livy's heart in her throat, when Clive caught Emily, fell backwards and landed on his behind. Shorty was there to take Emily from him. He ran away from the inferno with the child lying limp in his arms.

"Okay, Livy, get Ben," Clive yelled up to her.

She kneeled in front of the little boy. He was wheezing now, and his face was red. She hauled him up. Her knee almost gave out. She bit down on her lip and forged through the pain. Doing the same as before, she anchored her legs to the wall, held Ben while she kissed him on the top of his head, and dropped him, praying Clive would catch him too. Ben fell clumsily into Clive's outstretched arms. Both of them tumbled to the ground. Two men rushed over to pick up Ben then ran toward Shorty who was attending to Emily.

The house shifted sideways and, losing her balance, she grasped onto the window. The wood crackled and snapped, as the fire ate away at the two story structure.

"Livy, you have to jump," Clive yelled.

The heat from inside the house radiated through the air as smoke billowed from the window above her. Looking down, her head began to spin. If she jumped, she would have to leave the ranch—leave Ben and Emily. She had nothing left, and nowhere to go. She swayed, and almost lost her footing. She stared out across the chaos-filled yard. Ben and Emily needed her now.

"Livy, jump!"

She swung her legs over the windowsill. Her body shaking, She took a deep breath and jumped. Slamming into Clive, she sent both of them rolling on the grass.

"Are you okay?" Clive asked, lying next to her.

Her knee was pounding—the pain almost unbearable—and she was sure she had reinjured it. Trying her best to ignore the sharp stinging, she rolled over and coughed.

"Livy, are you okay?" Clive asked again.

"I'm fine," she rasped. The ashen taste in her mouth made her spit on the ground. Her sides were sore from hacking, and every breath felt like a hundred tiny needles stabbed her lower back.

"Here, take a drink." Clive handed her a tin full of cool water.

She wanted to pour it on her face, as her skin burned. Her hands still shaking, she took a sip of the cold liquid which doused her charred insides, causing her to cough some more. She stared at the house engulfed in bright red flames. Thick black smoke shot high into the sky, and an acrid smell permeated the air.

Ben and Emily! Frantic, she rolled over onto her knees, and cried out as pain shot up her leg. Pushing up, she forced the sore and aching knee to move as she ran over to the children. The light from the fire cast the whole yard in a red glow while some of the men stood in a line, passing down buckets of water to throw onto the house. Others soaked the grass around the home making sure the flames didn't spread to the other dwellings.

Ben sat on the ground. He was wrapped in a blanket and coughing loudly. His cheeks ruddy, and streaked with black soot.

"Ben, are you okay, honey?"

She crouched down in front of him.

"Yes." He took a drink of his water, and coughed into the cup.

She rubbed his back as she held him to her. "Thank God," she whispered, "I'm going to check on Emily. I'll be right back."

Leaving Ben, she moved over to his sister a few feet away. Her whole leg throbbed with such intensity she was sure she was going to vomit. She pushed aside the nausea and pain to get to the little girl. Shorty held her on his lap, and was rubbing her back vigorously. Emily whimpered in between loud barking coughs. Livy sat beside her, and when Emily saw her, the girl's arms flailed out. She ripped the girl from Shorty's lap, and cradled the child in her arms.

"She's coughin' pretty bad," Shorty said.

"Is she going to be all right?" Livy asked. The thought of losing Emily or Ben was too much to bear. She abandoned her reservations about God and prayed for them both to get better.

"I hope so. Her throat is a little burned from inhaling all that smoke."

"What can I do?"

"She needs to breathe clean air for a while, or at least until she stops wheezing."

Livy snuggled into Emily when she threw up in the grass. Crying softy and coughing, she pitched forward and vomited again. Livy gave her a drink of water, letting her rinse her mouth.

"It's okay, Emily," she hummed, rocking the child back and forth. Ben, with the blanket still wrapped around him, came over to sit beside his sister and Livy pulled him closer to her and placed an arm around his shoulders.

A thunderous sound came from the house, and Livy reassured the children that they were far enough away that they weren't in any danger. They watched as the second floor collapsed and falling hunks of debris shot sparks high, disappearing into the murky sky. Men yelled, dropping their buckets, running in different directions away from the monstrous inferno.

John was sitting by his campfire, thinking about Livy, when he saw a red hue brush the sky. When grey smoke shrouded the red glow, he realized that it was a fire, and it was close to his house. He scaled Midnight's back and leaned over his neck as the horse raced for home.

Uneasiness settled over him as he tried to catch his breath. Something was wrong, he could sense it. He thought of his children, Ben and Emily, praying that they were okay and that the fire was not burning the house down. Every step his horse took jarred John's sore back and tense muscles. He needed to get home. Fast. He needed to hold his kids, see Livy, and make sure everyone was all right.

As Midnight crested the hill, he saw the house. Leaning to one side, the whole structure blazed, swallowed up in massive, angry flames. Black smoke rose and curled from the roof waving him home. His heart lurched, and he kicked Midnight's side. "Yaw, yaw."

When he got closer he could hear the frantic shouts of his men as they tried to put the fire out. Midnight reared up, pawing the air with his front hooves when a ferocious sound came from the house, and the second floor caved in.

"No," he whispered.

The ruddy air smelled of charred wood and stung his nostrils. Jumping off of his horse, he ran toward the house, searching through blurred eyes for Ben and Emily. Coming up to one of his hands, he yelled, "Where are the children?"

"I don't know, Boss," he said, running to join the other men who were dumping buckets of water onto the grass, to protect the other buildings.

This can't be happening! Where were his children? Running from man to man, he asked for his children, but none of them knew where they were.

They have to be okay. They have to be.

He did a full circle. Chaos was everywhere, as men yelled over the sounds of the roaring fire, trying desperately to save the barns and the livestock.

"John," Clive shouted from behind him.

He sprinted toward his friend, his voice shaking, "Where are Ben and Emily?"

"They're safe, John. They're over here with Livy."

He embraced his friend in a hard, rough hug. "Thanks."

"C'mon." Turning, Clive ran toward the bunkhouse.

Relieved that his kids were all right, John raced after him. Livy sat holding Ben and Emily wrapped tightly in a blanket. His daughter was coughing and struggled for breath, when he fell to his knees in front of them. He took Emily from Livy's arms and held her close, kissing her head.

"Thank God," he rasped. Reaching over, he pulled Ben into his embrace as well—not wanting to ever let go of them again.

"John," Shorty stood beside him.

He twisted on his knees, without putting his children down.

"Emily's still quite sick."

He glanced down at his daughter, and could hear her wheezing when she took a breath. "Isn't there anything you can do for her?" he asked.

"I'm afraid not. She's inhaled a lot of smoke. Her lungs could be permanently damaged."

"Will she…?"

"I think she'll pull through, but we have to keep her coughing. She needs to get rid of all the soot in her lungs."

"Ben, how's Ben?"

"He'll be fine. He's coughed up most of it."

Emily began another coughing fit, and he pulled his daughter closer to his chest. Grey spittle smeared her tiny lips. He wiped her mouth with his sleeve. Tears threatened to fall from his eyes. "I love you, Emily." Then giving his son a squeeze, he kissed the top of his head. His hair smelled of smoke and was littered with ashes. "I love you too, Ben. You two are all I have. What would I do if I lost you?"

Livy's eyes misted as she watched John cling to his children. *You don't belong here.* Feeling as if she were intruding, she watched as the men dropped their buckets and stood staring in disbelief. The fire had eaten away the structure until nothing was left. The beautiful two story home was gone. Leveled to a pile of smoldering wood, and charred memories.

She took a deep breath and glanced over at John cradling his children. This wasn't her home. John had told to leave. He wanted her sent somewhere else, *put on the next stage to where ever.* His harsh words would forever be branded in her mind. Her heart ached at having to leave Ben and Emily, at not being able to say goodbye.

Dawn was approaching, and she knew that the children would be all right now that John had arrived. Not wanting another confrontation with him. Livy winced from the pain in her leg, as she got up and limped away. Not knowing which hurt more, her crushed soul, or her injured knee. With each step, she hoped John would call out her name and stop her from leaving. But the only sound she heard were the men as they began cleaning up some of the mess from the fire. With her shoulders slumped, and her head down, she limped on.

When she made it to the barn, she had to lean into the over-sized door to open it. She groaned, and her hand darted to her aching knee. She bit down hard on her bottom lip to keep from yelling out again, and pressed into the door once more. The musty smell of hay and horses welcomed her, and instead of covering her nose like she once did, she took a deep breath and sealed the scent in the back of her mind. She wanted to be able to call upon these memories whenever she grew lonesome for John, the children, and the ranch.

Limping over to one of the corrals, she spotted the same mare she'd fallen from. She was already saddled and left in her stall when the commotion drew her intended rider away. Opening the stall door, she ran her hand along the chestnut brown mane. "There girl, remember me?"

The horse shuffled her feet, and snuffed loudly.

"Think you can get me to town?"

The mare must've sensed Livy's need to leave, for she stood still while Livy figured out how to mount her. She didn't know when she'd started to cry, but her face was wet with tears and her nose was running. She picked up an empty crate and placed the wooden box beside the horse, stepped up, said a silent prayer that she'd not fall, and hoisted one leg up. Her knee rubbed the side of the mare. The pain unbearable, that she almost fell.

She clicked her tongue, and the horse trotted through the open gate and out the barn door. She pulled on the reins and stopped. She took one last look at the ranch. John's back was to her, and she couldn't control the sorrow that ripped through her. The love she felt for the Taylors would never go away. They had been her salvation, and she'd forever be grateful for them. She took a shaky breath, touched her hand to her lips and blew a kiss toward John and the children then kicked the mare's sides and trotted off toward the rising sun.

John said a silent prayer of thanks that his children hadn't been killed in the fire. Ben was curled up beside him, and Emily nestled on his lap, both fast asleep. Emily hadn't woken for over an hour, and he was relieved. His little girl had been up coughing all night and into the morning. She needed her rest in order to get better. He scanned the yard, looking again for Livy. She disappeared sometime last night, and he hadn't seen her since. She was probably in the bunkhouse, too afraid to be around him. Humph. Who could blame her? He had taken a strip off of her the other day. He rubbed his chest, heavy with guilt at the things he'd said, the words he'd used. He was ashamed of his behavior, and the whole thing left an awful taste in his mouth.

Clive rounded the corner of the bunkhouse and came toward him. "How are the kids?" he asked, rubbing his face.

"Ben's feelin' better. Em's finally settled down. She hasn't coughed in over an hour and she seems to be breathin' easier."

"Good to hear." Clive's hand gently touched the sleeping boy.

"Have you seen Livy around?" John asked. He looked out at the yard, hoping to see her familiar shape.

"Shorty told me she left sometime last night," he said.

Livy was gone? His chest burned. *I needed to talk to her.* He glanced down at Ben and Emily still asleep beside him, and he knew he couldn't leave them. "I need a favor Clive. Could you go find her? Tell her I need to talk to her?"

Clive smiled. "Thought you'd never ask. I'll head out right now." Tipping his hat to John, he left to saddle his horse.

He leaned against the wall of the bunkhouse, his back stiff from holding the same position for the last several hours. He'd decided not to take the kids inside. They needed fresh air and he would sit here until they felt better. He asked Ezekiel for more blankets.

He thought again of Livy. He needed to see her, needed to hold her. But most importantly he needed to tell her he was sorry. The musty scent of smoke still hung in the air and, blowing out a heavy breath, John couldn't look at where his house once stood. He couldn't afford to get caught up in trying to figure out how it happened, or why it happened, until Ben and Emily were okay and he had talked to Livy.

The sun, set high in the sky, warmed him. He closed his eyes and let the bright rays drape over him. Most of the men, tired after a night of battling the fire, were asleep inside the bunkhouse, but he knew a few were still up tending to the animals. What would he have done without them? They were what kept his ranch going, prospering. If it wasn't for them, he'd be dead by now, worked to the bone. He needed them, and he hadn't treated them very well these last few weeks.

He ran his hand through his hair. Those men saved his family, kept the fire from spreading to the tack house and other buildings. If they'd have burned down, he'd have nothing left. He didn't know if he could start all over again, or if he'd want to. The life he led was hard, gettin' up early and comin' in late. He sacrificed too much time working on the ranch when he should be with his children.

If Ben and Emily had perished in the fire—the thought alone making him sick to his stomach—he would have died inside. They were his life, his everything. Without them here, nothing would matter anymore.

Shaking his head and trying to swallow past the lump in his throat, he glanced down at his sleeping angels. The two had kept him alive after Becky had died, made him get out of bed in the morning, forced him to smile and laugh again when he thought he never would. John's mind wandered to Livy and what she must've gone through when her daughter died. The pain she must've felt, the anguish and torment—the guilt.

He flexed his jaw. He still couldn't believe the things he'd said to her. He showed no remorse, no feeling for how she'd felt, how she'd suffered, and could never imagine the hell she lived through without her child. He should've understood, or at least asked what happened. He should've listened to her explanations about Boyd. Instead, he acted like a fool, letting his temper get the best of him.

He let out a weary sigh. He dearly hoped she'd come back with Clive so he could apologize and make things right.

"John." Ezekiel stood in the door of the bunk house. "I have some warm soup broth for the young'uns, when they wake."

Sitting up straight, he said, "Thanks, Ezekiel. I'll let you know when they're up."

Ezekiel crouched down beside him, and stared out across the yard at the smoking house. "I've been wonderin' how it started."

Refusing to look over at the pile of rubble that used to be his home, he shrugged. "Don't know. I need to talk to some of the men. See if they saw anythin'."

"Can't right figure it out. All was calm here last night." Ezekiel said, before he disappeared inside the barn.

He didn't say anymore. He had no idea how the fire started. He hadn't really thought about it. He'd been too wrapped up in making sure Ben and Emily were okay. While he was out in the field, all he could think of was how Livy had deceived him, how she'd put his family in danger. But as darkness fell, his feelings changed to remorse. He didn't know if she should stay, or even if she'd want to, but he had to talk with her, listen to her. He needed to find out who she really was, and had decided to do so before he'd seen the fire.

When he rode into the ranch, he was scared, and worried that something had happened to Ben and Emily. When he'd found them sitting with Livy, he'd been so thankful they were alive that he'd ignored her, yanking them from her and smothering them with hugs. He could see now how his actions must've looked to her, how she would've felt. He knew that he'd cared for her—hell, he'd told her so—but did he love her?

Closing his eyes, he took a deep breath and pictured her in his mind. A smile spread across his face, and he dozed off.

CHAPTER TWENTY-SIX

Livy rode for hours before stopping to rest. Her pulse quickened when she spotted a rider coming over the hill and heading toward her. Fearful it may be Boyd, she searched the ground for a stick to use as a weapon. Cursing her luck—all she could find was a twig-like branch—she limped behind her horse and waited. Her grip tightened on the branch, and her heart hammered inside her chest as the rider came closer. She heaved a sigh of relief when she recognized Clive on top of the bay horse.

Coming out from behind her horse, she smiled weakly and waited for him to dismount.

"Mornin', ma'am," he drawled, as he took off his hat and smacked at the dust on his pants.

"Hello, Clive."

"How're you doin'?" he asked, as he looked with concern at her sore knee.

She glanced down at her injured and pulsing limb. It hurt like hell, and she had been favoring it ever since her fall last night.

"I've come to take you back to the ranch," Clive smiled at her.

Livy's heart leapt with joy and she peered around Clive to see if John was there.

"He couldn't come," Clive's eyes shifted, and he stared at the ground, "he sent me instead."

Her eyes stung with unshed tears, and her mouth went dry. She tried to swallow past her disappointment. "Oh, I see."

"Livy," Clive sounded desperate, and she wished again it was John who stood in front of her now. "He needs to talk to you." Reaching for her horse's reins, Clive gave them a tug.

She placed her hand on top of his gloved one. "Did he say that he loved me?" she asked, hopeful for the first time since she'd left the ranch.

Clive slowly shook his head. "I'm sorry, Livy."

Although she hadn't been surprised, Clive's answer sliced through her like a sharp knife. Her wounded ego was nothing compared to the sheer agony she felt deep within her soul.

"I can't, Clive," she whispered.

It killed her not to be able to see Ben and Emily, not to see John, but she was through sacrificing her soul for a sliver of happiness. She knew she was being selfish, but she refused to run back to John without hearing those three words directly from him. *And you never will.*

Clive nodded he understood. "Well, at least let me accompany you into town."

She appreciated his kindness, but she wanted to be alone. Riding into town with Clive may cause her to change her mind and race back to the ranch and to John. "No thanks. I'll head in myself."

"You sure?"

"Yes, just show me which way."

He lifted a gloved hand and pointed east, "Head straight that way, it'll take you into town."

Clive stared at her, and the pity she saw on his face made her cringe. She didn't want his pity. She deserved what had happened to her. She'd lied to John and his family and now she had to suffer the consequences. Livy didn't think her heart could withstand any more pain as she threw one leg up onto her horse.

Trying to stay strong, but feeling as if she'd crumble at any moment, she whispered, "Take care, Clive."

The horse trotted away, and she wiped at the tears flowing down her face. Her heart longed for John, her soul desperate to have a home—to belong. The realization of the past few days hit her like a ton of bricks. She'd never belong with John, and she'd never see the ranch again. *He doesn't love you. He never will. Everything you've ever wanted is gone, once again.* Hanging her head, she wept even harder.

An hour into the ride, her back ached and her knee pulsated with every step the horse took. After jumping from the window it hadn't felt the same, and she needed to ice the aching limb. Her knee was still swelling, and if it got any bigger she wouldn't be able to walk on it.

She took a deep breath. Having to tell Clive that she wouldn't return with him broke her in two. Defeated and exhausted she rode in the direction he had told her. The outline of Fort Calgary came into view after she'd come over the hill, and she breathed a sigh of relief. With no money, and nothing but the clothes on her back, she had already made the harrowing decision as to where she'd head first. Her stomach was in knots and her heart hammered in her chest, knowing what she was about to do.

The horse walked at a slow, steady pace into town. She figured it to be past noon the way people littered the streets. Averting her eyes, and wishing she'd thought to grab a hat, she tipped her head down, not wanting anyone to see her face. She was sure her red-rimmed eyes and uncombed hair looked frightful. The smell of baked bread hung in the air, and her stomach growled in protest. She hadn't eaten anything since yesterday.

Men and women walked the wooden boardwalks, and children scampered about yelling. She rubbed her chest to ease the wrenching pain that struck when she thought of Ben and Emily. She guided the horse straight for the saloon she'd seen when she had arrived in Calgary a month ago.

She swung her leg over the animal's back and bit her lower lip when she stepped onto the ground. Moving slowly, her body sore, she tied the horse's reins around the hitching post in front of the rundown bar.

"Thanks for getting me here, old girl," she said, patting the horse's side. She inhaled a deep breath and marched up the steps. She could feel the stares from the townspeople boring into her back as she pushed through the swinging doors.

The saloon was like all the other ones she'd been in. The uneven floor was splattered with bits of sawdust and cigarette butts left over from the night before. Tables were strewn with empty glasses and bottles of whiskey, and the musty scent of stale bodies and vile women hung in the air.

Trying hard not to gag, she headed straight for the man behind the bar. Her knee felt like it was about to explode, so she tried not to put too much pressure on her leg as she limped her way toward the bartender. Ignoring the looks from the men seated at the tables, she kept her eyes forward.

"Can I help you?" the man behind the long bar asked, glancing at her as if she were lost.

Straightening, Livy said, "I've come for a job."

She'd done this before, and loathed having to do it again. You had to be tough when you entered a bar. Had to show them nothing bothered you, that you could handle anything. And so, she pushed all her emotions from the last few days deep down inside of her, and took on a stern, confident air.

The bartender's eyes roamed over her attire, and she knew what he was thinking. "I don't need any more women workin' for me," he said, spitting into the glass he'd been holding before wiping it out with a dirty yellow cloth.

"I haven't come for that kind of job."

The man chuckled as he placed the glass down and picked up another one. "Well, what kind of job have you come for then?"

"I sing." Her voice sure, she stared straight into his eyes.

"Sing?" he echoed. "Look, lady, why don't you head on over to the church. They have a choir. I'm sure you could sing there." Dismissing her, he continued cleaning the glass.

"That's not the kind of music I sing," she said, determined.

He glanced at her again, and his blue eyes looked her up and down. "What kind of music do you sing?"

Livy needed this position, she needed to get enough money to leave, and she wasn't about to be pushed around by some low-life. "Look," she snapped, coming up to her full height, "I'm not here to play games with you. I know how to sing. And I know what to sing to fill your saloon with men and your cash box with money." She leaned over the bar so the man could hear her. "I've come for a job. Now if you can't find a spot for me to sing, I'll head over to the other saloon."

"You think you're that good, honey?" The bartender said. "What makes you so sure that you'll fill this place?"

She shrugged. "Hire me for one week, and you'll see if I'm tellin' ya the truth or not."

The man was quiet for a moment. "Fine. You have one week. But you're gonna have to find somethin' else to wear other than that," he said, pointing to her torn and stained dress.

Livy hadn't thought about what she'd wear. "I have nothing else."

"One of the girls might have somethin' that'll fit ya." He waved at one of the woman lounging beside a table.

"There's one more thing," she mumbled, hating to have to say the words, and hating the fact that she was even back inside a saloon. "I have nowhere to stay."

He glared at her.

"You can stay in one of the rooms upstairs, but it'll cost ya, and if you don't fill this place like you said, you're gone."

Relieved, she shook his hand in agreement.

CHAPTER TWENTY-SEVEN

"John." Clive nudged him. "John."

He opened his eyes and yawned. Sitting upright, he glanced around Clive. "Where's Livy?"

"She wouldn't come back."

He closed his eyes for a moment, and took a deep breath. "Did you tell her I needed to talk with her?"

"I did."

He sat silent. *Why didn't she come back?* He grew angry all over again. What a fool he'd been to think he could talk with her. She'd deserted them, him and his children—his sick children. She'd up and left without a care, without giving him a chance to explain. Frustrated, he ran his fingers through his hair.

"Well, she's made her decision," he growled.

"John."

"Save it. I don't want to hear it."

"She saved Ben and Emily."

He stared at Clive.

"I was sleepin' on the couch when the fire started. Livy and the kids were upstairs. The flames spread so fast that by the time I woke up, the whole kitchen was blazin'. I tried to get to the stairs, but they were already on fire. The house was heavy with smoke, and I couldn't catch my breath, so I ran out the front door." Closing his eyes, Clive continued. "The men must've smelt the fire, because by the time I'd caught my breath, they were throwing buckets of water onto the house.

"How did they escape?" he asked, as he pictured Livy frantically trying to save his children.

"I was runnin' from window to window, to see if I could see them, when I saw Livy leaning out her bedroom window, and screaming for help. She had the kids, must've gone and woke them," he said.

"How did they get out?"

"She had no choice but to drop them one by one, until it was her turn to jump." Clive hesitated. "She, uh, she reinjured her knee, judgin' by the way she was favorin' it. But once she'd coughed a few times, she was up and runnin' toward the children, makin' sure they were all right."

He stared at his foreman. "I know what you're doin'," he said, "and it doesn't change anything." Livy didn't want to come back and let him apologize, and he pushed any feelings he had for her to the side.

"And what exactly is that?"

"I am grateful she saved Ben and Emily, but she still lied to me. She still betrayed me."

"So you're still mad, are ya?"

"Why wouldn't I be?" He shot back. "She wouldn't even come back so we could talk."

Getting up, Clive glared at him. "Maybe she didn't want me to go and get her, maybe she wanted you to."

He moved away from Clive, dismissing him. "She's made her decision, like I said."

"She saved your children John, risked her life for them…"

"I heard ya the first time."

"If that doesn't warrant some kind of forgiveness, then I don't know what does." Clive rammed his hat down onto his head, and flexed his jaw.

He watched his friend walk away. He let Clive's words sink in. Regret gnawed at the corners of his heart, eating away the barrier he'd placed so carefully around it. He'd acted like an ass—again. Blowing out a frustrated breath, he didn't know how to fix the mess he'd made. And if the truth were to be told, he didn't know if he had enough strength left to try. Ben stretched, waking beside him, and he turned his attention to his son.

"Papa?" Ben said, his throat sounding dry.

He grabbed the cup of water beside him, and handed it to his son so he could take a sip. "Better now?" he asked, after Ben had swallowed the cool liquid.

"How's Em?" he asked, glancing down at his sister.

"She's feelin' better son." Staring at Ben's hair—messy and full of white ash—he felt a stab in his heart. He'd almost lost him.

Looking around the ranch, Ben asked, "Where's Miss Livy?"

He cleared his throat before answering his son. "She's gone."

"Gone where?"

He didn't like seeing the anguish in his son's eyes, and wished he didn't have to tell him. "She went back to town to catch the stage."

Ben's brown eyes filled with tears, and his bottom lip quivered. "She left?"

He closed his eyes.

"She saved us."

"I know, Son," he whispered.

Looking up at him, Ben whimpered, "I know why she left."

Surprised that he would know, he stared down at his son. "Do you now."

"She told us she lied to you."

He was surprised that Ben would know something like that. Livy must've told him.

"She told us she had a baby too and that it died." Ben's finger traced circles in the dirt at his feet.

His chest tight with regret, he couldn't look at Ben. "She told me that too."

Ben's eyebrows shot up. "She did?"

"Yes."

"Well, if you knew, why did she have to leave?"

Sighing, and rubbing the grit from eyes, he said, "There were other things, Ben." *And she doesn't want to come back here.*

"Like what?"

"You're too young to hear them," he said trying to end their conversation. He didn't want to talk about Livy anymore, didn't want to feel the piercing pain shoot across his chest every time her face appeared in his mind.

"I miss her already," Ben whispered.

Me too. "You've got me. I'm here."

He nudged his son.

"I know, but Miss Livy was almost like Mama."

His vision blurred and he whispered, "Son, I know you miss your mama, but she's gone."

"I don't miss Mama as much when Miss Livy's here."

He felt as tiny as a pebble on the ground, and he didn't know what to say to his son. He didn't know how to make everything better.

"Mama's keepin' watch over Miss Livy's little girl in heaven," Ben said. "So I don't think she's lonely up there anymore without us."

Ben sounded older than his seven years, and John was overcome with emotion at what a fine lad he was turning out to be.

"Miss Livy misses her little girl somethin' awful," he said thoughtfully.

"I'm sure she does." The memory of the things he'd said to her, the horrible words he'd used, came rushing back.

"She needs us Pa. We helped her with her breathin' attacks."

He remembered Livy having one the day Boots came to the house. He'd asked her why she has them, but never pushed her to explain. Now he wished he would have. Maybe things wouldn't have turned out the way they had.

"She needs us, Pa," Ben said again.

His hand lay on Ben's shoulder. "She's gone, Son, and she ain't comin' back." As much as he wanted to see her, run his hands through her hair, breathe her in, he couldn't go after her. This is how it was to be.

"You could go get her." His dark eyes pleaded with John.

"No, Son, I can't."

"Why not?" Ben asked, as tears streaked down his dirty face, smudging the ash and soot still on his cheeks.

"It's complicated," he said. *And she won't want to see me, not after what I said. What I called her.*

Ben's little head shook from side to side. "No, Pa. It's not," he continued, "I told Miss Livy I was sorry for all the bad stuff I did, and she forgave me."

"Bad stuff?"

Ben hung his head. "You're gonna be mad Pa, and I'm probably gonna get a whippin'. But I have to tell you."

"What did you do Benjamin?"

"I cut the cinch on the horse, and I told Miss Livy to go into the barn where the bad man was and look for you."

John's jaw clenched. What had Ben been thinking? Livy could've died. "Why would you do such awful things, Ben?"

"The bad man told me he'd kill you and Em if I didn't do as he said." Ben wiped his wet eyes.

"Boyd told you to do all of those things?"

How could he have not known his son was being blackmailed? He thought back and realized that the signs had been there. Ben hadn't been himself this past week. He was withdrawn, and always apologizing.

Ben nodded.

"You told Livy all of this?"

"She wasn't angry, Pa. You have to go after her," his son pleaded.

He laid his hand on Ben's shoulder, and tried to calm his son down.

"Please Pa, go get Miss Livy."

"Livy's made her decision to leave. Now let it be," he said.

"She loves us!" Ben yelled.

John's heart skipped at the thought. "Now how do you know that?"

"She told us last night and...and... I love her too, Pa." Sobbing, Ben got up and ran away.

Not able to get up and go after him with Emily still on his lap, he let his son go.

What the hell was he going to do? Damn it. He banged his head on the wall behind him. His son obviously cared for Livy, and glancing down at Emily, he was sure his daughter did too.

He didn't think he could get over everything that had happened between them. Besides, why would she leave without saying goodbye, without giving him a chance to apologize? He had his pride damn it, and he wasn't going to crawl after some woman.

A woman who left while Ben and Emily were still sick.

If she loved them like she'd said, then she'd have come back with Clive.

He surveyed his land, his home. Nothing had been the same since Livy arrived, and nothing would ever be the same now that she was gone. He ignored the dull ache in his heart, and pushing down all the emotions that ran rampant inside of him, he forced him mind to think of something other than her.

He was pleased when Emily woke up and the wheezing in her chest was gone. She was sitting on Alice's lap inside the bunkhouse, sipping on some of the broth Ezekiel had made for her and Ben. His son sat at the table carving at a piece of wood with his knife, pretending I wasn't there. He made several attempts to talk to him, but Ben ignored him, instead answering John when he needed to. Seeing his son's red-rimmed eyes tore him apart, and he'd hoped time would heal them all.

He got up from the table, asking Alice to keep an eye on the children, and then ventured outside. The sun was bright in the cloudless sky. He held his hand up to shade his eyes. The ranch was running as normal. And all of his neighbors had shown up over the last few days with food for him and the kids. Their wagons, heavy with lumber to build a new house, rolled into the yard. But he wasn't ready to rebuild, and had them pile it all next to the tack house.

He stared at the place where his house used to stand. Not yet strong enough to go over and have a closer look, he watched as his men hauled burnt wood and furniture to load onto three waiting wagons.

He looked at the crows cawing overhead. A dozen black scavengers were gliding in the air, and he watched as they dived, disappearing from his sight. They were circling something out in the field. One of the cattle must be down. He headed toward the tack house to saddle Midnight. Climbing up onto the animal, he took off to investigate, glad to get away from everything for a while.

As he got closer, he could see the birds pecking at something lying on the ground. Midnight startled them, and he watched as they flew away cawing and flapping their wings noisily, returning to their positions above. As he neared the carnage, he was startled to see a man lying in the grass next to the mud hole

Clive had fenced off. Wasting no time, he slid off of his horse and raced over. Worried, thinking it was one of his men, he became enraged when he recognized Boyd.

"You son of a bitch," he snarled, kneeling in front of Boyd and grabbing him roughly by the collar. Yanking him close, John's chest expanded with fury, as he glared down at Boyd. The man was taking quick breaths, and he noticed the way his body was laying. One leg, obviously broken, turned at an unnatural angle, and Boyd's face was a light shade of blue. He must've been thrown from his horse. He glanced up and scanned the field for the animal. All he saw was long stocks of yellow swaying in the breeze, and a coyote loping into some bushes.

"What're...you...doin'...alive...Taylor?" he rasped, out of breath.

"What are you talkin' about?" John asked.

"You...and your...whole...damn family...should've...burned," he sneered.

John's eyes grew wide. "You bastard." He punched Boyd's face so hard he broke his nose. He felt satisfied hearing Boyd yell out in pain. Blood flowed from his nostrils down to his mouth. Boyd spat it out onto his chin. John suddenly realized why Boyd didn't wipe the blood away with his hands—he couldn't move his arms! He didn't try to run, because he couldn't move his legs either.

"You're nothin' but a coward. A low-life. And if you didn't have a broken back, I'd kill you myself."

He took shallow breaths, staring up at John through deranged eyes. "Do you think I care? Kill me, Taylor." He spit again, coughing as he choked on the blood in his mouth. "I don't give a damn about you or your bitch of a wife. You can all go to hell."

He didn't care about his back or the fact that his face was already bloody and swelling. Boyd could feel from the neck up, so he hauled back and hit him again. But nothing would release the pent up anger boiling inside of him.

"You tried to kill my family," he shouted, his face an inch from Boyd's. "You blackmailed my son and you tried to rape Livy."

"No, Taylor," he whispered, his breaths short and forced. "I *did* rape her. Or hadn't she told you?"

The man smirked.

John stared at him.

"Before she came here, I slept with your woman, felt her body wiggle and squirm under me, as she cried and begged me to stop." Licking his bloodied lips, he leered at John. "It was luck that I ran into her after all this time."

"You're dyin'," he said his jaw clenched. "And I'm gonna sit back and watch it happen. I'll be the last thing you see before you go to hell." He wanted nothing more than to beat the life out of Boyd, but deciding to let the bastard suffer, he sat back and waited for him to take his last breath.

"I know you want to kill me, Taylor," Boyd egged him on. "C'mon, I know you...hate me." Blood slid from the corners of his mouth. "Hit...me...again."

John's fists scrunched open and closed beside him on the grass. He restrained his aching arms from fulfilling the strong desire to smash his fist into his ugly face one more time. A faint whistling sound escaped past Boyd's purple lips, and he watched as his head fell to the side and his lifeless eyes stared up at the sky.

Sitting up on his knees, he growled low in his throat as he rolled Boyd's body into the mud hole. Watching the man sink into the black abyss, he felt no remorse for the bastard who had tried to kill his family.

CHAPTER TWENTY-EIGHT

Six days after the fire, John stood in front of the black pit where his house once sat. He hadn't been able to come over and have a look until now. The scene was too overwhelming. But time had done nothing to ease the dull throbbing in his soul when he stared down at the wreckage.

His head down, he kicked at the bits and pieces of wood on the ground, when he saw something blinking up at him. Curious, he bent down and rummaged through the charred rubble, tossing bits and pieces to the side. He inhaled a sharp breath when he saw Becky's necklace. The heart-shaped locket, still attached to the chain, had been burned, melted and disfigured. He'd forgotten to put it in his pocket the day Livy was attacked. He let the chain caress his fingers, as it fell into his hand.

Closing his eyes, he brought the chain to his lips and fought back the tears that wanted to fall. Becky's house no longer stood. Her dishes, her clothes, her books, her sewing—all had perished in the fire. There was nothing left. Not a trace of her remained.

"John?" Clive knelt beside him.

"She's gone," he whispered, without looking at his friend. None of Becky's things were here for him to call upon when he needed to be close to her. He wouldn't be able to open the armoire in their room after a long day out in the fields—missing her so bad he felt as if his heart was broke in two—and bring her dresses to his face to inhale her scent. He would close his eyes, and it was as if she were there beside him, calming him, so he could get through another day without her.

Clive placed his hand gently on John's shoulder and squeezed. "She's been gone a long time friend."

A lone tear streaked down his face and he let it fall. "There's nothin' left of her. Nothin' left for me to hold on to."

"You were holdin' on to the wrong things, friend."

He gazed at the locket in his hand.

"She's here." Clive patted his chest.

"I built this house for her," John went on as if he hadn't heard Clive. "I kept her clothes, her sewing. I..." he choked, "I didn't want to let her go."

Somber, Clive nodded. "I know John. I know."

Overwhelmed by the anguish and pain he broke down and wept.

Clive squeezed his shoulder.

"I...loved her...so much."

"You'll never stop lovin' her."

He thought about his son. Ben hadn't so much as glanced his way ever since Livy left, and Clive had been keeping his distance from him as well. He was surprised that his friend had come over to talk to him at all, after what he'd done. "I've...pushed Ben away. I said things...to you...to Livy. I've been so cruel."

"It's okay," Clive whispered.

He shook his head.

"You have to let Becky go. You have to let her rest."

He looked through blurry eyes at his friend. "It's like she's died all over again."

"I know."

"I've held onto her memory for so long."

"Becky wouldn't have wanted that, John."

His wide shoulders shook as he wept, releasing all the anguish he'd kept inside for the past three years.

"She loved you, loved Ben and Emily. Becky would want you all to be happy."

He ran his hand over his eyes.

"And..." Clive said, "I think she would've approved of Livy."

John knew that Becky would always be a part of him, and every time he'd look at Emily he'd see his wife's face in hers. But was he able to put that aside and love another woman? He didn't know, and it scared the hell out of him to have to find out. Becky had been his life—his reason for living. He couldn't help but feel as if she'd been tossed aside and Livy took her place.

He looked at where his house used to stand, and found it hard to breathe. Becky's home was gone. The home he'd built for her, ravaged by fire, reduced to nothing but a pile of black wood. He had hammered every nail into the two story home, slaved for months so he could show her how much he loved her. But all that meant nothing now.

He ran his hand along his chin, Becky wasn't coming back, and he knew that. It had been three years, and he had to put her to rest, like Clive said. It meant he'd have to say goodbye, something he hadn't done yet, and it frightened him to have to let go.

"John," Clive asked, "do you have feelings for Livy?"

His thoughts had often wandered to Livy over the last few days. Her face haunted him every time he closed his eyes. He'd been a fool. He could see that now. But he knew there was nothing that could be done. Livy was gone.

Over the course of the week he'd tried to sway his heart that this was for the best, that he didn't care for her, and the children would get over her in time. But his chest had begun to ache, a slow dull pain, and he was as miserable as they were. His daughter asked for her every day, and Ben still hadn't spoken to him. He ran his hand through his hair and blew out a ragged breath.

"I feel like I'd be betraying Becky if I loved another woman." Anguish and torment oozed from his voice.

His hand still on John's shoulder, Clive spoke sympathetically. "You can still love Becky and love Livy at the same time."

He didn't see how that was possible, and shook his head. "No. I can't."

"You and Becky had somethin' special. She was your first love, the mother of your children. No one will ever take that away," Clive whispered, "but you and Livy have somethin' new, somethin' fresh and honest, and strong. They are two separate loves."

What Clive said made sense, but he didn't know if he could give his heart to Livy. "I don't know if I can."

"How will you know if you don't try?"

He shook his head.

"You have to try."

"I don't even know where Livy is."

"I do."

He stared at his friend.

"She's in town," Clive said, "singin' at the Prairie Dog Saloon."

He rubbed his tired, sore eyes. "How do you know that?"

Clive shrugged.

"A couple of the men went into town the other day, saw her singin'. Said she sounded like an angel."

She was in the saloon? He felt as if someone had punched him in the gut. The guilt made him feel sick. "She'll want nothin' to do with me." He lowered his head. "And who could blame her after what I said."

"Isn't she worth a try?"

"I pushed her to go back there. I forced her to leave." Disgusted, he stood.

"John, don't make the same mistakes I did."

"You did go after your wife, and she turned you down."

"Yeah, but I waited too long. I let my pride get in the way. Maybe if I hadn't waited so long, she'd have taken me back."

"I don't know."

"Don't wait, John. Don't do what I did."

He stood silent, thinking about everything Clive had said. He didn't want to be sitting here two years from now, mourning the loss of a second chance at love, wondering where Livy was and if she was okay.

"Clive, I'm sorry. For everythin'."

"It's all right John," he said, patting his shoulder.

He grabbed Clive and hugged him. Friends like Clive were hard to come by, and he was grateful that God had given him this one. Clutching the necklace in his hand, he had one more thing he needed to do.

A light wind blew over the prairies. John took off his hat and placed it on the ground beside him. Kneeling in front of the meager wooden cross he had nailed together, he let his fingers trace the grooves where Becky's name was. It was a peaceful place near the river. The grass, full and green, offered a blanket to sit on while he visited with her. A bouquet of daisies, her favorite, sat resting on his lap.

He closed his eyes and took a deep breath. "The house is gone, and it's time I realized that you are too." He pictured her in his mind, smiling up at him, happy. "You used to love this spot. Said you could see the whole ranch from here. I'll always love you Becky. That won't change."

Still holding the necklace, he gently hung it on the cross. "But I have to let you go. I have to let you sleep."

He placed a soft kiss on the cold metal heart, and taking the daisies from his lap, he placed them in front of the marker. "Goodbye, Becky."

"You're on in five minutes," Tom called from behind Livy's closed door.

Standing in front of the cracked mirror, she stared blankly at her reflection. She had filled the saloon, like she said she would, and had been allowed to stay. After her first night, the news had spread about a singing Angel inside the Prairie Dog, and the men came in droves to hear her. Tom paid her double what he'd originally offered, and she now had enough money to leave. Her ticket bought, she'd be taking the stage heading east in the morning.

She hated being back in a saloon. She felt sick to her stomach each time she stood up in front of all the dirty, unkempt cowboys who thought she'd offer them more than her voice. Last night was one of those nights. She shivered. After her ballad was done, she exited the stage and was caught off guard by a slobbering, drunken cowboy who decided he wanted her for himself. She kicked him hard in his groin and fled upstairs. Her room had no lock, so she slid the wooden dresser in front of the door and stayed awake all night, afraid that he'd come looking for her. She finally fell asleep at sun-up.

Relieved that tonight would be her last. She put on her makeup, dug the brass combs into her thick hair one more time, and slipped into the maroon colored dress she sang in. Her breasts were barely able to fit inside the low-cut bodice, and seemed as if they would burst out at any minute.

The slinky garment hugged her breasts and waist, leaving nothing to the imagination. Her shoulders bare, she couldn't wait to strip it from her body knowing she would never have to wear it again.

Her ticket sat on the nightstand beside her bed. Livy's eyes were drawn to the box sitting next to the ticket. The box Ben had given her. She wasn't ready to open it and see what was inside. The pain of leaving the ranch, leaving Ben and Emily, was still too hard for her to deal with.

She glanced at the mirror one more time before she opened her door and headed downstairs. She heard the cowboys, they were rowdy tonight. *John.* He was always on her mind. Her dreams, filled with images of him and the children, often woke her in the middle of the night, reminding her of the things she would never have. Her heart ached for them, yearned for one more glimpse of them. She missed the children terribly, and knew she'd never feel whole again.

She was tired of this life. Tired of singing in saloons. Tired of lying. This is what had caused her so much pain from the beginning, and she was determined to end it once she left here.

Since her arrival at the Prairie Dog, she had been holding on to the solace she found in the honest words of a child. Ben had told her his mama would watch over Emma in heaven. Whenever she thought of her baby, she took comfort in knowing that the woman who had raised such a fine boy was caring for her daughter, and the gnawing pain that had always been there wasn't as hard to deal with. Emma was a part of her, and she was grateful for the short time they had together.

Tom stood by the piano while he waited to introduce her. Al sat on the bench in front of the old music maker. The saloon was an unusually large building, with square wooden tables scattered about the planked floor. The bar, long and shiny, glistened with fine craftsmanship and was the one classy piece in the room. Liquor, mostly bottles of whiskey and moonshine, lined the walls behind the bar—the place Tom would be the rest of the night.

He had sectioned off a small area in the corner of the room where Livy could stand and sing. As he introduced her, the crowd—ranging from scruffy looking men, to men in well-tailored suits—sat cheering and whistling for her to come out. She took a deep breath, *this is the last time.* Her dress scraped the floor, making a swishing sound as she stepped to take her place. Clearing her throat, she forced a smile onto her face, turned and motioned for Al to begin. He took his cue and ran his talented fingers along the keys. The notes to "Clementine" echoed throughout the room.

John tied Midnight in front of the Prairie Dog Saloon. Pulling his hat low on his head, he pushed through the swinging doors and went in. The place was full of men all staring in the same direction. He joined them and was taken aback when he saw Livy standing beside the piano.

She was wearing a long dress, cut low and draped off her shoulders showing her creamy white skin and the cleft where her breasts came together. He was struck speechless at how she'd transformed. He made his way to the back of the room, and chose a table that shadowed him from her view. A voluptuous woman with blonde hair swayed over.

"What can I getcha, cowboy?" she asked, bending so he could see her bouncing breasts.

"Nothin', thanks," he said, smiling up at her.

Her chubby red lip stuck out as she pouted and stomped away. He ignored her, and watched Livy, mesmerized by her lovely voice and the way she brought each song to life, as if she'd written it. Amazed at how beautiful she was, how her hips swayed to the music, making him want her even more.

He'd been a fool to ever let her go, a bloody idiot to say the things he did, and he worried she'd want nothing to do with him. A light haze hung in the air, and he could smell the sweet scent of cigars wafting throughout the room. All his senses were tuned to Livy. Her body. Her lips. Her hair. Her voice.

Livy closed her eyes and let the music wrap around her, taking her to another time and place. She opened her mouth and let the words—charged with meaning—seep from her. She sang from her heart, as the crowd grew silent, listening. The grubby saloon, lit by a few kerosene lamps, had a calm, serene aura, and her body swayed back and forth in rhythm with the tune.

When the song ended, the men erupted in loud applause, hooting and hollering for more. Giving them what they wanted, she belted out "Yellow Rose of Texas", "Home Sweet Home", and "I'll Take You Home Again Kathleen". The last song affected even the tough guys, as they wiped a tear from their eyes. The cowboys tossed long-stemmed daisies, roses, and lilacs, to show their gratitude for the fine music she shared with them.

Holding an armful of the wildflowers—there were more at her feet—she asked the men to join her in her last song, "Home on the Range." They belted out the lyrics while clanking their glasses and dancing around the tables with each other. Carrying on well after the song had finished, the cowboys didn't notice as she slipped off to the side and went up to her room.

John was the exception. When her last song ended, he had to keep from jumping up out of his chair and rushing to where she stood. Instead, he waited impatiently for her to leave. His dark eyes followed her as she ascended the stairs, entered the third door on the left and closed it behind her.

He weaved his way through the crowd of boisterous men and climbed the stairs, two at a time, to her room. Taking a deep breath, he knocked.

"Who is it?" Livy called from the other side.

"It's John, Livy." He rammed his hands inside his pockets and then pulled them out again. He shifted his weight from his left foot to his right.

The door creaked open a crack, and Livy peeked out. Her eyes widened when she saw him.

"I…" He took a breath. "Livy, I have somethin' to say."

She stepped back from the door to let him in. She was still wearing the maroon dress, and he let his eyes roam over her. "You're beautiful," he whispered.

She blushed, and crossed her arms, covering her breasts from his view. "Why are you here, John?"

Swallowing past the lump in his throat, his face hot, he took off his hat and ran his hand through his hair. "I've come for you."

"Well…"

He held his hand up to stop her. "Please Livy, let me finish. I said some things to you that I shouldn't have. I-I didn't give you a chance to explain, and I'm sorry for that." He stared into her green eyes. "I didn't realize…I didn't know it then…"

She stood away from him. "Say what it is you've come to say, John."

"I love you, Livy," he whispered his eyes misting. He watched as her bottom lip trembled.

"What did you say?" she whispered.

"I said I love you, damn it." He went to her, pulled her into his arms and kissed her, softly, sweetly, holding onto her, not wanting to let go.

She wrapped her arms around his neck.

"I need you with me," he whispered against her mouth. "I love you, Livy, and I'm sorry—so very sorry."

"I-I love you too," she said.

He pulled away from her. "I want you to come home, darlin'. I want us to be a family."

Tears flowed down her cheeks.

He lifted her chin with his thumb. "Do you want to come home with me, Livy, and be my wife?"

"Yes," she cried, "yes, I want to come home."

He wasted no time scooping her up into his arms and walking toward the door.

"Wait."

She pressed on his shoulders so he'd let her down. She ran over to the nightstand, picked up the brown box Ben had given to her, and went back to John.

"What's that?" he asked, his arms around her again.

She glanced up at him, and he knew he'd never tire of looking into her beautiful green eyes.

"Ben gave it to me the night I left, but I couldn't open it."

"Well, open it now."

He watched as she lifted the lid off the box, and more tears fell from her eyes onto her cheeks.

"I can't believe it."

"What is it?"

She tipped the box, and showed him nestled inside, Ben's four-leaf clover.

He pulled her close. "Well, now, I have all the luck I need," he said as he brushed his lips on hers. "I have you, my shamrock-eyed Angel."

"And I have you," Livy whispered. "And Ben and Emily."

Standing on tiptoe, she kissed him with all her heart and soul.

Keep reading for a message from the author
and a sneak peek from LAKOTA HONOR, Book 1 in the Branded Trilogy.

MESSAGE FROM THE AUTHOR

Dear Reader,

Mail order brides have always fascinated me. In the 1800's women married for a sense of security, and financial stability. They were widows seeking help to raise their children, lost souls searching for independence.

In the early stages of writing *Chasing Clovers*, I laid awake countless hours mulling over how to develop this story into an emotional journey for my readers. I took the concept of Mail Order Bride and started asking myself questions. What if Livy came from an elusive past? What if she had a child who was her salvation from that past? And what if the child died? Destitute and alone, she needs to survive and marries a man she's never met.

As I wrote, Livy came to life. She burrowed inside of me, and soon I began to feel her pain, her sorrow, her guilt. I understood her anger and resentment toward others around her. A scorned woman, she longed to feel accepted, needed—wanted. John Taylor was that man. Proud and arrogant, he stepped into Livy's life and demanded she fit in with his family.

John and Livy are a very special part of me. Their story is one of faith and courage, and I will miss them.

I hope you enjoyed reading *Chasing Clovers*, and fell in love with John and Livy as I did.

Love,

Kat

LAKOTA HONOR
BRANDED TRILOGY, BOOK 1

1888, Willow Creek, Colorado

Nora Rushton scanned the hillside before glancing back at the woman on the ground. She could be dead, or worse yet, someone from town. She flexed her hands. The woman's blue skirt ruffled in the wind, and a tattered brown Stetson sat beside her head. Nora assessed the rest of her attire. A faded yellow blouse stained from the grass and dirt, leather gloves and a red bandana tied loosely around her neck. She resembled a ranch hand in a skirt.

There was no one else around, and the woman needed her help. She chewed on her lip, and her fingers twitched. *I have to help her.* She sucked in a deep breath, held it, and walked the remaining few feet that stood between her and the injured woman.

The woman's horse picked up Nora's scent, trotted over and pushed his nose into her chest.

"It's okay, boy," she said, smoothing back the red-brown mane. "Why don't you let me have a look at your owner?"

She knelt down beside the woman and realized she was old enough to be her grandmother. Gray hair with subtle blonde streaks lay messed and pulled from the bun she was wearing. Why was she on a horse in the middle of the valley without a chaperone?

She licked her finger and placed it under the woman's nose. A cool sensation skittered across her wet finger, and she sighed.

The woman's left leg bent inward and laid uncomfortably to the side. She lifted the skirt for a closer look. Her stomach rolled, and bile crawled up the back of her throat. The thigh bone protruded, stretching the skin bright white, but didn't break through. Nora's hands grew warm, the sensation she felt so many times before.

The woman moaned and reached for her leg.

"No, please don't touch your leg. It's broken." She held the woman's hand.

Ice blue eyes stared back at her, showing pain mingled with relief.

"My name is Nora," she said with a smile. "I am going to get help."

The wrinkled hand squeezed hers, and the woman shook her head. "No, child, my heart can't take the pain much longer." Creased lips pressed together as she closed her eyes and took two deep breaths. "Please, just sit here with me." Her voice was husky and weak.

She scanned the rolling hills for any sign of help, but there was no one. She studied the woman again. Her skin had a blue tinge to it, and her breathing became forced. *I promised Pa.* But how was she supposed to walk away from this woman who so desperately needed her help? She took another look around. Green grass waved in the wind. *Please, someone, anyone come over the hill.*

White daisies mingled within the grass, and had the woman not been injured, she would've plucked a few for her hair. She waited a few minutes longer. No one came. Her hands started their restless shaking. She clasped them together, trying to stop the tremors. *It would only take a few minutes. I can help her. No one would see.* She stared at the old woman, *except her.* If she helped her, would she tell everyone about Nora's secret? Would she ask any questions? *There were always questions.*

Nora's resolve was weakening. She ran her hot hands along the woman's body to see if anything else was broken. Only the leg, thank goodness. Lifting the skirt once again, she laid her warm palms gently on the broken thigh bone. Her hands, bright red, itched with anticipation. The leg seemed worse without the cover of the skirt. One move and the bone would surely break through the skin. She inhaled groaning at the same time as she placed her hands on either side of the limb. In one swift movement, she squeezed the bone together.

The woman shot up from the grass yelling out in agony.

Nora squeezed harder until she felt the bone shift back into place. Jolts of pain raced up and down her arms as the woman's leg began to heal. Nora's own thigh burned and ached, as her bones and flesh cried out in distress. She held on until the pain seeped from her own body into nothingness, vanishing as if it were never there.

She removed her hands, now shaking and cold from the woman's healed limb, unaware of the blue eyes staring up at her. Her stomach lurched, like she knew it would—like it always did afterward. She rose on trembling legs and walked as far away as she could before vomiting onto the bright green grass. Not once, but twice. She waited until her strength returned before she stood and let the wind cool her heated cheeks. The bitter taste stayed in her mouth. If the woman hadn't been there she'd have spit the lingering bile onto the grass. She needed water and searched the area for a stream.

Her mouth felt full of cotton, and she smacked her tongue off of her dry lips. She was desperate for some water. Had she not wandered so far from the forest to set the baby hawk free, she'd know where she was now and which direction would take her home. She gasped. She'd lost track of time and needed to get home before Pa did. Jack Rushton had a temper and she didn't want to witness it tonight.

"Are you an angel?"

She turned to face the woman and grinned. "No, Ma'am. I am not an angel, although I like to think God gave me this gift."

The woman pulled her skirt down, recovered from her shock and said in a rough voice, "Well if you ain't no angel, than what in hell are ya?"

Taken aback at the woman's gruffness, she knelt down beside her. *Here we go, either she understands or she runs away delusional and screaming.* "I… I am a healer." She waited.

The woman said nothing instead she narrowed her eyes and stared. "A witch?"

Nora winced.

"No, not a witch. I need you to promise you won't tell anyone what happened here today." Her stomach in knots, she waited for the old woman's reply.

"You think I'm some kind of fool?" She stood and stretched her leg. She stared at the healed limb before she hopped on it a few times. "People already think I'm crazy. Why would I add more crap to their already heaping pile of shit?"

Oh my. The woman's vocabulary was nothing short of colorful, and she liked it.

She smiled and stuck out her hand. "I'm Nora Rushton. It's nice to meet you."

The woman stared at her for a few seconds before her thin mouth turned up and she smiled. "Jess Chandler." She gripped Nora's hand with such force she had to refrain from yelling out in pain. "Thanks for your help, girly."

"I don't think we've ever met. Do you live in Willow Creek?"

"I own a farm west of here."

"How come I've never seen you?" *I never see anyone, Pa's rules.*

The wind picked up whipping Jess's hat through the air. "Max," she called over her shoulder, "fetch my hat."

The horse's ears spiked and he trotted off toward the hat. She watched in awe as the animal retrieved the Stetson with his mouth and brought it back to his master.

"I've never seen such a thing," Nora giggled and patted Max's rump.

Jess took the hat and slapped it on top of her head.

"Yup, ol'Max here, he's pretty damn smart."

"I'd say he is." She remembered the companionship she'd enjoyed with the baby hawk she'd rescued a few weeks ago. She'd miss the little guy. His feedings had kept her busy during the long boring days at home. "Miss Jess, I'm sorry to be short, but I have to head on home."

"Hell, girly, I can take you." She climbed up onto Max and wound the reins around her gloved hands. "Hop on. He's strong enough for two."

"Are you sure?"

"It's the least I can do."

She clasped Jess's hand and pulled herself up behind her. "Thank you, Jess, for keeping my secret." Placing her arms around the woman's waist, she gave her a light squeeze.

"Darlin'," Jess patted Nora's hand, "you can rest assured I will take this secret to my grave." She whistled, and Max started toward town.

Otakatay sat tall on his horse as he gazed at the lush green valley below. The town of Willow Creek was nestled at the edge of the green hills. He'd been gone four round moons, traveling to Wyoming and back. The rough terrain of the Rocky Mountains had almost killed him and his horse. The steep cliffs and forests were untouched by man.

On the first day in the Rockies, he'd come up against a mountain lion, a grizzly and bush thick enough to strangle him. He used his knife to carve into the dense brush, and his shotgun to defend himself. When he could, he stuck to the deer trails, and in the evening built large fires to keep the animals at bay.

He glanced behind him at the brown sack tied to his saddle. Inside, there were three. This time he'd ask for more money. His bronzed jaw flexed. He would demand it.

The sky was bright blue with smudges of gray smoke wafting upward from the homes and businesses. The weather would warm as the day progressed and the sun rose higher into the sky. His eyes wandered past the hills to the mountains behind them, and his insides burned.

He clicked his tongue, and his mustang sauntered down the hill. Wakina was agile and strong. Otakatay knew he could count on him always. Over the years Wakina had kept pace with his schedule and relentless hunting. The emerald stocks swayed and danced before him as he rode through. The grass brushed the bottoms of his moccasins, and he dunked his hand into the velvety green weed. He'd make camp in the forest outside of the mining town.

Wakina shook his head and whinnied. Otakatay brushed his hand along the length of his silver mane.

"Soon my friend, soon," he whispered.

The animal wanted to run down into the valley, but resigned himself to the lethargic pace his master ordered. Wakina tossed his head. Otakatay slapped Wakina's sides with the loose ends of the reins, and the horse took off down the hill clearing a path through the grass.

The rolling blanket of emerald parted as Wakina's long legs cantered toward the forest. Otakatay's shoulder-length black hair whipped his face and tickled his neck as his heart pounded lively inside his chest. It was rare that he felt so alive. His days consisted of planning and plotting until he knew every detail by heart. The eagle feather tied to his hair lifted in the wind and soared high above his head. For a moment he allowed himself to close his eyes and enjoy the smells of wildflowers and wood smoke. The sun kissed his cheeks and he tried to hold onto the moment, savoring the last bit of calm before rotten flesh and wet fur filled his nostrils.

His eyes sprung open. He pulled on the reins, and rubbed his nose to rid the smell, to push out the visions that saturated his mind. The scent clung to him burrowing deep into his soul and he mentally fought to purge it from his consciousness. He shook his head and concentrated on the fields, trying to push the memories away. He didn't want to do this, not now. He didn't want to see, feel, smell, or taste the memory again.

The rhythmic clanking echoed inside his head, and he squeezed his eyes closed. Sweat trickled down his temples. He clenched every muscle in his body. His hands skimmed the jagged walls of the damp tunnel. He stumbled and fell onto the rough walls, burning his torn flesh. He moaned. Every bit of him ached with such pain, he was sure he'd die. His thin body shook with fever. He reeked of blood, sweat and fear.

With each step he took, he struggled to stay upright and almost collapsed onto the ground. The agony of his wounds blinded him, and he didn't know if it was a combination of the sweat dripping into his eyes, or if he was crying from the intense pain. His back burned and pulsed with powerful beats, the skin became tight around his ribs as the flesh swelled.

He tripped on a large rock and fell to the ground. The skin on his knees tore open, but he didn't care. Nothing could ease the screaming in his back. Nothing could take away the hell he lived every day. He laid his head against the dirt covered floor. Dust stuck to his cheeks and lips while he prayed for Wakan Tanka to end his life.

LAKOTA HONOR is available now in a new 2018 edition!

Made in the USA
Columbia, SC
20 July 2018